Drowning on Land

Deep beneath the ground, the shells blew. The earth heaved around them, the trench they were in collapsing where the sandbag revetments had rotted.

Time-delay fuses, McCulloden thought. *Oh, shit.*

The ground heaved again and again—the sound of the explosions muffled, transmitted through the soil like ripples through water. Must be what an earthquake feels like, he thought, the ground beneath your feet no more solid than if you were walking on the air. The very air seemed to waver, turn brown, the dirt so thick it coated the lungs, that and the explosives choking out the life-giving oxygen.

Then a particularly close hit threw him bodily down, collapsing the walls around him, covering him with rat-infested sandbags, worms, the detritus of years of neglect. He was swimming in dirt, desperately trying to keep his head out of the constantly filling trench, praying to survive and knowing that if just one more hit close, it was over.

He had time only to register an explosion so impossibly loud that he knew even before the pain hit that his eardrums were probably gone. Then the world went black.

NAPALM DREAMS

A "MEN OF VALOR" NOVEL

By
John F. Mullins
Major U.S. Army
Special Forces (Retired)

POCKET STAR BOOKS
New York London Toronto Sydney

This book is a work of fiction. Names, characters, places, and incidents are products of the author's imagination or are used fictitiously. Any resemblance to actual events or locales or persons living or dead is entirely coincidental.

An *Original* Publication of POCKET BOOKS

A Pocket Star Book published by
POCKET BOOKS, a division of Simon & Schuster, Inc.
1230 Avenue of the Americas, New York, NY 10020

ISBN: 0-7434-7767-7

First Pocket Books printing April 2004

10 9 8 7 6 5 4 3 2 1

POCKET STAR BOOKS and colophon are registered
trademarks of Simon & Schuster, Inc.

Cover design and photo by James Wang

Manufactured in the United States of America

For information regarding special discounts for bulk purchases,
please contact Simon & Schuster Special Sales at 1-800-456-6798
or business@simonandschuster.com.

Dedicated to all the men, living and dead,
who served or are serving in the Special Forces.
John F. Kennedy told us to go out and "fight any foe,
bear any burden," and we did.

De Oppresso Liber

NAPALM DREAMS

Operations Order 25/72
B Company, 5TH Special Forces Group
(Airborne), 1ST Special Forces

1. SITUATION

    A. ENEMY FORCES.

    1: Weather--High temperature 105 degrees Fahrenheit, with a low overnight of 80. Partly cloudy, humidity 92 percent. Forecast calls for increasing cloudiness over the next twenty-four hours with the strong possibility of rain. Expect low overcast in the mountains, ground fog beginning at approximately 0300 hours, degraded visibility for flying operations.

    2: Terrain--Mountains rising to 5,000 feet a.s.l., heavily jungled, triple-canopy trees with some underbrush. In cleared areas expect heavy underbrush, elephant grass, wait-a-minute vines. Intermittent streams, most of which will be dry here at the end of the dry season.

    3: Identification--Captured documents and reconnaissance have shown the presence of the 66th and 28th NVA Regiments in the area, supported by elements of at least one artillery regiment. Local Viet Cong battalions likely in support.

    4: Location--Command headquarters likely across the border in Laos. Long-range artillery also likely there. Elements of both regiments have taken up positions from which they can easily mount an assault against Camp Boun Tlak. Signals intercept indicate the presence of antiaircraft artillery near the camp and located on the high ground surrounding it.

5: Activity—The enemy has moved its forward elements into covered and concealed positions within easy reach of the camp. Digging continues, despite frequent shelling from within the camp. Air observation shows communications trenches and forward positions being manned at all times.

6: Strength—Unknown with any certainty, however, the 66th and 28th are known to have recently crossed the border from rest and refitting in their sanctuaries in Laos after the mauling they took last year during Operation Bold Strike. Air strikes and other aggressive actions are unlikely to have degraded their combat ability to any great degree.

B. FRIENDLY FORCES.

1: Mission of next higher unit—Commander, Company B, and his combat staff will maintain a forward operating base at Firebase Esther and be prepared to maintain communications with all friendly elements able to support the mission.

2: Location and planned actions of units on the left, right, front, and rear—There are no units on the left, right, front, and rear.

3: Mission and route of adjacent units—There are no adjacent units.

4: Fire support available—Division Artillery, 4th Infantry Division, will provide fire support consisting of long-range artillery and aerial rocket artillery.

C. ATTACHMENTS AND DETACHMENTS—None.

2. MISSION—II Corps Mobile Strike Force (Mike Force) will move to reinforce Detachment A-228 at Camp Boun Tlak and assist the camp strike force in resisting the expected assault.

3. EXECUTION

A. CONCEPT OF OPERATION.

1: Scheme of maneuver—To be developed by Commander, II Corps Mike Force, and his staff.

2: Fire support—Operations in and around Camp Boun Tlak will be supported by Cobra gunships, with Air Force fighter support as backup.

B. COORDINATING INSTRUCTIONS—To be prepared by the Commander, II Corps Mike Force, and his staff.

4. SERVICE SUPPORT

A. RATIONS—Reports from within the camp indicate sufficient rations to support all reinforcements for the immediate future.

B. ARMS AND AMMUNITION—As per Mike Force Standard Operating Procedures (SOP).

C. UNIFORM AND EQUIPMENT—At the discretion of the battalion commander.

D. EVACUATION OF WOUNDED--Normal medevac procedures.

E. PRISONERS AND CAPTURED EQUIPMENT--Field interrogation of prisoners is authorized. Captured equipment is to be destroyed in place.

5. COMMAND AND SIGNAL

A. SIGNAL--Normal Signal Operating Instructions (SOI) in effect.

B. COMMAND--II Corps Mike Force battalion commander will assume command of all operations within Camp Boun Tlak upon his arrival on scene. Normal chain of command procedures will be followed.

The briefers, consisting of Company B command and staff personnel, asked for questions and, when there were none, left the tent. Remaining were the key personnel from the Mike Force battalion. Almost as one they looked at one another, and the expressions could be summed up in a couple of words.

Oh, shit.

Chapter 1

"So, what do you think?"

"I think we're gonna get our asses shot out of the sky."

Lieutenant Colonel Sam Gutierrez looked at the aerial photo again. The North Vietnamese zigzag trenches were clearly shown going right up to the wire of the beleaguered camp. If you squinted hard enough, you could see the blurry shapes of people. Lots of people.

"I think you might be right," he said. "See any other way of doing it?"

"Way I see it," Captain Finn McCulloden, commander of the First Battalion, II Corps Mike Force, mused, "is that we have three courses of action. Walk in from here. That way we could take the whole battalion. Get the battalion in there, Charlie isn't going to take the camp. Don't give a damn how many people he throws against us. Problem is, it'd take three days at best. That's if the NVA haven't ambushed all the avenues of approach, which they will have.

"Second, land right here," he said, pointing to a bald knoll, formerly an artillery firebase. "Never be able to get more than one lift in, the place is probably mined like hell, and the trails down off it mined and ambushed."

"So that leaves . . ."

Finn smiled. "It leaves coming in as fast as we can, landing right in the middle of the camp, which as we know is registered with mortar concentrations and rockets, has anti-aircraft guns all around it, and probably direct fire from recoilless rifles and RPG-7s. How do you like those odds, Captain Cozart?"

The helicopter pilot grinned back. "They suck." He looked around at the other pilots, seeing the young men, most of them warrant officers with less than two years in the Army, nod their heads in agreement.

"Then that's what we do?" Finn asked.

"No other choice, is there?" Cozart replied. "Your people are going to have to be unassing those choppers in a hurry. No room for more than a two-ship landing at a time. How many people are you going to try to get in there?"

"One company," Finn replied. "Eighty 'Yards, five round-eyes. The rest of the battalion will walk in. Maybe we can hold Victor Charles off until they get there."

Cozart called his pilots together to start planning the assault. Gutierrez pulled Captain McCulloden off to the side. "You know I wouldn't ask this, if I thought they could hold out one more day."

"Shit, Sam. I know that. Hell, I still owe you money from R and R, so I know you don't want me killed just yet." Finn McCulloden and Sam Gutierrez went back a long way, to their first tour in Vietnam when Sam was the captain commanding an A team and Finn was his junior medic. It was Sam, when he returned for his third tour and found himself commanding a C team in Pleiku, who had convinced Finn, also just starting his third tour, to take the newly opened position as commander of the Mike Force. They often needed new commanders, being the reaction force for A teams in trouble. There were no "walks in the woods" for the Mike Force. When it went out, there was a fight. The survival rate for the Americans who ran the Mike Force wasn't high.

"Don't suppose I can talk you into waiting, taking the main force of the battalion in?"

"You know better than that," Finn said. "Besides, you wanted me to take command, and I can't command from thirty klicks away."

Gutierrez nodded his head in assent. There had to be new command on the ground at Camp Boun Tlak. The team there, what was left of it, had lost confidence in the commander, First Lieutenant Bentley Sloane. Sloane had been the executive officer under Captain Stan Koslov, taking over the team when Koslov was killed on a local security patrol.

Thereafter Sloane had refused to let patrols go outside the wire, thus clearing the way for the NVA regiment now besieging the camp to make its preparations in relative safety. The more experienced members of the team—and there were damned few of them these days!—had argued with him to no avail. Now they blamed him for their precarious situation.

And Colonel Gutierrez agreed. This late in the war, Special Forces had been inundated not only with relatively inexperienced NCOs, but with officers who had no background in special operations at all. Some of those officers learned, and learned quickly. Others became casualties. Still others would probably never learn, and that type included Lieutenant Sloane.

Gutierrez recalled Sloane reporting to the C team for further assignment. He had wasted no time in letting it be known that not only was he a West Pointer, but that his family's military tradition was long and distinguished, starting with his great-grandfather, who had won the Medal of Honor at Cold Harbor. Gutierrez had marked him as a careerist, and an arrogant one at that. Getting his ticket punched with a short assignment in the combat zone, in preparation for moving up to bigger and better things. With the drawdown of conventional units and their increasing departure, SF was still the best place to get shot at.

Gutierrez had assigned him to Boun Tlak because Koslov was one of the best A team commanders still in II Corps, and what damage could the lieutenant do, under Koslov's thumb? Besides, Boun Tlak was next in line for turnover to the Vietnamese under Nixon's Vietnamization program, and the assignment wouldn't be for all that long, anyway.

Even shorter now, he thought.

Cozart approached. "Got a plan. May not be a good plan, but it's the best we can come up with at the moment."

"Let's hear it," Finn said. He had a lot of faith in John Wesley Cozart. Whatever anyone might say about the short-in-stature, arrogant aviator, you had to admit he had brass balls. You called him in, he was going to come in or die trying. Over the last six months that had happened four times.

"Way I figure it, we pack about twelve of your guys on each bird," Cozart said. The Huey was designed to carry six to eight American troops, but the Montagnards of the Mike Force were considerably smaller than their round-eye counterparts. Finn nodded. A heavy lift, but twelve they could do.

"Don't need much fuel, there and back," Cozart continued. "Keep door gunner ammo to a minimum—ain't gonna be much time for shootin'. That makes it an eight-ship lift.

"They'll expect us to come over this hill," he said, pointing to a piece of dominant terrain just to the east of the camp. "That way we'd be masked from their fire the maximum amount of time. Which means they'll probably have most of their antiaircraft guns sited here." He pointed to a patch of jungle just to the other side of the camp's cratered runway.

"So we'll trick 'em. We'll swing around, come in from the north, cross this ridge, drop down into the riverbed. Fly right on the water, pop up, be in the camp before they know it." He was grinning, clearly enjoying the thought of the flight.

Finn looked around at the young aviators, who would in the normal course of events be hanging out on the block back home or revving their souped-up cars up and down the main streets of a dozen small towns. Not one of them was over twenty one.

Smiling and laughing as if this were a training mission back at Fort Rucker.

An eight-ship lift, flying nose-to-tail rotor down a narrow riverbed, where the enemy would be able to shoot down on them. Where, if one ship went down, the following ones would have to make some hellacious gyrations to avoid running into it.

Where there wouldn't be a chance to autorotate if you lost power. You would fly right into the ground at 120 knots.

"Shitty plan," Finn said. "Let's do it."

His four NCOs thought it was a shitty plan too. "First two or three birds might get through okay," Sergeant First Class (SFC) Elmo Driver, platoon sergeant of the First Platoon, said. "Charlie's gonna be so surprised, seein' us come down that river, probably won't be able to get a shot off. After that, it's gonna be a shootin' gallery."

"I'll take ass-end Charlie," SFC Walter "Spearchucker" Washington, weapons platoon leader, said. "Always at the back of the bus, anyhow." Washington had won the hearts and admiration of Special Forces men everywhere when, shortly after Kennedy had awarded SF its distinctive headwear, he had been approached in a bus station by a little old lady, who had asked if he was one of those Green Berets.

"No, ma'am," he'd replied. "I'm a nigger. This here"—pointing to his hat—"is a green beret."

"Sorry 'bout that," Finn said. "You're up front. We need your machine gunners in that camp probably worse than anybody. Any other volunteers?"

"Hell, I figure ol' Elmo's wrong," Staff Sergeant (SSG) Andy Inger, company medic, said. "First birds ain't never goin' to make it through. They'll be piled up like a bunch a flies after the first frost. Gonna need somebody to come in, pull your sorry asses out of the wreckage. That might as well be me."

"Cheerful fuckin' bunch, ain't ya," Master Sergeant (MSG) George "Slats" Olchak, the American company commander of Company A, First Mike Force Battalion, grumped. Olchak was widely known as an equal-opportunity curmudgeon, who was reputed to have last smiled when the Japanese bombed Pearl Harbor.

"Ours is not to reason why," Andy Inger said. "If anybody around here stopped to reason why, we'd all be at home with our wives and girlfriends. Though not simultaneously, of course."

Finn laughed with the others. These few, these pitiful few, he thought, remembering the fragment of a poem by somebody or other. Once more into the fray, dear friends. Shit. Did anyone who wrote this stuff actually stand a chance of getting shot to pieces? Wouldn't have been so goddamn happy about it then, would they?

These four Americans were all that was left out of what had been a seven-man company command unit. The company XO, SFC Joe Pelligrino, had been killed just outside the old camp of Vinh Thanh. First Platoon leader SFC Tim "Backtrack" Volusio was back in the States, recuperating from wounds received on a downed-pilot recovery mission just south of Pleiku. Third Platoon leader SSG Harjo Spear had finally DROSed back to the world after having served three years straight in the Mike Force, swearing as he left that he was going to Washington to straighten out those assholes in personnel who wouldn't let you stay in Vietnam as long as you wanted to.

And the other companies were in worse shape, which was why he'd picked A Company to go in. Some of them were down to two Americans, and the line troops were severely understrength. The Mike Force had had a hard war.

"Weapons first," he said, breaking up the good-natured bickering that always went on before an operation. "First Platoon, Second, Third. Andy, you're right about maybe needing you at the rear. You ride the last ship. I'll go in with Walt. We go in light, individual weapons, a couple of grenades, basic load. Gutierrez tells me Koslov stockpiled a shitload of ammo, got it stashed in bunkers all around the camp, so we won't need any extra. The lighter those birds are, the better. Any questions?"

"Just one," Elmo said. "I guess it's too late to request a transfer to Nha Trang? Maybe run the Playboy Club? Sit around the bar with the other fat, old fucks and talk about how this war ain't nearly like it was way back in '65?"

"Maybe that would be a good idea," Olchak chimed in. "Some 'a those guys could probably make a soldier out of him. I've about given up on it."

"Damn," Elmo said, his face falling comically. "Is it that you're just jealous, Top? Of my manly physique? My obvious physical beauty? My mile-long . . ."

Finn left them to it. They'd been together so long and through so much that they acted more like a family than a military unit.

A family that was soon likely to be much smaller.

Within a few minutes they were outside, readying the Montagnard troops that made up the bulk of II Corps Mike Force. The 'Yards, as everyone called them, were an ethnic Indo-Malayan group who had settled in the highlands long before the Vietnamese came down from China. The Vietnamese scorned them as savages. They cordially returned the hatred, being perfectly happy to kill Vietnamese of any stripe, but in this case more particularly the North Vietnamese who came into their villages and pressed their people into labor as porters. The Special Forces had been working with the 'Yards almost from the beginning, following the example set by the French commandos who had fought their own war on the same territory.

Lots of SF called them "little people," with nary a trace of denigration. The average 'Yard stood about five foot four and weighed perhaps 120 pounds. But the Americans knew they were some of the best fighters in Southeast Asia. Absolutely loyal to the Americans, they would fight to the death rather than let the North Vietnamese (or Viet Cong, though there were few of those to be found these days) kill their friends.

Now they were forming up in ragged lines, shouldering weapons, complaining bitterly as the Americans made them leave behind the huge amounts of ammunition and grenades they habitually carried. Finn had, out of idle curiosity, once weighed the gear an average Montagnard carried into battle and had found that it outweighed its owner.

But it always left them with plenty of ammunition for the fight, an important factor when resupply, they not being an American unit, was problematic. Coming up against a Mike Force company was like being thrown into a buzz saw.

Finn wasn't too worried about the shortage of Americans. The 'Yard platoon leaders were certainly competent, having had the benefit not only of years of example from their American friends, but combat experience far beyond anyone now serving in Vietnam. Their only problem was language—if they got into a serious fight and needed air support, there was no one within the organization to call for it. But since they were going to be within the confines of Camp Boun Tlak, that wasn't an issue. There would be plenty of Americans to do that chore, and if there weren't, well, that would mean that everybody was probably dead, anyway.

His interpreter, Bobby, approached. "A good fuckin' day, huh, *Dai Uy*?" he said.

Bobby was half-Vietnamese, half-French, fruit of a long-ago liaison between a soldier of Groupement Mobile 100 and a bargirl from Qui Nhon. Shortly after Bobby had been born, his father was killed, along with most of the others of his unit, in a mile-long ambush in the Mang Yang Pass. Bobby had grown up shunned by both worlds, the Vietnamese looking down on half-breeds and the French abandoning the country. He'd lived by his wits and hard work, supplementing the meager income he made shining shoes on the streets of Qui Nhon with petty thievery. There he was found by a Special Forces sergeant, who not only took him in but started teaching him English to add to his already formidable French, Vietnamese, and Jarai (a Montagnard language). Over the years his instructors had continued to be Special Forces types, which was why he could not string three words together without one of them being *fuck*.

But he was a brave soldier and utterly reliable in the field. More American, some people said, than the Americans. Snaggletoothed, freckled, his features owing more to his French father than his Vietnamese mother, he could have passed for a darker-skinned American teenager.

His name was actually Robert, but in his hatred for the French, who had abandoned him and his mother, he disdained the pronunciation *Roh-bair* and had taken to the Americanization of his name with glee.

Finn shook his head. "You're gonna give the church ladies back home the fits," he scolded. "Gotta clean up your act."

Bobby grinned, unconcerned. "Yah, but I bet the girls will like it."

Finn had promised to look into getting him into school back in the United States, feeling fairly certain that with the drawdown of American forces, Bobby was going to have a lot of trouble with his own countrymen. And that was if the South Vietnamese were able to hold out.

If the NVA won, Bobby was a dead man, as would be all the people who had worked with the Americans.

"The girls," Finn said, "the nice ones anyway, will be shocked."

"*Dai Uy,* what would I do with a nice girl? I find me a nice young whore, we make lots of babies, call the first one Finn." Bobby interrupted the banter to shout a stream of obscenities at one of the Montagnard soldiers who had just dropped his M16 in the red dirt.

"Betcha he not do that again," he said, grinning at Finn. "Gonna be hot today, huh?"

"Maybe too hot. You stick close to me. Chopper goes down, we're able to get away, we'll E and E. We make it to the camp, we're gonna have a lot of work to do before tonight. I'll need your help."

"No sweat, *Dai Uy,*" Bobby said. "I stick to you like stink on shit. Kill a whole bunch a fuckin' communists, you and me. Just like always."

Gotta hope just like always, Finn thought. Luck is going to run out, one of these days.

Hope it's not today.

Captain Cozart sat in the cockpit of the Huey, going through the start-up checklist with his copilot. The whine of the turbine soon filled the cabin, and slowly the rotor blade started to turn. Within moments it was chopping through the air, filling the world with a sound that Vietnam veterans, years afterward, would hear and suddenly be transported back in time, the memories so sharp they would swear they could smell the exhaust.

He looked back over his shoulder at the passengers, Captain Finn McCulloden, his interpreter, radio operator, and eight Mike Force troopers jammed so tightly the door gunners had to stand on a tiny piece of floor. He pulled pitch and the chopper slowly, complainingly, lifted a tiny bit, allowing him to turn the nose down the pierced steel-planking runway. He moved forward, gathering the airspeed necessary to get the thing to fly. Normal helicopter takeoff was impossible with this sort of load; they were going to have to make a run at it.

The chopper slowly gained airspeed, and he brought up the stick a tiny piece at a time, finally getting just enough altitude and speed to clear the trees at the end of the runway, albeit by inches. Looking out the rearview, he could see the rest of the lift pulling in behind him, their formation not exactly what would be regarded as precise by the instructors back at Fort Rucker.

"Heading?" he said to the copilot, who studied the map strapped to his thigh and who, after a moment, gave it to him.

He swung the heavy bird in that direction, enjoying, as he always did, the rush of cool air through the opened window. Up here you could imagine you were in an air-conditioned office, far away from trouble of any sort, your only concern whether your bar tab at the "O" club was too high to allow you to drink as much as you wanted to.

The triple-canopy jungle below disabused you of that notion. At any moment it could erupt in green tracers, or worse, a stream of radar-guided 23mm shells. Then you could think about how painful it was going to be as they smashed through the thin Perspex under your feet, seeking soft flesh in which to embed themselves.

Just as it had been for many—all too many—of his friends.

Screw that, he thought. They want me, they got to catch me first. He keyed his mike, made contact with the Air Force forward air controller, now flying over the battle zone in a flimsy O-2 propeller-driven airplane. The O-2 had one propeller in the front of the fuselage and another pusher propeller at the back. The brass said it was to assure redundancy—if one prop went out, you could make it back home on the other.

The pilots and backseaters argued that it was so that if the front one didn't chop you up as it came whirling back through the fuselage, the rear one would make sure you looked like mixed salad.

" 'Bout ready for the festivities?" he asked.

"Got 'em stacked up," the FAC replied. "Fast movers coming in five, CBUs and nape. Four flights, two Air Force and two Navy, off the *Forrestal*. Snake escort will rendezvous at BR775420, go down the river with you, then pull off as you land, suppress fire around the camp. That do it for you?"

"Good as it's gonna get, ain't it?" Cozart replied. He looked over at his copilot, who was grinning in anticipation. "Tell the boys back there to get ready. Here we go."

Sam Gutierrez watched the last of the lift helicopters fade out of sight before walking back to the tactical operations center. He felt an ache in the pit of his stomach that was not altogether attributable to the indigenous rations he'd had for breakfast.

Damn, he thought. I should be up there.

He was not unaccustomed to sending men into combat. But it never seemed right not to be leading them himself. From the moment when, as a young second lieutenant in the Twenty-fourth Infantry Division, he had been given the mission of holding a critical mountain pass against the North Korean invaders, he'd been leading troops in life-or-death situations. And had found, much to his surprise, that he was good at it. His platoon had delayed the advance of the enemy for twelve critical hours, allowing the Americans and their allies to strengthen the Pusan perimeter the amount necessary to deny the communists final victory. For that action, he had been awarded his first Silver Star.

He'd also found himself assigned as a junior aide to the division commander, a job he hated. And when volunteers

had been solicited for something called the United Nations
Partisan Command (UNPIC), and he'd found out that it
involved guerrilla warfare and commando raids against the
North Korean rear, he had immediately volunteered. And
had been accepted, much against the wishes of the division
commander.

"You've got a fine career ahead of you," the general had
said. "Top of your class at the Citadel, excellent combat
record, maximum efficiency reports. You could be a general
someday. You want to piss all that away, running around
with a bunch of crazy assholes? If you don't get yourself
killed, which is very likely, you're going to be out of the
mainstream. Regular officers, and those are the ones on the
promotion boards, don't like people out of the mainstream."

It was a remarkably long speech for such a taciturn officer and affected Sam Gutierrez not at all. What the general
didn't realize was that Sam didn't necessarily want to be in
the mainstream. Even in the short time he'd been in the
Army, he'd seen the difference between those on the promotion track and those who did the job. The former were
always looking over their shoulders, worried that the next
action might put an indelible blot upon their records. So
largely, they did nothing at all, until forced into it. And when
they did do something, they made sure there was someone
else upon whom they could throw the blame.

The doers, on the other hand, didn't give a damn about
their records. And it often showed. Many of them were
World War II vets, some of whom had been company commanders and battalion commanders in Europe and the
Pacific, who had been reduced in rank to sergeant after the

war. Now that the country needed them again, they had been restored to former positions and were leading troops day to day in heavier combat than most had seen even during the bad old days of the world war.

After this war they would probably be reduced again, and most of them didn't really care. His old company commander had once told him that he believed he had the best, and most important, rank in the military. A captain had enough rank to influence the action, but not so much that he got pulled off into a staff somewhere. He would, he declared, be happy to stay a captain until the day he died.

He'd achieved that wish, his life cut short by a North Korean artillery shell only a few days later.

Sam Gutierrez had seen the truth in the general's statements in the years after the Korean War. His contemporaries had gone on to command companies, serve on battalion staffs, in a couple of cases even command infantry battalions. They had been decorated profusely by a grateful Army, while Sam had to content himself with the single Silver Star. UNPIC had been notoriously stingy with awards and decorations, the attitude being that everyone was doing things well above and beyond the call of duty, so how could you distinguish yourself from all the others in your same position? It was the same attitude he'd later found in the Special Forces.

Which he'd joined, almost as soon as it had been formed. His next few years were spent leading teams in Germany, Okinawa, South America. Always a captain, as his contemporaries were promoted well past. His regular Army commission saved him from the reduction in force (RIF) that decimated the ranks of the reserve officers throughout the fifties, a situation he found unfair in the extreme. The very best of the reserve officers were soon gone, and with them the leadership of the lower ranks, leaving the troops at the mercy of regular officers who couldn't hold a candle to their reserve contemporaries.

But that was the way it was, and he soon became resigned to it. He was having fun, doing important things, while the rest of the army was concerning itself with IG inspections, and CMMIs, and spit-shined boots, and changing the color of their uniforms.

He made his first trip to Vietnam in 1957, on a TDY tour from Okinawa. Had realized that, barring giving up, the United States was going to be heavily involved in the insurgency and had set about learning all he could about the country. Other TDY tours followed, sometimes teaching Vietnamese Ranger battalions tactics and weaponry, sometimes honing the skills of the men of what was to become the Vietnamese Special Forces, and finally building a fighting camp on the Cambodian border and leading Civilian Irregular Defense Group personnel against the Viet Cong and North Vietnamese who thought they owned the area.

Still a captain, he'd been surprised and somewhat dismayed when, shortly after that tour, he'd found himself promoted to major. The Army was once again needing experienced combat officers, and he was one of the most experienced of all. Two years later he was promoted to lieutenant colonel.

And was, finally, in a position he detested. Sitting behind, on the radio, as men he should have been leading left without him.

"You got commo with the camp?" he asked.

"I'll get it, sir," Lloyd Johnson, his operations sergeant, said. Ordinarily he might have made a wiseass comment. But something in the old man's demeanor told him it would be best to keep his mouth shut and do as he was told.

Colonel Gutierrez was a world-class ass-chewer. And today, Johnson suspected, anybody foolish enough to get into his sights was going to have a real problem.

Chapter 2

"Trung Ui Sloane, somebody on the horn for you," Sergeant Alvin Becker, the junior commo sergeant, said.

Sloane turned reluctantly away from the bunker embrasure, where he had been scoping out the surrounding terrain with the Zeiss binoculars he'd purchased at Abercrombie and Fitch, so many years ago it seemed now, though it had only been a few months. The excellent optics picked out flashes of movement, khaki-clad soldiers who never exposed themselves long enough for the sniper to get a shot at them. Sometimes they raised pith helmets on sticks, an old trick, but usually enough to get one of the Montagnard soldiers on the perimeter to fire at it, whereupon their own snipers opened up on him.

"I don't have time for that right now," he said. "I've got a battle to fight here."

"I think you better take it," Sergeant Becker replied. "It's Charlie Six."

Sloane scowled at the impertinence of the sergeant. He was yet another one who would be written up, once this was over. By now every surviving member of the team had a black mark against him in Sloane's little notebook. Insubordination, refusal to obey a legitimate order, insolence—the list ran into several pages.

But he thought it best not to ignore the call. He remembered the C team commander looking at him in disbelief and barely disguised scorn as he went through his litany of qualifications, finally silencing him with his own silence.

"That's very impressive," Gutierrez had finally said, his voice clearly indicating how little impressed he was. "But irrelevant. I'm assigning you to A-228, Camp Boun Tlak. Get out there, listen to your NCOs, try to stay out of the way. Maybe you'll learn something. Dismissed."

Sloane's face still burned at the thought of it. Damned Mexican, anyway. What did he know! Some things, he thought, should not have been changed from the old days, when officers came from one class, and other ranks included the Negroes and Irish and Mexicans and whatever other riffraff was necessary to throw into the mouths of the cannon.

"Bravo Tango, do you read me?" came the tinny voice over the radio, sounding irritated. Wordlessly, Becker thrust the handset at him.

"I read you Lima Charlie, Six," he said. "This is Bravo Tango Six, over."

" 'Bout damned time," the voice on the radio answered. "Operation Habu is under way. Be ready."

Sloane grimaced. He'd already insisted that the camp didn't need to be reinforced, that given enough airpower they could hold out forever if necessary. Gutierrez had overruled him. He'd opened his mouth to protest again, thought better of it. Lieutenant Colonel Sam Gutierrez could be quite profane when crossed. Just another sign of his ill breeding.

"Roger, Six," he said. "Estimated time of arrival?"

"Why don't I just tell you that, in the clear, so everybody can be ready," Gutierrez said, sarcasm heavy on his voice.

Sloane colored again, looked sharply over at Becker, who was trying to keep a smirk off his lips. "I understand, Colonel."

Over the handset came a truly inspired stream of profanity, the point of which being that you never gave someone's rank over the radio, that now Gutierrez was going to have to change his call sign, and that obviously Bravo Tango Six hadn't learned a damned thing since he'd been there. Sloane stood there and took it, there being no other choice with Becker watching him. To make matters worse, his nemesis, Master Sergeant Billy Joe Turner, came in just as it was trailing off. He knew the story would be all over the camp within minutes.

"Sorry, Six," he mumbled. Finally Gutierrez signed off with the admonition to not fuck this one up.

Becker started to say something, was stilled with a glare. "Mike Force is coming in," Sloane told Turner. "Get the troops ready."

"They never stopped being ready, sir," Turner replied in that laconic Tennessee drawl that seemed to take forever to get the words out. "We know how many?"

"More than we need, I'm sure."

Turner grinned. "Ain't you the feisty one." He turned to Becker. "See if you can get it arranged to take some of the wounded out on the last lift. We got about ten criticals, won't make it through the night."

"Got it, Sarge," Becker said, literally snapping to.

That was another thing, Sloane thought. Why didn't the troops show him the same respect they showed the old, barely literate team sergeant. Another notation for his book.

Turner looked back at him, the smile still curling his lips. "Ain't had enough fight yet, I take it?"

Not nearly enough, Sloane thought, not bothering to answer the question, turning back to the embrasure and lifting the binoculars. But I will. And not even high-and-mighty Mike Force can stop me.

Turner shrugged, raised his eyebrows at Becker, turned, and left the bunker. Outside the smell of burning wood mixed with feces was strong. During the last mortar barrage the shithouse had taken a direct hit. It was going to be slit trenches from now on.

Not that he thought it would be a problem. His asshole was so tight, he'd told the team medic, you couldn't have driven an eight-penny nail up it with a ten-pound sledge.

Turner, like most of the Americans in the camp, the new lieutenant being the only exception, was a multiple-tour veteran of Vietnam, plus had been on one of the old White Star teams in Laos. He'd seen his share of combat—more than his share, if you wanted to know the truth—and couldn't remember a time he'd been more frightened. Firefights in the jungle, you always knew that if you didn't get hit early, and if the enemy proved too strong, you could break contact and escape. When your own team initiated the firefights, it was because you knew you could win them. And on the recon missions he'd run across the border into Laos and Cambodia for SOG, the team was so small you could work your way around even the most determined of trackers and, if worse came to worst, call in enough air to keep them off your back until you could get emergency extraction.

Now there was no retreat, no way of breaking contact and escaping, no punching through the cordon of troops surrounding the camp. All exits were closed. Air helped keep them off you for a while, but the trenches were getting closer, and no matter how many strikes there were, there were always diggers to take the place of the ones who had been killed.

Uniforms from the bodies of those killed during the frequent probes indicated they were facing the Sixty-sixth NVA and Twenty-eighth NVA Infantry Regiments. There would be, Turner knew, an NVA artillery regiment in support. Though he had seen no evidence of it, he was also fairly certain there would be yet another NVA infantry regiment in reserve.

Over a division of enemy troops, against his pitiful force of four Civilian Irregular Defense Group companies, something like odds of nine or ten to one. The Mike Force company, if it managed to get in the camp in anything like good order, would help a little bit, but not much. Classic infantry doctrine said that the attackers needed a three-to-one ratio to assure victory against fortified defenses, but classic infantry doctrine wasn't worth a shit over here. Classic infantry doctrine assumed that even if the enemy did make a breakthrough, you could bring up your own reserves and pinch it off. There were going to be no reserves here.

He hunched down and ran from the command bunker to the 120mm mortar pit, where SFC Andy "Big Polack"

Stankow and his indigenous mortar crew were pumping rounds into "danger close" targets just outside the wire. The tube was pointed almost straight up. Smoke from the propellant had stained the big sergeant's skin so dark he looked like a giant Montagnard.

"Mike Force be here in twenty," he said.

" 'Bout goddamn time," Stankow grumbled, his accent heavy. "They miss fight otherwise, eh?"

"I'm sure they'd be real sorry about that," Turner replied, grinning affectionately at his heavy weapons specialist, who hadn't paused for a second. A line of Montagnard soldiers snaked its way to the nearby ammo bunker, daisy-chaining the heavy shells to the pit. Four of them were bandaged from shrapnel wounds, and one showed bleeding through the gauze. Turner made a mental note to have the medic come over and check him out.

"I'll give you the word to check fire," he said.

"Better not have to check too long," Stankow replied. "Dey be all over our ass, we don't keep shooting."

"How's your ammo supply?"

"Dat's de good news. Ve got enough to last two, maybe three more days. Not like old days when we shoot three rounds at Germans and run like hell."

Stankow had, as a teenager, joined the partisans fighting the German invaders, killing his first soldier when he was barely fifteen. He'd approached the soldier, who had been drinking wine stolen from a manor house, and had thrust a knife into his stomach. The soldier, barely older than he had been, asked only, "Why?"

It still bothered him. He'd told the story to Turner one

night when both of them had been drinking far too much, to explain why he hadn't killed a Viet Cong sentry when the man had been within easy knife range.

He had no trouble in killing at a distance, however. He dropped another round down the tube, the *whomf* of the propellant driving the air out of the chests of those standing near. Another round, a slight adjustment of the elevating and traversing mechanism, and another.

A rushing sound like an aircraft arcing across the sky, and Turner crouched low in the trench. The NVA shell landed not ten meters away, throwing up a huge cloud of dirt and rocks, the smell of high explosives so powerful it felt as if his nostrils had been burned right out of his head. He raised up, saw that the mortar crew had resumed their firing.

"Charlie gonna get your range, one of these times," he said.

Stankow grunted contemptuously. "Shitty goddamn gunners. Must have been trained by the Russians."

Turner laughed. If there was one thing that Stankow hated worse than the Vietnamese, it was the Russians. Get him started on that and he would hold forth all night.

No time for that. Turner passed through the mortar pit, took another trench, and headed for the dispensary. Going to have to let the medics know to get ready for casualties, he thought. Heavy casualties.

He just didn't see how the Mike Force was going to get in there without getting shot to pieces.

Lieutenant Sloane didn't either, and it didn't, frankly, bother him. Actually, he thought as he idly listened to Becker tap out confirmation of the LZ arrangements on the keypad attached to his leg, it might be better all around if there was a debacle.

It would just go to show how desperate the battle really was.

A warrior is judged by the quality of his enemies, he remembered reading somewhere. Probably something the instructors at West Point had tried to drill into the heads of the plebes. There was no glory in defeating someone who was clearly your inferior. They had to be almost larger-than-life, possessing either great advantages in numbers or being so wily that your own numbers didn't count.

Sloane was a student of history, but not of the history that the victors wrote. He liked to look beneath, to see the machinations of the writers, the biographers, the propagandists.

Such things were essential. After all, how could you win the requisite glory, for instance, in fighting a bunch of ragtag, half-starved Plains Indians whose numbers never achieved, even in their years of greatest triumph, anything like the numbers of soldiers against them. And yet the Plains Indians campaign streamers were proudly displayed on the guidons of the cavalry brigades, even to this day. And people still admired the soldierly qualities of Crook, the ruthlessness of Sheridan, and the doomed gallantry of Custer.

Here, he had it all. Nothing had to be invented. The North Vietnamese had a huge numerical advantage. They had the tactic of "hugging the belt," staying so close to friendly lines that the American advantage of airpower was in large part nullified. Their commanders were combat-seasoned through ten or more years of constant warfare. The press back home portrayed them as dedicated, almost fanatical fighters.

All the better then to win that which he must have. To prove to his father that he wasn't the weakling, the pansy, the useless piece of shit that dear old dad, especially when he had been drinking (and that was an almost constant in the last few years), was fond of calling him.

Sloane senior had been a tank battalion commander under Patton during the Battle of the Bulge. Had been in the race to relieve the embattled paratroopers of the 101st Airborne Division at Bastogne. Had missed being in the lead tank penetrating the perimeter only by a matter of minutes, being beat out by that goddamn, as he inevitably called him, Abrams. Had won the Distinguished Service Cross, three Silver Stars, and other combat decorations too numerous to count and had returned to the States a full colonel. Had later been promoted, below the zone, to brigadier general and then to major general.

And had then seen his career stall in a peacetime army that had no use for so many World War II generals. Even Korea didn't help a great deal, as he missed the entire war being stuck in a desk job in the Pentagon. Embittered, he'd turned increasingly to drink, which had only exacerbated the problem, and had gently been encouraged to retire.

Bentley's grandfather, who had made lieutenant general, had scorned his son's weaknesses. And Sloane senior had passed the favors on down to his own son.

That would soon end. Not since the Civil War had a Sloane won the ultimate prize. The starry blue ribbon that said it all.

That was soon going to change.

• • •

Billy Joe Turner was still in the trench when the rocket barrage came in. One moment he was crouched down, making
his way beneath a couple of logs, the next he had been
picked up and smashed against the log, dislodging one with
his head, and a moment thereafter he was sprawled in the
bottom of the trench gasping for breath. A second round
came in, and a third, each picking him up bodily and flinging
him back down. Loosened dirt cascaded down into his face,
and he had one brief, horrible thought of being buried alive.
He scrambled to his knees, only to be knocked down once
again as yet more rockets came in.

And then it was over, and the total silence at first convinced him his eardrums had been shattered. Sure enough
when he felt his ears, his hand came away with blood.

And then he heard a high, keening wail, from somewhere
behind him. Other sounds started to intrude, a couple of
shouts, a moan, and someone screaming for a medic. He
peeked up over the edge of the trench, was astounded by the
complete devastation. Clouds of dust obscured the perimeter, anything that had survived above ground was now gone,
and there were a couple of bundles of rags that he knew had
only minutes before been men.

The medical bunker had taken a direct hit, and it
appeared the roof had collapsed. It was from there that most
of the shouting came.

He measured the distance between his position and that
of the bunker. Close to a hundred yards, right out in the
open. But to get there following the trench line would take
him nearly a half kilometer out of the way. If the trench

hadn't collapsed in a dozen places, which seemed likely given the ferocity of the attack.

Screw it, he thought.

He scrambled up over the side of the trench, got to his feet, and nearly fell down again. Whatever damage had been done inside his head had thoroughly screwed up his equilibrium. He staggered forward, concentrating upon putting one foot in front of the other, realizing that he must look like a drunk trying to make his way home.

The snipers started getting his range, as he had known they would. The first round cracked just a few inches behind his head; another kicked up dust at his feet before whining crazily out across the camp. Better get a move on, Billy Joe, he told himself. How many times have you told people, these bastards never learned the concept of lead? Keep moving, zigzag a little, and the bullets will always be a little behind you.

Zigzagging shouldn't be a problem. Now run, dammit!

Sloane got up off the floor where he had flung himself when the first rocket had come in, staring in horror at the chunk of shrapnel that had come whizzing through the embrasure, still so hot it was scorching the sandbags into which it had embedded. If I hadn't ducked, he was thinking, that would have taken the top of my head off at just about the eyes.

Sergeant Becker was already on the radio, giving Gutierrez a sitrep. Approximately twelve rockets, he was saying, estimated to be 122 millimeter. Casualty report to follow.

He sounded absolutely cool and collected. Anyone on the other end would have thought he had nerves of steel.

Unless you were able to look into his eyes, Sloane mused. He's as scared as I am!

The thought was somehow comforting.

He looked back out the embrasure just in time to see Sergeant Turner hauling himself over the edge of the trench and watch as the first rounds kicked up dust around him. "Get back in the trench!" he screamed, knowing it was useless. The rattle of small-arms fire was becoming constant. Was this the attack for which they'd been waiting?

No, he thought. Not during the daytime. They wouldn't dare that, not with American air stacked up and waiting for targets. This was just another harassing attack, doing their best to soften us up, get us ready for the kill.

It looked like they were going to achieve at least a part of their goal. The bullets were striking ever closer to Turner, who had at least managed to accomplish a shambling run.

"Go, go, go!" Becker screamed, now at the embrasure beside Sloane. Becker turned, shouted that he was going to go out there.

"Stay here!" Sloane commanded. "That's an order. You stay on that radio."

Becker looked at him in utter contempt, for a moment appearing to be ready to defy the order.

"I'll do it," Sloane said, picking up his M16. "Anything happens, you'll be here to tell them about it." He left the bunker.

Becker watched him as he ran, hunched over, down the trench toward the spot where Turner had left it.

Maybe I misjudged him, he thought.

Nah! Just wants a fucking medal. He don't watch his ass, he's gonna get the CMH.

A Coffin with Metal Handles.

Turner was hit the first time not twenty-five yards away from the trench. Just at the moment he'd realized his equilibrium was coming back somewhat, and that he could chance running faster without the possibility of falling down.

He'd been panting like a dog from the effort, and that had probably saved his life. The bullet passed through his right cheek, cut a quarter-inch groove across his tongue, and smashed through the molars on the left side of his jaw. The impact broke the jaw, but worse was the damage done by the now-tumbling bullet and the tooth fragments turned into secondary projectiles. They tore a terrifying hole through his left cheek, spraying blood and bits of flesh like a blood-filled fire hose.

Had his mouth been closed the bullet would have taken off his entire lower jaw, probably including carotid arteries and jugular veins. He would have died within moments.

As it was, the impact spun him around, and for a confused moment he started to run back the way he had come. Then he came to a complete stop, turned around again, and with great dignity shot a defiant finger into the sky.

He started running again, the droplets of blood from his ruined cheek leaving a trail that was soon disturbed by the bullets hitting all around him. Thirty-five yards, then fifty. Jesus, would the place never get any closer? Maybe I should have gone back to the trench, let someone else take care of the guys in the bunker. I could be hiding down there right now, trying to get something around this hole in my face. There was no pain, a phenomenon he was familiar with from suffering the impacts of bullets and shrapnel before. Pain would come later.

If there was a later. Too late to go back to the trench now, buddy boy. Over halfway there. Run faster, steps now taking in feet rather than the inches they were when you started. You can make this!

The next bullet hit him just above the hip, barely missing his kidney. Its downward angle drove it through the pelvic girdle, puncturing the ball joint where femur attached to hip. Suddenly his left leg refused to work. Slowly, almost stately in its progress, his body sprawled facedown on the dirt.

Only one thing to do now, Billy Joe, he told himself.

You damned well better crawl.

Lieutenant Sloane reached Turner's jumping-off point at almost exactly the same time the sergeant was felled by the last bullet. He took several deep breaths, readying himself for the dash. His concentration upon the mission at hand was so fierce he did not at first notice the slackening of small-arms fire.

Sergeant Stankow, who had been coming from the other direction, did. He stuck his shaggy head up above the trench, glanced around, saw that the only fire at the moment was outgoing.

"Bait," he said.

Sloane looked at him, not fully comprehending what he was saying.

"Sniper could kill him now, he wants," Stankow said.

"Doesn't want. He's waiting for somebody to come out, try to help. Gets two or three that way." He mused for a moment, thinking back to the bad old days in the forests near Warsaw.

"Same thing we used to do to the Germans," he said.

"So what do we do?" Sloane asked, realizing for the first time just how far out of his depth he was.

Stankow grinned. "Same thing we were gonna do. Only fast."

Turner forced himself to dig his elbows into the dirt, using them and his good leg to move slowly, achingly forward. Now there was pain, from the jaw, from the hip, from everyplace, it seemed, on his body.

Easier just to lie here, let it happen, he thought.

No! That's just what they want you to do. They know somebody is going to try to come and get you. You lie here, they'll end up killing someone else.

Crawl, damnit!

A round smacked into the dirt two inches in front of his face, kicking dirt into his eyes. Then another, and a third, all three within an inch of one another. Slow, measured shots.

Playing with me now, Turner thought. Telling me he can take my head off, anytime he wants. Telling me to lie still, don't move.

"Fuck you, Jack," he tried to say, his swollen tongue filling his mouth so thoroughly it came out as a grunt.

He crawled forward.

Staff Sergeant Benjamin "Bucky" Epstein finally reached the gun position toward which he'd been crawling. The

Montagnard crew was nowhere in sight. Probably in a bunker, he thought, waiting for the next attack. Don't blame them. The position was terribly exposed, as it almost had to be to be effective.

He was relieved to see that the 106-millimeter recoilless rifle—stolen from the First Cavalry Division—seemed to be unharmed. The 106, a direct-fire weapon, was mounted on a little hill at almost the exact center of the camp. It had to be mounted high to be able to clear the structures around it both for its trajectory and because the backblast when it fired would rip the top right off a bunker or tear a man in two. The lower part, along with ammunition stores, was shielded by a triple wall of stacked sandbags, and it was behind these that he now took cover.

In successive bobs, looking like a duck continually diving beneath the surface of a pond, he determined that the .50-caliber spotter rifle was loaded, and that a round of high explosive was in the tube of the 106.

Now, he sent his thoughts out to the unseen sniper, where the hell are you?

"Ready?" Sloane asked.

Stankow grinned. "Vy not?"

Sloane took another deep breath. Stray thoughts ran through his mind.

Is this going to be it? Am I going to die here on this godforsaken piece of ground, trying to help a man I don't even like? Will anybody recognize what we did here? Will anyone care?

Will it get me what I want?

And the answer came back, a resounding NO!

Then best I don't die, he told himself, even as he scrambled up over the edge of the trench, barely aware that Stankow was only fractions of a second behind him.

It was like one of his nightmares, the one where he was fleeing some unknown enemy that sometimes took on the look of his father, the one who, if it caught you, would do some unimaginable evil. And you were trying so hard to get away, but your legs felt like they were moving through thick molasses, feet sticking to the ground so hard you had to use all your strength to pull them out, and all you wanted to do was lie down and let it happen, but you couldn't, and you kept going simply because there was no other choice, and OH, GOD, here it comes. . . .

The sniper, well hidden under a canopy of freshly picked leaves and branches some six hundred meters out, cursed as he tried to track the runners through the relatively small field of view of the scope on his Dragunov rifle. He wished he had the Leatherman scope they'd shown him back in school, captured from a Marine sniper outside Da Nang. But the Russian instructors had used the Leatherman only to show how superior was their own technology. And truly, the optics had seemed better. But only when shooting at stationary targets.

Not against people like this, who seemed to have wings on their feet.

His first round went somewhere that he could not see, and his spotter told him he was inches—inches!—behind the bigger one.

Never mind. Another round was already in the chamber—the advantage of having a semiautomatic rifle instead of the bolt actions the Americans favored. And there were eight more behind that. All he had to do was hit one of them. Then the other wouldn't be able to pull both men to safety. He would have to either abandon the attempt or pull them one at a time out of the exposed zone.

Either way, he would win. One more American-Killer medal. More whispers around the campfire, the other soldiers eyeing him with almost superstitious awe. He sighted through the scope again, this time allowing for six inches more lead. He pulled the trigger.

This is it, Sloane thought as they reached Turner. No way in hell is he going to miss again.

Six rounds had been fired at them since they'd entered the open area. Each one getting closer and closer. The only reason, he supposed, they hadn't already been hit was that Stankow and he were varying their pace, moving as erratically as possible. But now they'd have to try to scoop up Turner and make the other twenty-five yards to the safety of the nearest trench.

They'd never make it. One or both of them was going to take a bullet, and then it would all be over.

He considered his options. Keep on running seemed to be the best. No one could blame him for refusing to die for no reason. Turner was a goner. He would shortly bleed to death. Did it make any sense for them to join him?

With a groan he grabbed Turner's left arm just as Stankow grabbed his right. The sergeant seemed impossibly heavy.

Was he already dead? Was all this going to be for nothing?

Turner groaned in pain as they hoisted him, each wrapping an arm around his shoulders, moving forward as quickly as possible as they did so.

It wasn't going to be quick enough.

Now! the sniper told himself as he centered the reticle on the head of the heavy one, then moved it two inches forward. His concentration was so intense that he paid no attention to his spotter, who screamed in fear as a heavy round smashed into the tree inches above their heads. A puff of white smoke, for a second obscuring his vision. He cursed, again took up the sight picture.

It all ends here, he thought.

Bucky Epstein had finally caught the muzzle flash of the sniper rifle. He centered the spotter scope on the spot, fired the .50-caliber spotter round. The tracer arced outward, seemingly slow in its passage but in reality moving at twenty-six hundred feet per second. It finally hit a tree just above the spot where he'd seen the flash, the white phosphorous smoke bright against the green.

Good enough for government work, he thought, and fired the main gun.

Sloane and Stankow heard the roar of the recoilless rifle, followed shortly thereafter by the far-off impact of the high-explosive shell. They were dragging Turner toward the nearest trench, both tensed against the impact of the bullet they knew had to be on its way.

Ten feet, fifteen, twenty. And still no bullet. For a moment Sloane allowed himself just a little bit of hope.

Then came a scattering of small-arms fire, kicking up dirt in random patterns around them. Not out of danger yet.

But this was not the precision fire that they'd been waiting for. It was a bunch of NVA, cheated of their prize, trying by barrage to take it back. This was chance fire. And chance was all they needed.

And suddenly it was there. He dropped down into the trench, pulling Turner gently in behind him, as Stankow did the same from the other side.

It was over. The firestorm died almost as quickly as it had started.

He would have laughed in joy, but didn't have enough air left in his lungs.

Chapter 3

Though he had done it many times, it never ceased to amaze Finn McCulloden how quickly you could get chilled riding in the open door of a Huey. Down in the jungle, hundreds of feet below, it would be so hot you'd suck the bottom right out of a canteen after walking a couple of hundred meters, your tiger-stripe fatigues blossoming with white salt stains. Here, the wind whistling by at over a hundred knots, you always cursed yourself for not wearing a sleeping sweater.

No matter. He'd be back in the heat soon enough, and probably wouldn't have had time to take the sweater off and store it anyway.

He wondered how many hundreds of North Vietnamese troops were watching the flight overhead, watching and waiting. They wouldn't be potting any stray shots, not unless they were fairly certain it would do some good. The "snakes," Cobra gunships that accompanied the formation, made sure of that. They just loved to swarm on some poor, unsuspecting troop who made such a foolish mistake.

A patrol had once found a shot-up North Vietnamese

lieutenant, still raging about the stupidity of his troops. "I told them, no shoot at skinny helicopter," he told his captors. "But they no listen. Now look." And he pointed to a wiped-out platoon, bodies already swelling from the jungle heat.

No, the danger wasn't here, not at least unless the NVA had managed to move in some of the radar-guided ZSU-23s that were increasingly showing up. In such a case, the first they'd know about it would be when the first round exploded somewhere under the Plexiglas of the cockpit, with the rest of the burst walking down the fuselage. In which case, there wouldn't be time to worry about it anyway.

No, the danger would come when they swung around, dropped altitude, and started flying down the riverbed. The snakes would be providing suppressive fire, but if the enemy was dug in, as they were likely to be, the suppressive fire of rockets and miniguns wasn't going to do all that much good.

He couldn't imagine that they were going to make it unscathed. The only question was, could they make it at all?

Somewhere deep in his brain was the question, should we be doing this? Some might have argued that the camp was lost anyway, that one Mike Force company wasn't going to do much to help. Why send good after bad?

It was a measure of how things were, and how they'd always been among the members of the Special Forces, that such things were kept to the back of the brain, like some dirty little secret. Your friends were in trouble, you went in to get them. That's just how it was. No matter if the "friend" you were going in to help was a complete stranger, or as had happened at least once, it was someone who had been caught screwing your wife back at Fort Bragg.

The ship banked a hard left and started losing altitude. His gut tightened up as it always did, muscles squeezing the diaphragm so tight he had to forcibly gasp for air. The Montagnards sitting next to him, almost as one, tucked the Buddhas they wore around their necks between their teeth. If you died with Buddha in you mouth, they had told him, you were assured of reaching nirvana.

Often he wished he had his own religion in which to believe. Unfortunately, he didn't. The Southern Baptist preachers of his youth had permanently turned him off anything to do with God or the hereafter. He'd told one particularly persistent chaplain, there to bless the troops before a combat operation—never mind that there wasn't a Christian in the bunch—that of course he believed in the hereafter.

I plan to be live so long, I'll be here after you're gone, he'd said.

False bravado. Now he was as frightened as he'd ever been. He didn't want to die, felt that the universe simply couldn't exist outside him. The thought of not-being jangled with his here-and-now, with no room for compromise.

Down now, almost on the treetops. The chopper had to flare up to miss a particularly tall one, scattering the monkeys inhabiting the upper branches into chittering flight.

I know how you feel, he told them.

And then they were down into the riverbed, the trees now flashing by on both sides, the chopper fire-walled. Hell, he thought, they don't have to shoot us. All it would take would be a good strong wire strung across the stream. No way to see it in aerial photos, no time for the pilot to avoid it even if he did catch a glimpse of taut-strung metal. Down they'd go, the crash killing them all. Then the fuel would go, which would cook off all the ordnance. All a Bright Light team would find, assuming they could ever get in there in the first place, would be chunks of tooth and bone. He knew. He'd had to recover remains of just such crashes often enough.

Behind them the other choppers dropped down into the riverbed. Smart guys, he thought of the NVA who must now be taking them into their sights, attempting to judge the necessary lead to bring down the fast-moving choppers. One ship might get through, but the ones following are sure to run into the burst. Get one, and the others are going to have to try like hell to avoid it, there being scant seconds to pull pitch and get up over the wreckage.

And still he hadn't heard the telltale *spang* of bullet meeting sheet metal. He wasn't much of a gambler, but would have bet a couple of months' pay that they would be taking heavy fire by now.

Up front Cozart looked for all the world as if he were taking a pleasure trip, stick held loosely in his hand, swerving just in time to match the winding course of the river, his mouth moving in a steady stream of conversation with the other pilots.

Finn knew just how deceiving the impression was. He'd gotten drunk enough with Wes Cozart to know he was as scared as anyone else there. His hindbrain would be chattering in fear, just as Finn's was now. But what he called his "manual override" would be in charge, doing exactly the right thing at exactly the right moment. You didn't have that, he'd said to Finn, your fear will take over. Then you'll make a mistake. And it will be your last one.

The snakes were holding fire, conserving ammunition while they waited for a target. If it hadn't been for the wind roaring through the door and the whop of the blades, it would have been eerily quiet.

Finn recognized the characteristic bend in the river that marked the halfway point, flashing by underneath as Cozart neatly banked the chopper. Maybe, just maybe, Wes had been right. Maybe the NVA commander wouldn't have thought anyone so foolish as to come up the riverbed.

Which meant, of course, that they would be concentrated around the camp. Right under where they'd have to come up and over the trees to get to the LZ. And by now the watchers who were absolutely sure to be beneath them would have radioed the warning.

The easy way is always mined, he remembered an old team sergeant saying. Never more true than today.

He saw the final checkpoint coming up just as a stream of green tracers reached up toward the chopper, the gunner quickly adjusting for lead. Here it comes, he thought.

A Cobra pilot who just happened to be in the right place at the right time centered the spot in his sights and let go a burst of minigun fire, the sound like an elephant fart. Every fifth round was a tracer, the gun shooting so fast that it looked like a hose of fire. The last green tracer winked out just behind the tail boom.

And amazingly, there was no other willing to take the chance. Scared them enough? Finn wondered.

Not likely. He had a great deal of respect for the men down beneath them, particularly when it came to discipline. Likely they would be just as frightened as he, but they would hold their positions, obey their orders, until they could not.

Just like him. Just like the troops he led.

Nope, he thought. They're just waiting. Likely that last gunner didn't get the word and paid the price for it. Always that 10 percent.

Cozart was pulling pitch again, the chopper straining to come up over the trees. Finn caught his first glimpse of the camp, looking more like a derelict refugee village than a fighting institution. Fires flared here and there, and a heavy pall of smoke obscured the south perimeter. Two hundred meters to the wire, he estimated, and another hundred to the LZ. Zigzag trenches everywhere outside the wire, with hundreds, or perhaps thousands, of rifles, machine guns, and rocket launchers pointed directly at his scared ass.

He realized he was, inexplicably, smiling.

Stankow cocked his head, listening. "Choppers coming in," he said. He bent back to his work, trying to splint Billy Joe Turner's leg so movement wouldn't cause any more damage.

Sloane listened. Sure enough, there was the whop-whop of an approaching Huey.

He could only hope that the team, what was left of it, would take care of the matter. Right now he couldn't do much. No radio, no means of communication at all, unless perhaps you wanted to sprint across that open ground again . . .

No. His bravery was gone, emptied out of him like water from a broken crock. He was content to stay here in the trench, help Stankow with Turner, try not to think about what might come next.

"Ve'll have to get him to the LZ," Stankow said. "Get him out of here. No more fighting for you, my friend."

Turner glared at him with the one eye that wasn't covered by the clumsy bandage Stankow had wrapped around his head in an effort to stop the profuse bleeding from his mouth and jaw. His tongue was far too swollen to say anything, though it was clear that he wanted to.

They'd gotten Turner into the shelter of what was left of the trench leading from the medical bunker, only to find the entire building had collapsed. Stankow had rooted around long enough to find morphine, serum albumin, and an assortment of bandages. Turner had asked with his eyes about Otis Matthesen, the senior medic, whom he had heard crying for help.

Stankow just shook his head. Matthesen's arm had been taken off at the shoulder by a fragment of the rocket. He'd bled to death while they had been in the race with the sniper.

If Turner had been standing right next to him, Stankow knew, he wouldn't have been able to help. There was simply not enough limb left to put a tourniquet on.

But he also knew that Turner would forever blame himself for not getting there in time. As he would probably have, himself. That was just the way things were.

He looked up over the trench again, this time seeing the bulbous nose of the Huey approaching, not a hundred yards out. Becker ran out of the command bunker and popped a yellow smoke. The pilot adjusted for wind direction, then quickly set the bird down, followed within seconds by another chopper. The skids hadn't touched the ground when the people spilled off. Stankow spotted a tall figure.

"Dai Uy," he yelled, "over here!"

The man came running over. Stankow now recognized him beneath the camouflage paint, and the recognition came as a great relief. Finn McCulloden had a reputation in II Corps. A reputation for never, ever, leaving anyone in the lurch.

"That Billy Joe Turner under there?" Finn asked. "God-damn, Billy Joe, you look like shit." He grinned at Stankow. "Been too long since I was a medic. Think I lost my bedside manner. How many others you got, need to get out of here?"

"Had ten, before the rocket attack," Stankow said. "Now I don't know how many."

"Get 'em ready," Finn said. "Bastards didn't shoot at us on the way in, can't imagine why, but I ain't gonna look a gift horse in the mouth. Billy Joe, you're leaving right now." He hoisted the sergeant by one arm, Stankow taking the other. Together they half-carried, half-dragged Turner to Cozart's chopper. From every portion of the camp, it seemed, came a stream of wounded men. Within seconds the chopper was loaded to maximum, as was the second. Wes gave him a thumbs-up, pulled pitch, and was soon no more than a speck in the distance. Long before he had cleared the wire the second two choppers came in, spilling their loads and taking on new ones. McCulloden let his NCOs deploy the troops—hell, he thought, they've been doing this as long as I have—as he helped with the medevac.

The more seriously wounded were being carried out now, borne on improvised stretchers, many of them already with that gray look that told of impending death. Most wouldn't survive the ride back to the launch site, far less make it to a hospital.

Didn't matter. The people watching would know that every effort to help them would be made, should they be in the same shape. Finn thought he owed it to them. After all, he'd owed them his life, often enough.

The second lift took off, and right on schedule the third one came in. He allowed himself a small sigh of relief. There had, even now, been only sporadic and ineffective fire coming from the outside. Maybe this part wasn't going to be so bad after all.

As they were loading the last of the wounded on the final bird, a Vietnamese in the uniform of a lieutenant of the Luc Luong Dac Biet (LLDB) came running up.

"I need go too," he screamed. "I wounded!" He waved a bandaged arm at the crew chief, who seemed inclined to block him to let one of the more obviously wounded Montagnard soldiers ahead of him.

He screamed something in Vietnamese, roughly pushing the Montagnard aside.

Finn looked into his eyes. In there was the stare of a frightened animal. Nothing there except fear so overwhelming it swamped out all other human qualities.

"Let him go," he told the crew chief. "No use to us, anyway."

The young specialist fourth class shrugged, allowed the Viet to get on the bird, where he trampled one of the stretcher cases, eliciting a moan of pain from the downed man.

"Cocksucker," the crew chief said, spitting the word out.

"Yeah, but he's our cocksucker. Now get the fuck out of here," Finn said. "Good luck!"

The crew chief snapped his smoked visor down, grabbed

the spade handles of the M60 machine gun. "You too, Cap'n,"
he shouted over the whine of the turbines. "Think you'll need
it more than I do."

McCulloden and Stankow ran toward the command
bunker, reaching it just as the telltale rush of incoming mortar
rounds filled the air. Three of them erupted with a crashing
roar near where they had been standing only seconds before.

"Guess they got tired of waiting," Stankow said.

"Impatient bastards, aren't they?" Sergeant Olchak said
as he came sliding over the side of the trench. "Got first platoon on the south wall, second on the east, third gonna be a
mobile reserve, keep 'em next to the ammo bunkers. That
okay?"

"Weapons platoon scattered where they'd do the most
good?"

"Way I figure it, Victor Charlie ain't gonna come across
the open ground to the north," Olchak replied. "So I put 'em
reinforcing first and second."

"Sounds good. I'll take a walk-around in a few minutes.
Sergeant Stankow . . ."

Finn's voice was drowned out by the roar of automatic
weapons fire, most of it seemed directed at the last chopper,
just now a hundred yards outside the wire. Tracers reached
up like long green fingers all around it. At least some of the
rounds had to be hitting it, he thought.

Sure enough, a cough of smoke came from the turbine,
and the chopper soon started losing altitude. The firing died
down; someone, Finn was sure, having given the order to let
them come down halfway intact. That way there would be
prisoners to take.

For a few moments they watched the chopper struggle to maintain altitude, and by sheer force of will and more capability than the designers of the bird had ever imagined, it seemed it was going to.

Not that it mattered. Maintaining altitude wasn't enough. The camp was in a bowl, with mountains all around. Flying at the same altitude would only result in the inevitable crash.

Then, incredibly, a figure was jettisoned from one of the doors, thrashing and flailing all the way to the ground. The chopper, relieved of even that small amount of weight, fairly leaped up. Within seconds it was over the top of the lowest mountain, albeit probably by inches.

"Reckon that LLDB lieutenant sacrificed himself for the good of the others?" Stankow said, keeping his face perfectly straight.

"That'd be my guess," Finn replied. "Come on, let's see what kind of rat fuck we got going here."

Son of a bitch not only didn't say hello, Sloane thought, he didn't even acknowledge I was here. Looked right through me.

His fury at the slight was complicated by his shame, the thought that the Mike Force commander was justified in his scorn. He had sat right there and allowed them to expose themselves to the terror of the open ground, carrying Turner to the helicopter so slowly that any halfway decent sniper could have taken their heads off at leisure.

He simply hadn't had it in him to go once more into the danger. The deliberate bravery he'd shown in going out there in the first place had flown away like the leaves in autumn.

It reopened the deep, dark well of insecurity so skillfully built by his father over the years of his childhood. Was the old man right, after all? Would he never amount to anything worthwhile? General Sloane had constantly compared him to the great men he had known: Patton, Bradley, even that midget Texan, as the old man had called him, Audie Murphy. You'll never come close to them, Sloane junior had been told, so many times he could have recited the speech verbatim. No one will. Their like shall not come this way again.

No! It won't happen that way. I can't let it. I'll do what I set out to do. Just isn't time yet. After all, wouldn't make much sense to piss my life away before it happens, would it? Bide your time, Sloane, he told himself. It will come.

But now he faced the daunting task of reestablishing his authority, under a man obviously determined to ignore it. To do that he had to get up out of this trench, face the dangers once again. Sheer force of will got him to his feet, and a burst of automatic weapons fire directed at something nearby almost put him down again.

Which vastly amused Sergeant Andy Inger, who had been busy taking care of the more minor casualties with which the camp seemed to be filled and was now coming down the trench to see what he could salvage from the ruined dispensary. That boy's a little gun-shy, he thought.

"You okay, *Trung Ui*?" he asked.

"About time somebody got over here," Sloane snapped. "Come help me. There could be other bodies under this wreckage."

Inger stifled the sharp retort that was just behind his lips.

The lieutenant was obviously under some strain, looked close to breaking. He'd speak to Captain McCulloden about it later. Best now to do what he'd intended to do in the first place, which coincidentally coincided with the lieutenant's demands.

He wormed his way past the collapsed doorway, to be met by the sight of Otis Matthesen's body, his blood—more than it seemed any man should carry—pooled on the hardpacked clay and already covered by flies. Matthesen had been one of his instructors in the Special Forces Surgical Lab, back at Fort Bragg. Back then Matthesen was a rarity, an SF medic who had never been in combat. This had earned him a reputation as a REMF, a Rear Echelon Mother-Fucker, and had even his students talking about him behind his back. What the hell does he know about gunshot wounds? they would ask. He's never seen one.

It wasn't his fault. Every time he'd volunteered for Vietnam, his request had been rejected. We need you here to teach the young medics, he had been told over and over. Besides, you're a master sergeant, and if you got to Vietnam, you'd be stuck in a C team somewhere, way back in the rear. Only combat you'd see would be with the MPs down in the ville.

Matthesen had finally solved that problem, with the simple but elegant solution of punching out the next officer who told him that. Whereupon he had summarily been reduced in rank to sergeant first class and had then told the company commander administering the punishment that he would do it again to the very next person who told him he couldn't go to Vietnam.

Now, in that cosmic game of chance that combat often is, he had been unlucky enough to have been standing in the entrance to the bunker when the first rocket came in and hit directly in front of it. The Chinese-made 122s were notoriously fickle. Some never exploded at all. When they did, their cases generally didn't fragment in any predictable pattern. You could be standing right next to the impact and, other than losing your eardrums from overpressure, suffer no more ill effects than that of concussion. The casing might break into two or three large pieces or split right down the middle and bury itself in the ground or, if the ground was particularly muddy, expend all its energy upward.

Or one of those huge, jagged chunks of metal, traveling at twenty-six hundred feet per second, could come straight at you. Lopping off a limb as quickly and effectively as would a red-hot guillotine.

Sorry 'bout that, Sergeant Matthesen, Inger silently told him. Hope you like it, wherever you are.

He heard the sounds of barely suppressed retching behind him, as if someone were having his breakfast come all the way up past the Adam's apple and being swallowed, with effort, back down again.

Inger knew how he felt. No matter how many times you saw violent death, it always came as a new shock. What had once been a man was now an empty sack of rapidly decomposing flesh, all his hopes and dreams and plans now gone to who knew where?

All the assholes back in the world, he thought, who talk about the glory of war, the honor of dying for one's country—they should see this. No glory. Certainly no dignity. Just sad.

To avoid embarrassing the lieutenant even more than he was already embarrassed, Inger occupied himself by taking his poncho from the indigenous rucksack all the Mike Force troopers carried and quickly covered the body. "We'll pick him up later," he told Sloane. "Get him out when all this is over."

Sloane stiffened his face, realizing that he was being handled. But there was little he could do about it. What was he going to do, chew out the medic for doing something he should have done?

"We could shore up this entrance," Inger continued. "Rest of the bunker looks okay. We may need the space before it's over. Can you get me some of your 'Yards to help?"

Grateful for something useful to do, Sloane acquiesced. Outside the bunker he took in a great draft of explosives-contaminated air, then fell into a fit of coughing. Which then brought up the breakfast he had been trying at such cost to contain.

God! he thought. I hope nobody's watching this.

"Stankow told me what happened," McCulloden said. "Good shooting, Bucky."

Sergeant Epstein acknowledged the compliment with scarcely a change of expression. He was still pissed that he hadn't seen the sniper earlier, before Turner had got hit in the first place.

But he took some solace in the memory of a sniper rifle spinning slowly through the air, like the baton thrown by a twirler at a Fourth of July parade.

He'd occupied himself after that shot by sending round

after round of high explosive at any target that showed
temerity enough to put another shot into the camp. He was
fairly certain he'd managed to hit at least one of the machine
guns that had shot up the last chopper.

Now, he was fairly certain, it would be time to move the
gun. The NVA forward observers had had plenty of time to
see where the fire was coming from, would have registered
the big guns on it, and would blast him right out of this
bunker if he stayed there much longer.

He said as much to the Mike Force captain, who agreed
with his assessment.

"I'm sure you have alternate positions planned?"

Epstein looked at him as if he had been insulted. Which,
of course, he had been. He was a weapons man, for God's
sake! Even some dumb-assed demo man would know to do
that, much less an eleven-bravo.

Ah, well, he told himself, dog-ass officers had to ask
questions. Made 'em think they were important. Even mus-
tangs like McCulloden, who, he had heard, was a pretty
good guy. For a dog-ass officer.

"Four," he said, deciding to humor the captain. "None of
'em have the fields of fire of this one. North side, partially
masked by an ammo bunker. South side is so low, you can
really only shoot in one direction. Leaves the one covering
the front gate and the one on the east, covering that ravine."
He gestured toward a rift in the slope. "Figure that's their
best-covered and concealed avenue of approach."

Finn nodded. "Need some help getting it over there?"

"Nah. Me and my 'Yard crew, we got it down to a sci-
ence. Ksor Drot!" Epstein yelled. A squat, little Montagnard

sergeant emerged from the ammo bunker, where he had been inventorying the stock. Epstein rattled off a stream of Jarai, and the sergeant soon had a four-man crew disassembling the weapon and packing the pieces through the trench system. Two of them were bowed under the weight of the barrel, two others wrestled the folded-up tripod, and Ksor Drot proudly carried the sight.

McCulloden was surveying the ravine Epstein had indicated, his expression not at all happy. "Who the fuck let that place get overgrown like that?" he demanded.

Epstein shrugged. "LLDB told us to stop burning it off. Said they had complaints from Saigon, fires were getting out of hand, crossing over the mountain and getting into some Frenchman's tea plantation."

"Same LLDB lieutenant, took the header out of the Huey a couple minutes ago?"

"The very one," Epstein said, smiling for the first time. "*Trung Ui* Tang didn't like to upset the applecart around here."

"Didn't like to patrol much, either, I understand."

"So I was told. Course, that kind of stuff ain't the concern of us enlisted swine. So I was also told."

McCulloden's expression was grim. He had held himself back from bracing Lieutenant Sloane at the outset, had been glad for that decision when Stankow had told him of the lieutenant's willingness to risk his own life to save that of Billy Joe Turner. Now Finn wondered if he had made the right decision. Might have been better to have relieved him on the spot, made him get on the chopper and face Sam Gutierrez's wrath.

Everywhere he looked were signs of neglect. Neglect of the most basic kind. The overgrown ravine was only one part of it. Weeds had also been allowed to grow in the wire surrounding the camp, making it difficult if not impossible to tell if everything was still intact. The moat that marked the final protective barrier before the bunkers was half-filled with trash, and the bamboo punjii stakes that had once lined it were rotted and askew. Here and there were well-beaten trails through the wire where 'Yards, taking the path of least resistance, had been accustomed to making their forays into the surrounding jungle.

At least the NCOs seemed to maintain a modicum of professionalism. Sergeant Epstein certainly seemed to have his situation in hand. "Any beehive?" McCulloden asked.

"Ten rounds at each position," Epstein replied. "Figure, there's so many of 'em they can get through ten rounds of that stuff, we're shit out of luck, anyway."

McCulloden agreed, though he couldn't let his facade of false optimism slip enough to show it. Beehive rounds contained thousands of inch-long steel fléchettes, little finned darts. Unlike the old canister rounds, which were essentially large buckshot-dispersing devices that started spreading right out of the barrel, beehives stayed whole until a set distance, at which they would disperse in a patterned group. The resulting storm of high-speed fléchettes whining through the air sounded like a huge swarm of angry bees, thus the nickname.

The pattern ensured anything exposed or behind even light barriers in a cone that started at dispersal and going out as far as a hundred meters, and at its maximum extension reaching another hundred meters across, was going to be hit with one of the fléchettes. Probably a lot more than one. The first time McCulloden had seen it used, from another 106 recoilless, the assaulting force had from the front looked as if they had a bad case of measles. The fléchettes had the nasty habit of tumbling after penetration, however, and from the back the victims looked like so much raw hamburger.

Finn started to say something else, then paused to listen. "Out of here!" he screamed, leading the way at a full run down the trench.

Bucky Epstein, having heard the same sound, was right behind him. The far-off cough of artillery, and from a direction that ensured it wasn't friendly. You don't move your ass, he told the captain silently, you're gonna have my boot tracks right up your back.

They'd made it perhaps a hundred yards, and more importantly, past two doglegs in the trench, before they heard the freight-train sound of the shells coming in. The first one hit, the impact shaking the ground under their feet, but strangely accompanied by no explosion. For just a moment McCulloden allowed himself to think that perhaps it was a dud, or maybe the gunners hadn't set the fuses— wouldn't that be funny!—and then it did go off, deep beneath the ground. The earth heaved around them, the trench collapsing in places where the sandbag revetments had rotted.

Time-delay fuses, McCulloden thought. Oh, shit.

The ground heaved again and again—the sound of the explosions muffled, transmitted through the soil like ripples through water. Must be what an earthquake feels like, he thought, the ground beneath your feet no more solid than if you were walking on air. The very air seemed to waver, turn brown, the dirt so thick it coated the lungs, that and the explosives smoke choking out life-giving oxygen.

Then a particularly close hit threw him bodily down, collapsing the walls around him, covering him with rat-infested sandbags, worms, the detritus of years of neglect. He was swimming in dirt, desperately trying to keep his head out of the constantly filling trench, praying to survive and knowing that if just one more hit close, it was all over.

He had time only to register an explosion so impossibly loud that he knew even before the pain hit that his eardrums were probably gone. Then the world went black.

A direct hit on the ammo bunker.

Chapter 4

From far away, someone was calling his name.

He ignored it. Couldn't they let him rest, for a little while at least? It was warm and snug where he was. Nice and dark, just as he liked it when he slept. Leave me alone! he wanted to tell them, but found that he could not talk. Something was blocking his mouth.

No matter. He'd had dreams like this before, nightmares really, when he couldn't move, couldn't talk. This one too would pass when he woke up.

The voices were becoming even more insistent. Irritating. Damn it! Usually when he had these dreams, there was fear, sometimes abject terror as the nameless thing that was always in pursuit came closer and closer and he was trying to escape but could only wait for the rending jaws, the annihilation.

But this was just plain irritating. Go away! Let me sleep.

Then a great blow to the center of his chest, and he came up coughing and sputtering, heaving up great clots of dirt.

"Thought you were a goner for sure, Cap'n," Epstein said.

He blinked the dirt out of his eyes, saw that he was in a shallow trench where it was obvious that Epstein had been clawing away at the soil covering him. His legs were still buried deep.

"All's I could see was your hand stickin' up," Epstein said. "Twitched a couple of times, so I figured you still had somethin' goin'. Had to give you a good smack, get you started breathing again."

He helped McCulloden dig himself the rest of the way out. Except for a great tiredness and a huge ringing in his ears, he seemed to be otherwise uninjured.

"You okay?" he asked the sergeant.

Epstein grinned. "Hell of a ride, wasn't it? Guess I better get back to my troops. By the way, don't think we're gonna use that position anymore." He gestured back toward the spot they had just occupied. It looked like the photographs of a place he had once seen, called Verdun.

Master Sergeant Olchak came up, grinning at the sight of his dirt-covered commander. "You 'bout tired of playin' in the mud, sir? Somebody wants to talk to you." He handed McCulloden the handset of the radio he was carrying.

Finn ran his tongue in around his teeth, found more dirt, spat it out. Olchak offered him his canteen. Finn accepted gratefully, finding the lukewarm water as delicious as French champagne.

"The radio, sir," Olchak said, gently reminding him of what he was supposed to be doing. "FAC, call sign Shooter Two-Zero."

Finn stared at the handset for a second, feeling strangely befuddled. What was happening to him? Usually he brushed off such insults as that his body had just suffered. He'd been, in the course of three tours, wounded twice, suffered severe concussion three times, and had fallen thirty feet from a helicopter hovering over too-tall elephant grass. Each time before he had gone on about his business. Now all he wanted to do was lie back down again.

It had been so nice and warm and dark.

With a physical effort he shook it off, dislodging yet more dirt, some of which was taking up residence in the crotch of his tiger fatigues. His grandma would have said, "You could grow potatoes in there, boy."

Damn near joined you, Granny, he silently told her.

"Cowboy Six, this is Shooter Two Zero," came the voice from the handset. Finn realized it was at least the third time he had heard it.

"This is Six," he said. "Go."

"Got a flight of fast-movers burning up gas," the FAC said. "Where do you want 'em?"

"Arty been working us over down here." Finn's head was clearing somewhat, now that he had something positive to do. "I figure one-five-sevens. Way it came in, had to be a battery." He looked critically at the craters. There was an ever-so-slight slant, pointing back toward the west. "My guess would be they got 'em somewhere across the line. You see anything back that way?"

"Wasn't looking," the FAC said. "Wouldn't do much good if I had. We don't have clearance for strikes over there, unless we get permission from Saigon first."

Finn silently raged at a policy that would allow the enemy sanctuary while exacting no revenge for his violations of international law. But it had been that way since his first tour, down on the Cambodian border, and would probably remain so until the war was finally over. The politics of it were obviously more important than the lives of mere men down here on the ground.

"Fine," he finally said. "What ordnance are your fast-movers carrying?"

"Nape and Rockeyes," the FAC replied, signifying napalm and cluster-bomb units (CBUs). The latter were particularly good for troops in the open, scattering hundreds of bomblets over a wide area where they fell and exploded, filling the air with shrapnel.

But he didn't see any troops in the open. At least not at the moment. And the CBUs were fairly useless in heavy jungle, a lot of which had not been cleared to the distances he would have liked around the camp.

"Roger," he said. "Give me the nape starting fifty meters from the wire, west-east axis right up the ravine you see there. Burn off some of that crap, maybe we can see something. Then I'll think of something to do with the Rockeyes."

"Good copy, Six. By the way, got several more flights that want to get in on the action. Rest of the country quiet for a change. You game?"

Finn smiled, finally feeling himself now that he had something useful to do. "I expect I can find 'em something to do. Bring 'em on."

Spearchucker Washington was setting up a .50-caliber machine-gun team to cover the ravine when the first fast-mover came in. "Down!" he yelled, having already been told over the command net what was to come.

The Montagnard soldiers unquestioningly flattened themselves against the clay, one so close to Washington his merry brown eyes were staring into his own. The expression changed when the first *whoosh* of a napalm canister struck just outside the wire.

Glad I'm wearing a hat, Washington thought as the blast of searing heat struck them. It was like opening the door to a furnace, the heat seeming to penetrate to the bone. My hair would be even frizzier than it is.

One after another they came in. By turning his head slightly he could see them as they arced up over the mountain, the droop wings of the F-4 Phantom easily identifiable. To get as low as they needed to be for precision work, they then had to pour the coals to it to rise above the surrounding terrain. Dirty black trails of smoke marked their passing, pointing up into the sky like accusing fingers.

The shifting valley winds brought back to him the smells: burning gasoline, woodsmoke, and underlying it the unmistakable stench of charred flesh. Someone was out there, he thought. Poor bastards.

He'd had as much war as anyone in Special Forces, had been in situations that, except for the valor of his troops and a great deal of luck, would not have been survivable. Had seen men ripped apart by the effects of high-speed metal chunks tearing into their bodies. Had wallowed in his own blood after taking one of those pieces of metal himself.

But he couldn't even imagine what it must be like to always be expecting the death from the skies. How the hell they managed it, kept on fighting despite the losses they must have been taking, was beyond him. He didn't know if he could have done it.

He had a grudging admiration for them. Very grudging. The same troops who could withstand such treatment, who stood fast under years of privation, near starvation at times, who could expect not much more than a long and lingering death should they become seriously wounded, were capable of such casual cruelty that it sometimes took your breath away.

On a previous tour he had served with Project Delta, a long-range reconnaissance unit based out of Nha Trang. Delta had the unenviable mission of sending small teams of men into the most closely held Viet Cong and North Vietnamese sanctuaries, there to gather intelligence and direct artillery and air strikes against lucrative targets.

Washington was too big to be on one of the reconnaissance teams (the commander had taken one look at him and said, "Hell, you can't be on a team. You got wounded, they'd have to quarter you to get you out"). The other choices were rear-area make-work, or joining the Ranger company that served as the reaction force. Washington had, of course, chosen the latter.

As a platoon leader of the company, he was sent in to find a team with whom they had lost all radio contact. They hadn't been hard to find. They still sat at their last reported position, the four Montagnards lying in a semicircle around the three Americans. Almost as if they had been placed there for some barbaric religious ceremony.

One of the Americans had obviously been killed early in

the engagement. His body, except for being stripped naked, was untouched except for the hole where an AK round had taken off the back of his head.

The other two hadn't been so lucky. One had been bayoneted at least a hundred times. From the blood that had flowed from the wounds, it was obvious the thrusts had been carefully calculated not to kill.

The other sat against a tree, sightless eyes staring out into the jungle. His pants had been pulled down around his ankles, and his genitals were missing. There were no other wounds.

The claw marks on the trunk of the tree to which his hands had been tied were mute witness to his suffering.

So, while Washington had a grudging admiration for his adversaries, he didn't have much sympathy.

"Burn, you cocksuckers," he said as another flight of Phantoms came in.

Finn was glad to see the napalm causing a brush fire that quickly ran up the ravine, charring everything in its path. The monsoon rains had been late this year, the grass and underbrush were as dry as they would ever be—ideal conditions for a conflagration.

Finn hoped it burned down the whole goddamn plantation on the other side of the mountain. The Frenchman there had long been suspected of being a Viet Cong supporter. So far, no one had been able to prove it.

On his last trip to Saigon, Finn had run into an old friend, Captain James NMI Carmichael, who was now a Provincial Reconnaissance Unit (PRU) adviser in Thua Thien Province.

The PRU, explained Carmichael, trying to recruit Finn, was
the action arm of the Phoenix Program. Its results-oriented
mission was to eliminate the Viet Cong infrastructure, wherever it could be found. Gather the appropriate intelligence,
locate the target, capture him if possible, and if not . . .

Finn suspected that the Frenchman wouldn't have lasted
long in Jim Carmichael's province. Maybe, he thought, I
was wrong to turn him down when he tried to get me to join
the PRU. Maybe on another tour.

First you have to survive this one, he told himself.

He directed the FAC to have the Phantom flight drop
their Rockeyes on the trench complex to the south of the
camp, opposite the ravine. Not, he suspected, that they
would do a lot of good there. Charlie was well and truly
dug in, and it would only be by chance that a piece of
shrapnel would catch an unwary victim. But if they didn't
drop it, they would fly out over the ocean and pickle the
bombs before returning to base, no one particularly liking
to set one of the big birds down with live ordnance still
attached to the wings. Better to cause some hate and dis-
content among the ranks than to kill a few innocent fish, he
told himself.

The first bird made its pass, the cylinders dropping from
its wings right on target. They looked like standard iron
bombs in flight, until at a predetermined altitude the canister
ripped open and hundreds of bomblets, each about as big as
double-clenched fists, spread like snowflakes. As soon as
they exited the canister, fins popped out, stabilizing the
bomblets and orienting them nose downward. The spin
imparted by the fins also armed the firing circuits. Long

before a bomblet hit the ground, it would go off if it so much as encountered a leaf wafting through the air.

The bomblets went off with a rippling roar, black explosives smoke coating the ground, soon to be swallowed up by the dirt chewed up by the shrapnel. A subnote of the explosion was a long-drawn-out moan, that of hundreds of thousands of pieces of metal cutting the air. And anything else they might encounter.

The next bird came in, and the next, and the next, each neatly planning its pattern so that it slightly overlaid the last. Damn good pilots, Finn thought.

"Cowboy, this is Shooter."

"Go, Shooter."

"How you like them apples?"

"Just like the bridegroom said to his new wife," Finn said.

"How's that?"

"Honey, I think you've done this before!"

He heard the FAC chuckling over the air. After a moment he said, "Yeah, but that doesn't make me a slut, does it?"

"If it does, you're my slut. And I still love you too many, GI."

"Bet you say that to all the FACs. Anyhow, you ready for something else?"

"Surprise me."

"Hell, it surprised me. Got a call from Sandy, over somewhere you don't want to know about. Pulled a team out and didn't get shot up nearly as bad as they expected. Heard about your problems with the arty, said since they were in the area, anyway, might as well help. You want to give me an azimuth on where you think it came from?"

"Two-seven-five degrees. Given the range of the one-five-seven, figure anywhere from ten to twenty-five klicks from here. Big area, ain't it?"

"Well, they say they don't have anything else to do for fun, and you know how long those guys like to hang around, so they'll be buzzing around, see if they stir up anything." There was a pause, a lot of dead air, and then the FAC said, "You know, it would be a hell of a lot easier if they shot at you again."

"Gee, really like to help you out. You want me to paint a bull's-eye on my ass?"

"Only if you think it'd help," Shooter Two-Zero said.

The Sandys he had been talking about were Korean War–era A-1 fighter-bombers. Prop driven. Low and slow, they liked to say. Not like the afterburner crowd. They had tremendous load capacity, the ability to loiter for hours, and pilots who weren't afraid to get down and dirty. You called for danger-close from a Sandy, and you'd damned well better be tucking your head between your legs, because he could put a five-hundred-pound bomb virtually yards from your position. Sandys worked over the Ho Chi Minh trail from the other side of the border, often supporting reconnaissance teams from SOG, still more often providing the necessary air support when one of the afterburner crowd was down on the ground, crying for help.

Finn hoped they could find the artillery, but didn't count on it. More likely the next barrage was going to be just before the attack. Which was going to come, he was sure, sometime during the night. Best they could do would be to keep the gunner's heads down during the day, preventing another barrage at least for the moment. Which was enough to be grateful for, he supposed.

"Appreciate the help, Shooter," he said. "I'll be talking to you again."

"That's what they all say," Shooter said, making a mock sigh. "You keep well down there, you heah?"

"We're gonna try."

Stankow was showing Olchak the perimeter defenses. "Five layers," he said. "Straight five-wire barbed-wire fence to the outside. Keeps the goats and pigs out of the minefield. Twenty-five yards behind that is triple-strand concertina. That marks the minefield. Standard layout, one antitank, five M-14 antipersonnel. All marked on the map, here."

"Think any of them still work?" Olchak asked.

Stankow scowled. He didn't like Olchak very much, hated him, in fact. And now the arrogant son of a bitch was questioning him!

Learned his trade under the cocksucker Germans, he thought.

Olchak was Ukrainian. Had been brought up under the Reds, fell under the spell of the so-called Ukrainian nationalists, had at their urging joined the German Army shortly after it took Kiev.

In other words, they had been sworn enemies since 1940. Not that such situations were all that unusual in the Special Forces. The Lodge Act had encouraged "freedom fighters" from all over the world to come to the United States, there to combat totalitarianism no matter what it called itself. And the situation wasn't as virulent as many had been. After all,

Olchak's unit had never served in Poland, being sent instead to fight and die outside Leningrad. Far worse was the case of the Nowak brothers, one of whom had been a Czech partisan, the other having joined the SS.

But, Stankow thought, Olchak was still a cocksucker. Stankow's favorite word for anyone he didn't like. And Olchak was questioning the defenses.

What made it worse was that Stankow had to reluctantly agree that it was likely that few of the mines would still be operational. Since the new lieutenant had taken command, they had been forbidden entrance into the minefield. Too dangerous, Sloane had said. And true enough, it was difficult to check the field without taking one or two casualties.

But that was the way of it. And if you didn't check, didn't look for freshly dug earth, how were you to know that Viet Cong sappers hadn't been inside the wire, clearing a path for the assault troops?

Stankow just grunted in answer, trusting in the cocksucker Olchak's experience to tell him what the grunt meant.

"Another triple-strand concertina behind that," Stankow continued. "Twenty-five yards of tanglefoot, then a row of claymores. Moat, which you've already seen, another triple-strand concertina. This one is new, made from that razor wire we just got in."

Tanglefoot was single-strand barbed wire, strung ankle to waist height in symmetric patterns, covering the entire space between the row of concertina and the claymore mines. Its purpose was to delay, if not stop, any attackers. You could crawl under it, but it was a slow process. You could step through it, but you were also slowed, and terribly exposed. Not a good place to be when you were confronted by a bank of claymore mines. The latter sprayed a pattern of steel ball bearings in a cone-shaped pattern, making certain anyone caught in the zone was going to be riddled.

"Control of the claymores?" Olchak asked.

"Two control centers. One at the company command post for each sector. Second is at the CP in the inner perimeter. They can be fired individually, in a ripple, or all at once."

"How often do you check the firing wires?"

"We run a continuity check at the beginning of each shift. Other than that, we can't do much. Wires are buried. They weren't, we wouldn't stand much chance of keeping them whole under a mortar or artillery barrage."

"So, someone could conceivably go out and stick a pin through the firing wire, short it out, but it would still show a complete circuit on continuity check, am I right?"

Stankow grudgingly admitted that. It was something he had worried about too. But there seemed to be little they could do about it.

"We blow one at random, a couple of times a month," he replied. "So far we've only had one failure. And that was because one of the 'Yards opened it up, took the C-4 to use for fishing."

"Grenades weren't good enough for him?"

"Said he wanted some bigger fish."

Olchak pointed to a well-worn trail leading from the bunker line out past the outer perimeter. It had quite obviously been blazed by someone familiar with the camp defenses. In the minefield it first took a sharp right, then back toward the outer perimeter, then right again, on and on until the minefield was cleared.

"When we first got here, all the 'Yards had their families living in the camp. Captain Koslov didn't like that, thought there was too much chance some of 'em were on the other side. Made them move out. They set up some longhouses down the valley. Of course, their husbands and fathers thought it ridiculous they'd have to go out the main gate to see them. We started getting these trails all over the place. Tried to stop 'em; only thing we did was make 'em cut the wire in other places."

"Should have shot a couple," Olchak said.

You would say that, you Nazi-loving bastard, Stankow thought.

"When the NVA moved in, the problem went away," he said. "Families took to the hills. Lost a couple of soldiers with them, I expect because they needed some security. Not as many as I would have expected, though. We got a pretty good crew here."

And we'd have lost them all, if we'd started shooting one or two, *pour l'encouragement des autres,* he thought.

"But you've still got the trails," Olchak insisted.

"Somebody tries to use one now, they're gonna get a hell of a surprise. In fact, I wish they would come that way."

He had helped Stan Braxton, the demolitions specialist, bury the surprises. Fifty-five-gallon drums filled with a homemade napalm, beneath which were command-detonated shaped charges. Flame fougasses, they were called. When set off, they would burst spectacularly, cooking anyone within a twenty-five-meter radius so thoroughly you wouldn't have to stick a meat thermometer in them to see if they were done, Braxton said.

Despite the looks of the place, with the trash and all in the moat, they were probably as prepared as they were going to get to repel a ground attack. Which wouldn't mean a hell of a lot, Stankow knew, when the sappers got into the wire. He'd never liked sitting behind fixed defenses. For every defensive measure you took, there were a half dozen ways of getting around it. A bunch of SS troopers outside Warsaw could have told you that. If they had still been able to say anything at all, after he and a couple of his partisan friends had wriggled through the wire, thrown grenades into the bunkers, and shot any survivors.

Where were you? he silently asked Olchak. Nazi bastard.

"You can go back to your mortar pit," Olchak said. "Keep up the H and I on all major trail junctions. Who knows, maybe we'll get lucky. Kill a battalion commander, or something."

Or maybe we'll just piss away some more ammunition, Stankow thought. Oh, well, it got him away from Olchak. Who he was seriously thinking about strangling.

Sloane was sitting in the command bunker, nursing his anger. Captain McCulloden *still* hadn't seen fit to talk to him.

It didn't help when Becker took a radio call from Colonel Gutierrez, asking for the captain. "I'll talk to him," Sloane told the radio operator.

Becker looked embarrassed for him, further fueling his rage. "Ah, he was pretty specific about wanting to speak to Cowboy Six, sir."

"Well, goddamnit, go get him then!"

Becker knew he should stay with the radio, didn't really trust the lieutenant to operate it properly. The big Collins single-sideband that was their only voice link to the outside world was notoriously temperamental. If it went out, they'd be limited to CW—Morse code tapped out on a keypad.

By the lieutenant's own admission he wasn't even cross-trained in commo! How you could be a Special Forces officer without having at least a little cross-training was beyond Becker. Maybe like the older NCOs said, it was because Sloane was summer help. Weren't enough of the older officers, the ones who had served their apprenticeship at Fort Bragg or Bad Tolz or Okinawa, to go around. They'd been killed, suffered disabling wounds, been promoted well past the rank necessary to serve on an A team, or had just thrown up their hands and quit in disgust.

So you ended up with people like Sloane, who obviously intended to serve his one tour in SF, get the requisite I-been-there badges, and go on to bigger and better things. The hell of it is, Becker thought, you give him a few more years at this, knock that ego down a peg or two, and he might just turn out all right. Certainly didn't suffer from cowardice— the run to save Sergeant Turner had shown that. He'd watched the entire episode from the safety of the command bunker and had wondered if he would have had the courage to do it himself.

Best not to piss him off any more, he thought. The lieutenant looked ready to blow.

"Be back in a couple, sir," he said, grabbing his M16 and slipping on his load-bearing equipment (LBE). The belt was salvaged from an old Browning automatic weapons belt, had six integral pouches, each of which held four twenty-round magazines of 5.56mm ammunition. On each side, behind the magazine pouches, hung a one-quart canteen, kept topped off. In front was a first-aid pouch with bandages, and on the other side was an older model of the pouch, which contained five Syrettes of morphine, a bottle of dextroamphetamine, and a few aspirin. Rolled on the rear was a poncho and poncho liner. On the harness itself he had strapped an Air Force survival knife, haft down on the left-hand side. To the back was strapped a tube containing serum albumin blood expander. Finally, there was a pouch containing a strobe light.

The whole rig weighed in at something over twenty pounds. He'd made the mistake once of leaving the bunker without it, thinking it silly to encumber yourself while you were inside the camp. Sergeant Turner had seen him and had administered a truly inspired ass-chewing.

"Suppose we get hit," the sergeant had said. "And you're on the opposite side of the camp. You've got a rifle with one magazine. No water. No extra ammo. No way to signal you need help. You have to stay in a bunker all night, no way to get warm. Better yet, you get cut off, have to E and E, spending your nights out in the jungle for a week or two. You think this shit would be too much to carry then? Put it on, dumb ass."

And he had, and he always would. Turner was gone, but the truth of his statements lingered on. Especially now.

They were in deep shit. Best be prepared for whatever came.

• • •

Finn McCulloden was helping Sergeant Washington dig deeper into the red clay, siting one of the many M60 machine guns with which the weapons platoon was equipped. From his inspection of the perimeter Finn had noted that it was already fairly well equipped for grazing fire along the final protective line (FPL), with an older 1919A6 .30-06 machine gun placed at each point of the star shape in which the camp was laid out. The FPL position, used as the last resort when the attacking force was close enough to justify it, interlocked fires between machine guns, creating a line through which no one could cross without the high probability of being cut to pieces. But, he knew, the NVA would already have plans to take out one or more of the machine gun positions, creating dangerous gaps in the line through which they could pass without worrying about more than direct fire.

Washington had placed his M60s in alternate positions, far enough away from the original sites to guard against their being taken out by any direct or indirect fire aimed at the former, close enough to take over FPL duties when they were taken out.

Finn looked up at the surrounding hills while he was helping to dig the U-shaped position, wondering just how many forward observers were scoping out their every move. Who the hell picked the spot for this camp? You would have thought that no one had ever heard of the tactical advantages of high ground.

It was the same throughout South Vietnam. His first camp, Loc Ninh down in III Corps, had been even worse than this one. The hills around it had been so high and so close the VC had been able to look down into every single bunker. Originally the camp had been proposed up the hill to the west, not only on high ground but next to the old French airstrip that had been their only link with the outside world. But that ground was covered in rubber trees, and the French who still ran the plantation had protested bitterly to the Diem regime, who had then directed the camp be built where it wouldn't harm the precious rubber.

Late in that tour, when the camp had been hit by a couple of Viet Cong battalions and then-Captain Gutierrez had directed air strikes and artillery at positions the enemy had dug throughout the rubber plantation, the question had been rendered moot. The French had soon moved out, the camp was relocated up the hill, and the tactical situation had been vastly improved.

Finn had taken as much pleasure in that as he had when seeing the fire from the ravine roar over the mountain, hoping that it would burn out the Frenchman there.

There wouldn't be a relocation of this camp, no matter what happened. Either it would be overrun, in which case it would be abandoned, or it would be turned over to the South Vietnamese in the so-called Vietnamization program. Many of the border camps had already been, the Special Forces advisers moving out and the LLDB taking over the task of trying to run things.

Sometimes it worked. You had Vietnamese who were the equal of anyone he'd ever known—brave, conscientious, smart. Those who had absorbed the combined knowledge of the years of American advisers with whom they'd been teamed. Outfits led by them, Finn thought,

could be put up against anything the North Vietnamese had
to offer.

All too often, however, you had LLDB like the unfortu-
nate lieutenant who had just taken the long jump from a helicopter. Lazy, venal, full of bluster when it was safe, happy to
hide in bunkers or run away when it was not. Their attitude
had been, the Americans are here, let them fight the war!

Such attitudes were why a lot of American Special
Forces people called the LLDB Low Life Dirty Bastards, or
Look Long, Duck Back. But for better or for worse, it was
soon going to be their show.

He was afraid it was going to be for worse. Much worse.

As they finished digging, the Montagnard gun crew
came back dragging some six-by-six-inch wooden beams
they had managed to scrounge. Finn didn't want to ask them
from where. Usually when the 'Yards came back from a
scrounging trip, they were followed by the highly irate former owners.

He helped them stack a triple layer of sandbags to the
rear and sides of the position, then place the beams across
the top. They'd already located some pierced-steel planking (psp), which would now cover the beams and, once in
place, hold up yet another four or five layers of sandbags.
If they had time, they would then try to find some tin roof-
ing to put on top of that, positioned with an air space
between tin and sandbags. If mortar or artillery rounds
came in, they would detonate on the tin instead of burying
themselves in the sandbags, where they could do a lot more
damage. Such measures were only good for a couple of
rounds, the tin quickly being blown away, but sometimes

that was the difference between ears ringing and being buried alive.

Having just been buried alive, Finn couldn't recommend the experience.

He straightened up, back aching from all the work, to see Sergeant Becker approaching.

"Looks like I'm needed elsewhere," Finn told Sergeant Washington.

"Knew you were going to crap out on me sooner or later," the black man said. "White boys can't stand that manual labor, can they?"

"That's why we need a Mexican or two."

"How's that?"

"For that Manuel labor, of course."

Washington chuckled. He looked up into the surrounding hills, face growing serious again. "Shitty spot."

"Only one we got, though."

"Yeah. Say, I was wondering. You think we just surprised 'em this morning, getting in here without being shot up any worse than we were?"

"Been thinking about that too. No, I don't think we surprised them."

"How come they gave us a free ride?"

"I think some NVA commander is sitting out there, dreaming about the medal he's gonna get. For not only taking this camp, but wiping out a Mike Force company in the bargain."

Chapter 5

"That's it?" Gutierrez asked.

"That's it," the division artillery officer for the Fourth Infantry Division replied.

Gutierrez studied the overlays again. Square blocks indicated the planned barrages available along the route of march for the remainder of the Mike Force battalion. They were pitifully few.

"We're down to damn near skeleton crews," the DivArty commander, a lieutenant colonel like himself, said, his voice apologetic. "Division getting ready to rotate back to the States, they haven't been supplying us with replacements like they should. Practically all the newbies are going to the units that aren't leaving until next year."

Gutierrez had seen the truth of that statement in his jeep drive through the base. The once-hustling area now looked almost abandoned, and those who still remained walked around in an ill-shaven, uniform-neglected, shambling stupor.

It had been like this ever since the administration had declared that the war was virtually won, that the Vietnamese could now handle the bulk of the fighting, that we were at long last going to bring the boys home. And worse than the lack of replacements was the attitude of the soldiers and officers. The war was over. Hadn't you heard? Would you like to be the last man to die in Vietnam?

Combat units had been pulled back into base camps, where they rotted. Now that there was nothing productive to do, soldiers in time-honored ways found lots of unproductive activity. Drug use was rampant. Disobedience to orders was almost universal. Any officer with the temerity to insist upon soldierly behavior was regarded as unbearably chickenshit and subject to having a frag grenade rolled under his bunk.

Worse still, from Sam Gutierrez's viewpoint, was the scarcity of artillery ammunition! It was still rolling in at the ports of Da Nang, Cam Ranh Bay, and Saigon, but was now being siphoned off to send to the Vietnamese artillery units. Ordinarily the route of march of the Mike Force battalion would have been bracketed by nearly continuous artillery plots. Now they were down to planning the plots only on those areas considered particularly dangerous, and the barrages themselves were held to three rounds per gun.

It infuriated him. It infuriated him even more given the trip he'd already made to the Vietnamese division responsible for the area. There he had politely been given tea, offered a beer if he wanted it, and turned down flatly when he asked for support. The Vietnamese had their own operation going, he had been told, and would need all the artillery they could get to save their own bacon.

The Vietnamese operation, he already knew, would consist of pushing out a couple of infantry battalions a kilometer or so, simply to clear the surrounding area of infiltrators and keep the base camps secure. If they were unlucky enough to make contact with anything more than a company-sized unit, they would break contact and scurry back to base with the artillery putting down barrages behind them. Blowing up yet further a lot of empty jungle.

Not that they would have given the Mike Force a lot of support even if they hadn't had their own operation going. The Mike Force was made up of Montagnard soldiers, and the Vietnamese and Montagnards hated each other with a mutually intense passion. He had been told in confidence once, by one of the few LLDB officers he trusted, that even if the South Vietnamese managed to hold on to the terrain they had, and if by some miracle the North Vietnamese honored any truce the negotiators in Paris managed to come up with, the war would still not be ended. The Viets intended to teach the increasingly confident Montagnards of the Central Highlands a lesson, one they would not likely forget over the next couple of centuries.

Thus the loss of a battalion of their best-trained and motivated troops was not to be regarded with any dismay. Fewer of the tribesmen to resist later.

Though obviously the very polite Vietnamese colonel commanding the artillery would never have said such a thing. After all, they were all in this together, were they not?

The attitude did not surprise Gutierrez, though it did make him so angry he could spit. From the first, when he'd been an adviser down in the Delta trying to recruit the Hoa Hao sect, through his first experience setting up an A camp in III Corps with ethnic Cambodians as the strike force, on to the battalion he'd led of the overseas Chinese known as Nungs, and especially with the Montagnards, he had fought the general attitude. That all except the ruling Vietnamese were beneath contempt. That the country would be a great deal better off without them. That extermination of minority groups was not only allowable, but would be an acceptable solution to a problem that had plagued the various rulers for the hundreds of years since they had invaded the country from their original home in southern China. In this the North Vietnamese had the same attitude as did their southern kin, though their propaganda was much better at keeping the fact hidden.

"And the camp?" he asked, shaking away the anger and concentrating upon the matter at hand.

"Only thing we can reach them with is the one-seven-fives," the DivArty commander replied.

"Shit!" Gutierrez swore. The 175mm cannon had tremendous range, dropped a shell containing over a hundred pounds of explosive, and with its largely automated firing system could pump out those shells rather quickly. It had originally been designed for the European battlefield, its primary purpose the delivery of tactical nuclear shells into the Russian tank battalions the planners continually expected to sweep across the plains of northern Germany. And therein lay the problem.

Tactical nuclear shells, obviously, had a tremendous damage radius. It wouldn't matter a whit if the impact point for such a shell was hundreds of meters off that which was planned, if you were going to destroy everything within a kilometer radius anyway. Thus the designers and manufacturers hadn't had as a first priority the accuracy of the weapon.

Put quite simply, you could not depend upon the one-seven-five for close-in work. Call it within fifty meters of your position, as you often had to do since the North Vietnamese had long since come up with the tactic of "hugging the belt" of their adversaries, and you were as likely to have it drop on your own position as you were theirs.

This meant, of course, that the camp defenders could not depend upon artillery to keep the attackers out of the wire. Its only use would be to pound rear areas, in the sometimes forlorn hope it would hit something vital. Unlikely in the extreme, he knew, since the NVA would be thoroughly burrowed into secure caves in those rear areas.

"Sorry," the DivArty lieutenant colonel said. He was well aware of the limitations of the piece. Way back, when he had been a young forward observer, he had seen firsthand the effects of trying to call in a one-seven-five strike as danger-close. Some of the shells had hit where they were supposed to. Some had blown up empty jungle. And one had landed squarely upon the command element of the forward company. He had been lucky enough to be on one of the outposts. Otherwise he would not have been there at that moment.

Not that he was pleased to be. He was as frustrated as the Green Beret commander. He supposed he should have been grateful for the position, a lieutenant colonel in what was usually the slot occupied by a full bull, or even a brigadier general. But with the drawdown, those officers were studiously avoiding positions so pregnant with the possibility of disaster.

If everything went right, it would be a bright spot on an

already distinguished record. If it went wrong, as was completely likely, he would never make O-6, much less flag rank.

Worse than that, men like himself, men who still thought the profession of arms was honorable, who continued to put themselves in harm's way, would die. He might live through not making general. He didn't think he would ever get over knowing something like that was his own fault.

"What about ARA?" Gutierrez asked.

"That I can help you with." ARA, the Aerial Rocket Artillery battalion, was made up of heavily armed Huey helicopters. Each bird carried twenty-four 2.75-inch rockets in pods slung under each door and could fire the rockets individually, in a ripple, or in salvos. And the ARA battalion had been kept up to nearly full strength, someone in the command structure realizing that with the drawdown they had to have something to guard against disaster.

"Only one problem," the DivArty commander continued.

Gutierrez's expression was wary. What now?

"Weather's supposed to turn to shit tonight. Meteo is calling for zero-zero."

Gutierrez shook his head. One thing was just piling atop another. Not that he was surprised. It took no feat of logical thinking to realize the North Vietnamese would know about the weather as well. The monsoon season was already late, which meant when it came in, it would do so with a vengeance. Once the clouds closed in around the mountain camp, they wouldn't open up again for weeks or perhaps months. The choppers, of course, had no integral radar capability, couldn't fly in conditions like that without the very probable result of crashing headlong into a mountain.

"Shit," Gutierrez said.

That about neatly sums it up in one word, the artillery-man thought. Shit.

Finn McCulloden, now back in the command bunker, received the news from Gutierrez. "Well, ain't this just ducky!"

"I'm still working on it," Gutierrez said. "What else can I get you? Ammo, rations, water? Best try to get it in before the weather closes in."

"How about calling up God and getting us some pre-plot lightning," Finn replied. "Failing that, let's go back to yesterday and start all over again."

"I'll see what the chaplain can do," Gutierrez said, and they both laughed. Chaplains didn't go out where the Mike Force went. Bad for their health.

"For the shape we're in, we're not in bad shape. Everything's dug in, the perimeter defenses look reasonable, we've got plenty of ammo, chow, medical supplies, water. We can hold out, they don't throw any real shit in the game."

Finn wished he was as confident as he was trying to sound. In truth, if the NVA came at them in waves, as they tended increasingly to do these days, they'd be within the wire in seconds, crossing past the claymore belt atop the bodies of the fodder they would have put in the first ranks. Once past the claymores, it would be every man for himself, little battles that would decide the overall outcome breaking out all over the camp.

Policy was to retreat to the inner perimeter at that point. That would consist of the command bunker and the concentric fighting positions surrounding it, all protected by yet more razor wire and another band of claymores.

And if they got past the inner perimeter?

Sorry 'bout that, he thought.

What the hell, Finn, he told himself. Who promised you that you were going to live forever?

"Even if the weather does close in," Gutierrez was saying, "we can still do Sky Spots. B-57s out of Tan Son Nhut are standing by, got five-hundred-pounders."

That was something, anyway. Every camp in South Vietnam was registered on the Sky Spot system, had reflectors placed in strategic locations, reflectors that would show up loud and clear on the airplane radar systems. The man on the ground would give a reference, tell the plane azimuth and distance from this or that reflector, and soon a bomb would come whistling down. In earlier days the system hadn't been completely perfected; bombs might come down on you as easily as they did on someone else, but over the years the system had been fine-tuned. If you didn't have too many wind shifts caused by unpredictable currents in the mountains, if the humidity didn't affect the trajectory of the bomb, if you had a sharp pilot and bombardier, it could be very effective. Within a certain distance, that was. No one in his right mind was going to call in a Sky Spot on danger-close.

"Rest of the battalion jump off yet?" Finn asked.

"Yeah," Gutierrez replied. "So far, so good. Very light resistance—not even enough to call it delaying tactics."

"That must be making Charlie Secord feel good." Secord was Finn's second-in-command, a junior captain who had earned his bones with Delta Project. And the comment was sarcastic. Light resistance certainly meant that the NVA were conserving their forces for a big fight. They'd shadow the battalion with spotters and trail watchers, firing signal shots to indicate direction of travel and proximity. Secord could expect a big ambush somewhere along the way. But he would know that.

"He's making haste slowly," Gutierrez said. "Said he knew you'd understand."

Indeed Finn did. It would do little good to rush the other two companies to the camp only to have them destroyed along the way. Killing a lot of people to save a few had never seemed a good tactic to Finn McCulloden.

"So you think they're going to try it tonight?" Gutierrez continued.

"Hard to say. What you told me about the weather makes it likely, but we haven't had any artillery or rocket barrages for the last couple of hours. Seems like they'd be trying to soften us up more. Occasional mortar round comes in, just to piss us off, that's about it."

"Maybe the air is keeping their heads down?"

"Shit! Be the first time it stopped them. Up at Khe Sanh, they kept shooting even when the B-52s came in. Any chance of a little Arc Light, by the way?"

Arc Light was the code name for B-52 bomber strikes. The B-52 carried 108 five-hundred-pound bombs, and each strike consisted of six planes flying in staggered formation. An Arc Light strike saturated an area the size of the Washington Mall from the Potomac to the Capitol. Finn had participated in a number of bomb-damage assessment (BDA) missions, flying into the strike zone while the ground was still smoking. If they were lucky enough in their targeting, catching the unwary enemy above ground or in shallow defensive positions, there would be virtually no survivors.

Too well he remembered the sight of loops of intestine hanging from shattered trees, like bloody ornaments. Anyone not caught by shrapnel was generally killed by concussion, and those few who were far enough away to suffer the latter to a lesser degree wandered around like zombies.

Of course, if the NVA commanders had seen fit to burrow into the ground, as they increasingly did these days, many of the soldiers would be virtually untouched. And they would come swarming out like a hill of disturbed ants, eager to exact vengeance on the BDA team.

Not that Finn blamed them. He thought he'd probably feel the same way.

"I'm told no. Rumor has it, they're busy up north. Bringing the North Vietnamese back to the negotiating table, they say. And a merry Christmas to all."

Damn, Finn thought. I'd completely forgotten it was Christmas.

Back in the World, people would just now be settling in on couches, complaining about how much they'd eaten. Staring dully at the detritus of ripped-up wrapping paper, wincing at the noise of the toys, trying to find something good on television.

And that evening Walter Cronkite would be on, with the latest film from Vietnam, the latest statistics on killed and wounded. Sounding appropriately magisterial and disapproving of the whole effort.

And unless the viewers had someone actually involved in the fighting, they really wouldn't give a shit. After all, those people were soldiers, they would be saying. They knew what they were getting into.

And some of them, Finn hoped it was only a few, would be nursing their own hatreds. Hoping that even more of the warmongering bastards would die, that the ever-valorous and brilliant North Vietnamese would cause such terrible damage to the war machine that it would never recover. These were the ones who would spit upon a man in uniform, call him a baby-killer, rejoice in the sight of missing limbs, tell the man they wished it had been worse.

Finn had, despite warnings from the processing detachment in San Francisco, chosen to wear his uniform home on leave, the last time he'd been back to the States. Mostly he'd just attracted hateful stares. But one particularly aggressive young man, his hair long as was the fashion of the times, his eyes clearly showing the effects of his drug of choice, had pushed his way through the crowd, hacked up a great clot of phlegm, and spat it upon Finn's ribbons.

Luckily, the policemen who had pulled Finn off him had been veterans. They'd suggested in the strongest possible terms that the captain get himself to the airport and out of the city, and to avoid passing through it on his way back to Vietnam.

His own father and mother, back in Arkansas, would be wondering what he was doing, hoping he was okay. Wondering, as they always did, why he kept going back over there, when anyone could tell he'd done his duty, and more, a long time ago.

Pressed to explain it, he couldn't. Not even to himself. The closest he could come was that there was a war on, and his friends were busily fighting it, and if he were to quit now, he would always wonder if he should have done more. Intellectually, it made little sense, and he could admit that.

But intellect had little to do with it when a friend died. Too many of them already had. More would. Perhaps he would too.

No time to think about that now.

"Anything else you need?" Gutierrez was asking.

"A Christmas miracle?"

"Fresh out of those. Good luck, my friend. God be with you."

I've had enough of this, Sloane thought. Captain McCulloden was still ignoring him, seeming lost in thought after signing off his conversation with Colonel Gutierrez.

"If I might have a word with you, sir?" he said, forcing himself into McCulloden's reverie.

"Lieutenant Sloane," Finn said. "I've been intending to get around to you. Come walk with me."

He turned and left the bunker, giving Sloane no choice but to follow. Does he know how much I hate him? Sloane wondered. And not only him, but all of them. Treating me like a child, like a know-nothing. Just because I didn't serve in Bad Tolz or Panama or some other godforsaken place, didn't have to hump an ANGRC-109 radio, didn't get drunk on ouzo in Greece, or any of the other damned things they keep talking about.

He often felt like a very junior member of some exclusive club, a club moreover, that didn't really want him as a member, but had to put up with him for a little while until they could get rid of him.

I'm just as good as any of you! he wanted to shout. His freezing up at the thought of going once more into the sniper's killing zone was now forgotten. They didn't need me at that point, he had told himself. After all, if McCulloden had been killed helping Turner to the chopper, who would have taken charge? They taught you that back in West Point—never sacrifice all the command element. That these people would ignore such a basic tenet just showed again how superior he was to them.

McCulloden stopped a little down the trench, turned to face him. A small smile curled on his lips. "Wanted to tell you, I thought you did a good job, you and Stankow. Billy Joe would have been a goner. He and I go back a long way—hate to lose him."

Sloane, disarmed, stopped the complaint he had been formulating. So someone did appreciate him, after all! It was a strange feeling.

"You probably know that Colonel Gutierrez wanted you relieved," Finn said. Sloane opened his mouth to protest, was stopped by a gesture.

"I don't think we need to do that," Finn continued. "There were some stupid things done here, things that got us in the position we're in now, but I don't know that all of it is your fault. I did some stupid things as a lieutenant, but I always had a couple of the senior NCOs keeping me out of trouble. Looks like that didn't happen here. Don't know if they didn't try, or you didn't listen. Going to give you the benefit of the doubt. You agree with that?"

Sloane indicated that he did. He was almost pathetically grateful. Almost grateful enough to tell the captain, who he suddenly realized was only a couple of years older than himself, the truth.

But not quite.

• • •

McCulloden, after giving Sloane his orders and responsibilities, had also considered telling him the truth. That the only reason he hadn't been relieved was that they were going to need every rifle they could put on the line. Sloane didn't seem to lack for bravery—only good sense. Finn had already decided to put both him and SFC Stankow in for the Bronze Star for valor for their actions with Turner. If he lived long enough to write up the citations.

He looked at his watch, shaking it to make sure it wasn't stopped. Looked up at the sun to confirm the reading, though it didn't seem possible. Yep, not even at zenith.

It seemed impossible that so little actual time had passed since the briefing that morning. It should have been days, but was only hours. Heat waves shimmered off the runway, a harbinger of things to come. The jungle beyond rippled like a live thing, green and full of menace. If you looked hard enough, you could see the jaws, waiting to rend.

Or you could see the spots where the bombs had struck, the shattered timbers, the yellowed vegetation that you thought looked like cat's eyes.

It was easy to give rein to superstitions in this country. The local Montagnards, animists for the most part with a thin veneer of Christianity overlaid by French Catholic missionaries, believed everything had a life of its own. The trees spoke to one another, whispering of times gone by and the puny efforts of the worms below. The jungle cats, grown fat with the leavings of war, howled at night with the voices of the dead. Even the ground seemed to have a life of its own, producing fungi that would quickly overwhelm the left-behind corpse, making it nothing more than a bump in the forest floor.

The leavings of a thousand years of war called to you, asked you to join them in the eternal rest you so richly deserved.

Would it be rest? Or would you be forever condemned to fight the battles over and over, skeletal shadows eternally clashing, destroyed, rent to shards, only to begin again upon the next celestial day.

Finn shook himself. Didn't pay to have too much of an imagination in this business. You dealt with facts, with the things you could touch, hear, see. The things you could put a bullet into.

"Cap'n?"

He turned to see Washington and Inger. "Got something going here," Washington said. "You need to come and take a look."

Finn struggled to understand the excited soldier, the Jarai speaking so fast that his guttural language was virtually incomprehensible. It didn't help that in his excitement he threw in bastard French, American profanity, and even a couple of words of German learned from some long-dead Legionnaire.

"He say he goddamn be digging deeper, have hand come up from hell, try to take him back down," Bobby the interpreter suggested, trying to be helpful.

"I got that much," Finn said. "What the hell does it mean?"

Washington wordlessly pointed to the hole in the bottom of the trench. Shovel marks from the Jarai soldier's entrenching tool marked the first couple of feet, disappearing into a hole that in its darkness seemed to reach down into the very bowels of the earth.

"He step down in hole," Bobby said. "To see if it deep enough. Fall in."

The Montagnard burst into another spate of excited shouting.

"Say the gods come to take him away," Bobby translated. "He know this place is accursed."

"Hush!" Finn commanded. A couple of words from Bobby and even the Montagnard complied.

From somewhere beneath them came the faint sounds of scraping.

"Shit!" Finn swore. "Washington, you find any shaped charges while you were looking around?"

"Whole bunker full of fifteen-pounders," Washington replied, immediately getting the message. "Be back in a minute."

While he and Inger went to fetch the charges, Finn explained through Bobby what was happening: "They're digging under the camp. That's why the artillery stopped. They got far enough, they were afraid of a strike collapsing the tunnel. Or tunnels. Bobby! Get around the perimeter, tell everyone to stop what they're doing, listen. They're going to have more than one of these."

As Bobby scurried away to do as he was told, Lieutenant Sloane came up, eyes wide. "I heard," he said.

"That's what happens when you let 'em get too close to the wire," Finn said, ignoring the look of hurt, almost as if he had taken a physical blow, that came over the lieutenant at the implied rebuke. "Find something to probe with—any long rods you can drive into the ground—start probing everywhere around the perimeter. Some of the tunnels are probably already finished—'Yards won't hear 'em digging."

Sloane stood there for a second, trying to formulate a response to the rebuke. His face had reddened, angry words building up like a fountain behind his tongue.

"You understand English, Lieutenant?" Finn said, his voice a low hiss. "Get moving!"

As the lieutenant hurried down the trench, Washington and Inger came up from the other side, the former carrying a wooden box filled with shaped charges, Inger lugging firing wire, a blasting machine, and a box of electric detonators.

"Blow me a hole right down the center of this," Finn instructed.

Washington pulled one of the charges from the box. It was a tube of fiber, filled with fifteen pounds of Composition B molded into a cone shape at the bottom. At the top the cylinder tapered to another cone, with a firing well for the detonator. The shaped charge used the Monroe effect, named for the engineer who had discovered its properties. Demolitionists had long known that no explosion is instantaneous in all parts of the explosives they were using. Instead, the propagation wave moved from the point of detonation to the farthest reaches of the explosive at a rate equal to that of the detonation speed of the medium. It was, with modern explosives, faster than could be recorded by anything less than the most rapid of high-speed photography, but it was still there.

They had also known that the lines of force from detonating explosives were directed exactly ninety degrees from the surface of the explosive medium. Much explosives force was dissipated harmlessly into the air in this way. Monroe, a Scottish engineer, had discovered that, once the lines of force were on their way, they could be redirected. Two lines of force, if they collided at exactly ninety degrees, tended to cancel one another out. But if they intersected at a lesser angle of incidence, they actually added to the force of one another, pointing themselves in a direction that could be manipulated depending upon the angle of the original surface of the explosives.

What this meant in practice was that if you built your explosive into a cone shape at the bottom, and started the propagation at the top, the cone directed the augmented lines of force into a pencil-point of virtually unimaginable energy, the heat it produced almost as hot as the surface of the sun. This principle allowed relatively small antitank rounds to punch through several inches of homogeneous armor, and linear-shaped charges to cut plate metal so cleanly it looked as if it had been subjected to an acetylene torch wielded by a master.

The fifteen-pound shaped charges Washington was now setting up had been designed for the combat engineers and were used primarily for digging holes. If you wanted to destroy a road, you put the charges into a pattern, blew the holes, and then planted cratering charges made up of a much slower explosive into the resulting pattern. Exploding the cratering charges, whose ammonium-nitrate/fuel-oil mixture created a heaving, rather than the shattering effect of higher-speed explosives, dug holes that even the best-designed tank couldn't negotiate.

And of course, the resourceful Special Forces demolitions men who had experimented with them had found all sorts of other uses. Buried upside down and command-detonated under a tank, they would send the turret spinning into the air like a thrown saucer. Washington had once built what he referred to as the world's largest claymore, placing one of the charges on its side, in front of that standing a roll of barbed wire, and in front of that a fifty-five-gallon drum of fougasse. When detonated, the shaped charge ripped through the barbed wire, sending it out in whirling masses of white-hot shrapnel. The force of the shaped charge, barely attenuated by the barbed wire, then punched through the fougasse, igniting it into a roaring fireball that consumed anything in its path.

He'd had the chance to use it on an attacking VC squad, intent upon forcing their way into the front gate of the camp he was defending. There was little to pick up and bury the next day.

While Washington and Inger were setting up the charge, Finn stripped off his web gear, keeping only the Browning Hi-Power pistol and a couple of fragmentation grenades.

"You're too damn big for that, *Dai Uy*," SFC Elmo Driver, whose First Platoon had responsibility for this sector of the perimeter, said.

Finn looked down at the diminutive sergeant, who, some said, wouldn't have weighed enough to open a parachute were it not for his enormous balls. Driver stood barely five foot four. Truth be known, he was probably slightly shorter than that, but a sympathetic recruiting sergeant had fudged the measurements slightly to allow him to get into the Airborne in the first place.

Legions of bigger men had found to their sorrow that Driver's being small did not mean that he was a pushover. As one six-foot-four sergeant had said after a run-in with him at the NCO club in Okinawa, "It was like fighting a goddamn buzz saw."

Wordlessly, Finn handed over the pistol and grenades. He hadn't been all that eager to go down the hole anyway. Closed-in spaces had never been his favorite places. He tried to tell himself he wasn't claustrophobic, but every time he had to go into a cave or down a tunnel it felt as if his diaphragm were pushing his heart right out his ears, where it thundered with each beat.

"Get clear!" Washington ordered, running the firing wire around a couple of jags in the trench. Finn and Driver went the other way, huddling down behind a substantial earthen berm.

"Fire in the hole, fire in the hole, fire in the hole!" Washington shouted. He twisted the handle of the blasting machine, sending enough current down the line to initiate the firing sequence in the detonator. The current was just enough to send a spark across the gap between two wires. That spark set fire to a mixture whose flash point was extremely low. The fire then heated the initiating mixture, a tiny amount of extremely sensitive explosive, usually lead styphnate, which contained only enough force to begin detonation in the slightly larger intermediate charge, which then detonated the main charge. All this was contained within a slim cylinder of aluminum slightly smaller in diameter than a pencil.

The final detonation was powerful enough to begin the explosives propagation wave in the relatively insensitive

Composition B that made up the shaped charge. Military explosives were by nature insensitive, since they were subject to all sorts of insult by bullet, flame, or just extremely careless handling. You didn't want a truckload of explosives to go off just because someone shot a sniper round into it.

But all that was quicker than the senses could detect. The people close to it felt the earth shudder, the sound of the explosion muffled by the sandbags Washington had packed around it for tamping. A great black cloud of explosives smoke mixed with red dirt gouted up, covering Finn and Driver with a layer of grit.

They ran over to the hole before the last clods fell to the earth. Finn was glad he wasn't going in. It looked distinctly uninviting.

Driver was grinning. "Alice ain't got shit on me," he said, then dropped down into the hole.

Chapter 6

Driver paused only long enough to extract two cigarettes from the pack he always carried in his blouse pocket, rip the filters off, and insert them into his ears as field-expedient earplugs. He'd learned his lesson on that early on. The first time he'd fired a pistol in a cave, down in War Zone C in III Corps, the noise and concussion came close to stunning him.

The tunnel was thick with explosives smoke, the acrid chemical burning his throat and nasal passages with each breath. But, he noticed, it was wafting away from him, indicating that the tunnel was unblocked in that direction.

He'd moved only a couple of steps before he came across the first body, partially covered by dirt from the explosion. He could see no marks on the flesh and concluded that the digger, who wore only a pair of black shorts, had died of concussion. A few feet farther and two more bodies, one who appeared to have been some sort of an official. He was dressed in khaki and had officer tabs on his collar.

It was completely silent in the tunnel, which, to his surprise, was fairly roomy. In tunnels down in III Corps he'd had to crawl and wriggle his way through. Here he could move in no more than a slight crouch.

Twenty feet from where he'd entered, a slight bend obscured his field of view. He cautiously approached it, pistol held close to his body. An old tunnel rat had shown him that trick. People tended, when they were frightened and wanted to be ready to shoot, to hold their pistols out into the firing position. Which meant that the pistol was the first thing to come around a corner, long before you could see what might be hiding there. The tunnel rat had demonstrated how easy it was to take the pistol away, grabbing it and the pistol hand, twisting sharply on one direction or the other. You were then confronted with the choice of trying to hold on to the gun and getting your arm broken, or letting it go. Neither was a particularly good option.

The moan, followed by a shuddering breath, hit his senses with a blow that was almost physical. He could clearly feel the surge of adrenaline shooting from the glands just atop the kidneys all the way through his circulatory system—like a river of liquid fire.

With an effort he slowed his breathing from the short, shallow gasps the adrenaline produced. Slowly he sidestepped, weapon covering each section of the cave as it appeared. Cutting the pie, it was called. The theory was that you could be ready to take out any adversary the moment he appeared, more quickly than he could react.

Driver had no idea if it worked or not, never having had to use it when actually facing an armed adversary. But it sounded good and was a lot better than the alternative, as far as he was concerned.

The alternative was the buttonhook, so named because you hooked your entire body around the corner, again depending upon your speed and your enemy's slow reaction time. Both techniques had been taught by a British Special Air Service (SAS) operator seconded to the Tenth Special Forces Group at Bad Tolz while he was there.

And what if there's more than one guy on the other side? The question had been posed by Sergeant Major Clive Howard, himself a veteran of OSS operations in World War II.

"Then you'd bloody well hope they're all bad shots," the SAS man had replied.

Driver didn't think he wanted to trust his life to a lack of marksmanship training on the part of the North Vietnamese Army.

He saw first a leg, badly mangled, and as he sidestepped farther, the rest of the body. The man's black, chop-cut hair was coated in red dirt; his eyes stared at Driver with the look of one who knew his time on earth was going to end with the sight of flame coming from the muzzle of the gun that was pointed unerringly at his forehead.

Driver saw no weapon, and the man's hands were clear. A quick glance on down the tunnel showed no danger at the moment. He came to a snap decision, tucked the pistol into his belt, and grabbed the wounded man under his arms, dragging him quickly back around the corner and then to the entrance hole.

"Got a prisoner down here," Driver yelled, seeing Captain McCulloden's face appear quickly above. He handed an arm up, felt the weight being lifted as if the Viet were nothing more than a bag of straw.

Shit, he thought. Now I'm gonna have to go back and clear that section again. Probably should have slit his throat, kept going.

He justified his actions, at least for the moment, by thinking that perhaps they could get some useful information from the prisoner. But somewhere deep inside he knew the real reason was that he simply didn't have the stomach for killing an unarmed man.

Getting soft in your old age, Driver, he told himself.

"He say he just a digger," Bobby translated. "Dig caves all over. Nobody every tell him why, they just say, dig. He dig."

Inger glanced up from where he was applying bandages to the man's leg. "Broken tibia and fibula, no major blood vessel involvement. He's not going anywhere anytime soon. You think he's telling the truth?"

Finn grimaced. "What difference does it make? We know he was digging a tunnel. We know they're planning to attack this place."

"We kill?" Bobby asked, already thumbing his holster open.

"No, you bloodthirsty little bastard, we don't kill." Finn looked at Bobby with real fondness. Despite his being a vicious little shit, he was a pretty good kid.

Bobby's face fell. Then his habitual cheerfulness made its inevitable way back to the surface.

"Oh, well," he said. "He probably die with all the rest of us, anyway."

"And thank you, Pollyanna!" Inger said, finishing the bandaging and selecting a piece of wood for a splint.

Bobby looked mystified. What the hell was Pollyanna? The Americans were always making obscure references, using slang that never appeared in his Vietnamese/English dictionary. He never knew if he was being insulted or complimented. He resolved to find out at least what Pollyanna was. If he ever got the chance.

Sergeant Epstein came up, out of breath from running the entire way from the other side of the camp. "L-T Sloane found another one," he gasped. "North side. Looks like a big one."

"What's he doing about it?"

"Resting right now," Epstein said, grinning. "Been working his ass off."

"Bobby, get four out of Driver's First Platoon down there to back him up," McCulloden commanded. "Andy, finish up with this guy and then turn him over to whoever's commanding the rest of the LLDB detachment. Then come on over."

Slats Olchak came up, bearing the news that they had found yet another, a hundred meters to the south of the one they were standing on.

"Busy little rats, ain't they?" Finn said. "Why don't you see if you can find us something that'll make a big boom. I'm getting about tired of this."

Driver was just getting up the nerve to go around the corner where he'd found the wounded man when he heard a noise behind him. He whirled—and was faced with the gold-toothed smile of Nic, his Montagnard platoon sergeant.

"*Dai Uy* Finn tell us we come and help," Nie said. "Bring Frick and Frack."

Driver grinned, glad for the company, indeed. Nie was the most dependable man he had, veteran of a French *groupement mobile,* had been with the Mike Force almost since its inception. Frick and Frack were so named because they were twins and no one (even most 'Yards) could pronounce the names their superstitious mother had given them. They lived together, slept in the same hammock while in the field, and had never been known to consort with women, Montagnard or otherwise. But then, they didn't do much socializing with the men either, being entirely self-contained, it seemed, within themselves.

What mattered the most was that they were good soldiers. Incredibly brave, quite smart, even innovative. In a just world they would have been on their way to at least field-grade rank. Here they would be lucky to make sergeant.

Driver pointed to his left rear, Nie automatically taking up position there, Frick and Frack slightly behind him, ready to provide covering fire. Once again Driver cut the pie, and this time the tunnel was clear.

He took a deep breath and inched his way down the tunnel. They had to be here somewhere. There had been plenty of time for them to recover from the explosion, set up an ambush, or form a raiding party. They'd spent too much time digging this thing to just give it up.

He felt Nie's hand on his shoulder, stopped, and looked at the Montagnard, who was signaling that he heard something. Shit, Driver thought. He pulled the filter tip from one ear and could now hear it himself. Chattering. In Vietnamese. A lot of it. And it was coming closer.

He hurried to the next bend in the tunnel, flattened himself against the wall, took out a frag grenade, and pulled the pin. Beside him, Nie did the same. At Driver's signal both let the spoon fly, the click of the striker hitting the cap so loud it seemed impossible for the people around the corner not to hear it.

One one thousand, two one thousand, he mouthed, Nie watching him closely. Finally he tossed the metal orb around the corner, followed closely by Nie. They'd "cooked off" the grenades, allowing the fuses to burn for two seconds of the three to four seconds they were supposed to take before they exploded. Made it far less likely that someone was going to be able to scoop them up and throw them back.

"Du ma My!" someone screamed just before the grenades filled the world with chest-crushing concussion and black explosives smoke.

Driver whirled around the corner before the survivors could recover their senses, double-tapping a cursing North Vietnamese soldier who was trying to get his gun up. The man went down like a stone, exposing another, whom Driver also shot.

Nie opened up with his M16, impartially hosing down everyone in his path. The racket was earsplitting, the acrid powder smoke clogging the nostrils, mercifully overpowering the smell of blood, shit, and fear.

Within seconds it was over, Frick and Frack rushing by Driver as he reloaded the pistol, happily shooting down the few enemy soldiers who had survived the initial onslaught. Frick motioned him forward. Just ahead was daylight.

"Hold this position," Driver told Nie. "I'm gonna go get something to close this little subway down."

• • •

Sloane had hit upon the happy expedient of driving lengths of one-inch-diameter steel reinforcing rods into the ground at two-foot intervals through the outer perimeter trench. The rods had been shipped in months ago, intended for use in reinforcing the concrete of a planned series of bunkers, but the cement itself had never arrived—probably scammed off for some South Vietnamese officer to build a house, Billy Joe Turner had sourly surmised. The rod had laid in a stack, quietly rusting, until Sloane, looking for something with which to follow Captain McCulloden's directive, had remembered them.

Driving the rods was easy, given the fury that possessed him. With each whack of the sledgehammer he fancied he was crushing the captain's skull. How dare he speak to a fellow officer that way! Especially in front of the enlisted men. He had seen their barely suppressed smiles, the amusement that crinkled their foreheads. They were probably even now laughing at him. *Boy, the captain really dug in ol' Sloane's shit, didn't he?* In their inimitable crude way, they would be dreaming up all sorts of tales to tell.

It wouldn't look good, afterward.

Reputations were such tenuous things. He remembered a crude joke told in the team house by Turner, about a French painter. Who had complained that, despite his having painted a thousand pictures, some of which now hung in the finest collections in the world, no one called him an *artiste*. But, and here Turner had adopted the worst French accent Sloane had ever heard, *I suck one little dick, and everyone calls me a cocksuckaire!*

Would his actions with Stankow this morning be enough

to offset his reputation with the men? Probably not, especially when McCulloden, after a promising first start, had gone back to treating him like some unpleasant substance he had to scrape from his boot.

Whump—and the piece of reinforcing rod he had been hammering against the fierce resistance of the dry earth suddenly disappeared. "Give me another piece of rod!" he commanded the Montagnards, his voice excited. He drove it down two feet to the right of the first, this time being a bit more careful, and when it too had gone in three feet, the resistance stopped.

Without a word, Bucky Epstein, who had been following the probing crew at a distance, amused at seeing Lieutenant Sloane engaged in the first physical labor he could remember the officer doing, left to inform the command group of the find.

Sloane sat down, aware for the first time that he was sweating profusely. He greedily swallowed down half a canteen of water, looked ruefully at his ordinarily spotlessly clean tiger fatigues. They were covered in red dirt, sweated through at crotch, armpits, and chest, the sweat already drying to encrusted-salt white.

It felt good. His shoulders were already aching, he knew his hands were blistered, his head felt as if it were going to explode, but it felt good. He'd always scorned physical labor, felt that such efforts belonged to the "common man," that people such as himself should be doing the supervision of such things. There was no dignity in digging in the dirt, and dignity was all-important. How could you lead men if they thought you were just like them?

Perhaps it wasn't so bad after all. Epstein, who had been following the group—ostensibly to provide security—had for the entire time worn that mocking smile that was so much a feature of his demeanor. With the finding of the tunnel his manner had suddenly changed. Was that just the slightest hint of respect?

Another idea hit him. "Get shovels," he told the interpreter. "Let's find out who's down there."

Olchak hadn't been able to find the cratering charges he would have preferred, but did locate a bunker with cases of engineer demolition packs, what some people called satchel charges. Each was an olive-drab satchel, about the size of a large lady's handbag, containing four two-and-one-half-pound slabs of TNT. Good enough, he thought.

He organized a carrying party, each Montagnard hefting a wooden case with four of the units inside. They weren't particularly happy about carrying them, especially now that someone outside the perimeter was once again directing sniper fire at any exposed targets. Since Olchak didn't think he'd have time to explain to them that a stray round wouldn't detonate the TNT, and since even if he had, he wouldn't have known how to put it in Jarai, he fell back on the expedient of cursing and shouting and the occasional boot to the backside to get them moving.

Give me my old squad anytime, he thought as they hurried down the trench. They never questioned orders, never hesitated, never showed fear. Of course, they were now all dead, their bones entombed somewhere in the vast Russian wastes where they'd fallen. He'd been the only survivor, of that and of other squads, the ones in the last years of the war no more than children. He hadn't, he realized now, been much more than a child himself, sixteen when levied by the German occupiers, only nineteen when he'd had to make his way alone, through hundreds of miles of Silesian forests, Russians everywhere, to make it back home.

And what was waiting for him when he got there? Ruined towns, piles of corpses hastily buried and methodically dug up by the forest animals looking for food. The few survivors hating him, blaming him along with the Germans for what had happened to them. Threatening to come and slit his throat in the night.

His sense of survival told him that he would be far better off in one of the prisoner-of-war camps down the road, the ones run by the Americans or British. To go to a Soviet PW camp was to disappear, vanish as so many had into the vast slave labor camps somewhere the other side of the Ural Mountains.

He had, of course, lied about his unit to the young American interrogator at the nearest camp. He'd been merely a foot soldier in an infantry unit, he said, impressed by the Germans against his will, sent off to fight and threatened with execution if he did not. Since the story matched so well that told by thousands of his countrymen, and since by the time he'd joined his unit they had abandoned the practice of tattooing the blood group on the inner forearm, he had gotten away with it. SS *Standartenführer* Georg Olchak became *Privat* Georg Olchak, one more victim of the Nazis.

Since he'd never been allowed to come home on leave, and since all who had known him in the military were now dead, he was easily able to carry it off. He had been out-processed, and because of his command of English imparted by his schoolmaster mother, also now dead, had found work as an interpreter for the occupation forces. From there it had been a simple matter to emigrate to the United States, particularly when his home country was swallowed up by the communists. By then the Allies had realized that their old friend Stalin was now their new enemy, and anyone willing to fight the minions of godless communism was welcome.

He'd never regretted the move. Killing one communist was as good as killing another, no matter what color the skin or shape of the eyes.

McCulloden's eyes lit up when he saw the boxes. "Just the ticket. How many of these do you need, Elmo?"

Driver, exhausted and not really willing to go back down into the dark hole that stank of death, shrugged his shoulders. "One box ought to do it. So give me two."

"Spoken like a true demo man," Olchak said, grinning at the sergeant. "Calculate the charge, double it, then add ten percent."

"Creative destruction," Driver replied. "Nothing like it in the world."

He dropped back down into the hole, grabbed a handed-down crate of explosives, and dragged it to where Nie was still holding the fort. Elmo had to bump across the bodies to do so, one of them moaning as his foot pressed down on the stomach. Expelling gases, Elmo knew, but it freaked him anyway.

"One more back there," he told Frack, not willing to walk across the bodies any more than he had to. "Go get it while I rig these."

The 'Yard looked unhappy to leave his brother, but followed orders anyway. Soon he came back dragging it. "Make big boom," he said. "I like."

"Me too." Driver stacked the satchel charges in two piles. From the kit that went along with the charges he took out four nonelectric detonators and a roll of detonating cord. He cut four three-foot lengths of cord, then crimped a detonator to each one. Into the firing well of the TNT of the bottom satchel in each stack he inserted two detonators, double-priming them, in the parlance of demolitionists. The trailing ends of the detonating cord he then tied together with yet another piece of det cord, stringing the latter back six feet. Finally, he taped two electric detonators to the cord and ran the firing wire back to the mouth of the cave, where he handed it back up to Olchak.

He sat back for a moment to survey his work, visualizing the effect. When he got back to the surface, he would hook up the blasting machine to the firing wire. A twist of the handle and an electric charge would course down the wire, where it would set off the electric detonators. Even if one was a dud, the other would go off. That was why you double-primed. The explosion would begin the explosive propagation of the detonating cord, a plastic-covered PETN explosive. PETN detonated at a speed of thirty two thousand feet per second—far faster than the eye could see. It was, for a military explosive, also fairly sensitive and was used only in small amounts in things like det cord.

The det cord would carry the explosion to the detonators crimped to it. He could simply have run detonating cord in a couple of loops through the TNT and depended upon it to set off the main charge, but why take chances. This way he knew he'd get a good detonation.

The detonators, in turn, would begin the propagation in the TNT, itself relatively insensitive. Part of the explosive force would dissipate out the mouth of the tunnel, part of it would blow though the entry hole, but with eighty pounds of it sitting there, it should be more than enough to do the job.

He exited the hole finally, marginally satisfied. Ammonium nitrate would have been better, but you used what you had. A combat demolitionist couldn't be a perfectionist.

With a flourish, Olchak handed him the blasting machine.

"Glad you don't owe me any money," Driver said, wiring the leads to the terminals on the machine. "You might have decided to cancel the debt while I was down there."

"Depends on how much money," Slats Olchak replied.

The hell of it, Driver thought as he yelled fire in the hole the necessary three times, is that I don't necessarily think he's joking.

He twisted the handle and was rewarded with the feeling of a huge thump somewhere beneath them, powder smoke and dirt whooshing out the hole like the exhaust from a rocket.

"Holy shit!" he heard Epstein exclaim, and lifted his head above the trench line to see a huge plume of smoke erupt from the other end of the tunnel. Slowly, almost majestically, the ground just outside the perimeter wire collapsed into a sizable depression.

"Don't think they'll be using that one anymore," Finn McCulloden said. "Now let's shut up the rest of them."

• • •

Sloane's shovel broke through the top of the tunnel. "Stand back!" he commanded the 'Yards who were helping him dig. He pulled the pin on a frag grenade and dropped it down the hole. The explosion shook the ground only slightly, smoke pouring from the hole.

"Dig!" he said. "Quick!"

He was like a man possessed, dirt flying from his shovel, doing as much as any three of the Montagnards. This was his prize, and by God he wasn't going to let anyone else exploit it. McCulloden and the others were even now blowing up the tunnel discovered on the south side of the camp and would soon be making their way around to his.

Finally there was enough space for him to drop down inside. He grabbed a pistol belt equipped with more frag grenades and extra magazine pouches for the M-1911 Colt .45 pistol he habitually carried, the one he'd had modified to include mother-of-pearl handles. That and a flashlight completed his kit.

Now or nothing, he told himself, steeling for the ordeal. He'd never been in a tunnel before, expected tight confines, rats, or worse. He'd heard that the Viet Cong sometimes suspended cobras from the roof. He hated snakes. Wasn't too fond of tight places, either.

Be a man! He could visualize his father, standing there beside him, exhorting him to shape up, quit being such a pussy, get back out there and fight it out!

Here's to you, you old bastard, he thought, and dropped down into the hole.

He fell much farther than expected, almost automatically putting his body into a parachute landing fall (PLF), twisting quickly erect and covering front and then whirling to the rear, pistol held stiffly out before him.

"Jesus Christ!" he breathed. This wasn't a tunnel, it was a goddamned thoroughfare! He could stand without crouching or even bending his head to avoid the low-wattage lightbulbs that lit up the place. The frag grenade had destroyed the ones nearest the entry point, but as far as he could see in both directions, they lit up the cavern with an eerie blue-white glow.

This wasn't some spur-of-the-moment tactic dreamed up by the North Vietnamese when they decided to attack this particular camp, he thought. This thing had been there for a long time. The floor was hard-packed, showing the impression of dozens of feet. Weak spots were shored up by timber and plywood. It sloped gently downward, toward the perimeter, to allow seepage from monsoon rains to drain out.

It was easily capable of accommodating two men at a time, shoulder to shoulder. He could imagine an entire company coming through, only to appear behind the defenders at the worst possible time.

And I found it! That should be worth something, even with McCulloden.

He looked up to see the round faces of the Montagnards, staring down at him in astonishment. "Get a squad down here," he told the interpreter. "Cover my rear. I'm going to see where this thing comes out."

The North Vietnamese, obviously aware of the disaster that was befalling their painfully gained tunnel system, had brought in a new team of snipers. To expose yourself, even for a moment, was once again to take the chance of a bullet through the head.

"Think you can do your magic again, Bucky?" Finn asked.

"Do better than that, sir," the sergeant replied, eyes lighting up. "Last time I visited Pleiku, I happened across an M-21 Sniper System. Traded an NCO from the Fourth ID, was getting ready to DROS, out of it and a case of Lake City .308. You get the troops spotting where the fire's coming from, I'll put a round right down their barrels."

Finn had no doubt it would be true. Epstein had been a corporal in the Israeli Defense Forces during the Six Day War, was rumored to have stacked up the better part of an Egyptian infantry company with a weapon far less capable than the M-21. After the war he had gotten bored with patrolling Sinai, left Israel, and joined the U.S. Army with the specific goal of coming to Vietnam. The Army had, in its usual inimitable manner, sent him not to an infantry unit, but to a maintenance battalion in the 101st Airborne. It had taken him almost the full year of his first tour to effect a transfer to the Special Forces, being accepted as a recon sergeant in Studies and Observations Group. Wounded on his first trip "across the fence," he had recuperated in Japan, returned at his own request to Vietnam, and, it being felt that he was still not sufficiently recovered to run recon yet, was assigned to Boun Tlak Special Forces Camp.

Funny how things sometimes worked out, Finn mused. No novelist would have conceived of the roundabout way that had put a trained sniper exactly where he was needed.

As Epstein ran at a crouch through the trenches to find

his weapon, Finn turned back to supervise the destruction of the second trench. Once more Elmo Driver and his crew were below, this time facing no resistance. Whoever commanded the NVA facing them had obviously come to the belated realization that trying to push through enough people to overcome a determined adversary in such a confined space was a waste of time and men.

Within a few minutes Nie, Frick and Frack, and finally Elmo Driver came storming up out of the cave. Elmo had decided it was too risky to try to detonate everything electrically. Too much chance of the NVA coming in behind them and cutting the wire while they were setting up.

He'd hit upon the expedient of rigging several different nonelectric circuits and hiding them within the explosives. The detonators were crimped to precut pieces of time fuse, the length selected to provide only exactly enough time to clear the tunnel once the fuse lighters were pulled.

Within only a second of Elmo's feet clearing the hole came the *whump* of the explosion. Once again the ground lifted just outside the wire, settling into another depression.

The depressions were bad, would give the attacking NVA a place to shelter themselves from direct fire once the main attack came, Finn thought. "Sergeant Stankow, you think you can put us some mortar concentrations on those?"

"You have to ask?" Stankow said, acting hurt.

"Probably not." Finn grinned. This was what was nice about dealing with professionals. You seldom did have to ask.

The probing teams had so far found no more tunnels, leaving only the one Sloane had reported. Finn and Driver's team headed through the trench complex to the north side, hearing the crack of sniper bullets as a steady drumbeat marking their passage.

Halfway there, the way was blocked by a group of Montagnards huddled around one of their own. It was immediately obvious there was nothing to be done for him. He'd obviously been unwary enough to expose himself for just a fraction of a second too long. The round had taken off the top of his head as neatly as one would use a can opener on a container of brains. The brain itself looked surprisingly undamaged, but Finn knew that beneath its seemingly unmarred surface the blood vessels would have exploded from the overpressure. The man had been dead before he could hit the ground.

Bobby yelled at the Montagnards to get the hell out of the way and they obeyed in stunned silence.

It was often that way. One moment you were standing there talking to a man, the next he had essentially ceased to exist. No matter how many times you saw it, it always came as a shock. If you were yourself engaged in combat you could continue to function, your survival instincts taking over and protecting the organism. Only sometime later would you have to face it, often when you least expected it.

That was the pernicious effect of snipers. There really wasn't a lot you could do, other than to take cover and face the realization that it could have been you, lying there with your brain steaming in the air.

"Get this body out of here," Finn instructed. "Tell the rest of them to dig this trench deeper. And to keep their goddamned heads down."

In truth the trench was probably deep enough, but only in

action could the thrall be broken. It was easy to destroy morale, and thus fighting effectiveness, if you just stood there and did nothing. The mind did terrible things.

One of the Montagnards yelled back at Bobby, getting up in his face. Both were gesticulating wildly, seeming ready to come to blows. Good, Finn thought. Anger is good. Anything was better than the apathy that came over you at such times. He knew. He'd been there.

That matter finally resolved after much shouting, they hurried on down the trench. Another sniper round struck close, showering dirt down on them, this time answered by the heavy boom of a weapon somewhere inside the camp. Finn smiled. Obviously Bucky Epstein was at work.

Finn came around one of the corners in the zigzag trench, finally seeing a group of Montagnards gathered around a hole. "Ask them where *Trung Ui* Sloane is," he told Bobby.

Bobby chattered for a moment in Jarai, a look of astonishment suddenly coming over him. Bobby had sized up the lieutenant much earlier on, judged him to be like so many he had seen—a know-nothing who by virtue of rank still tried to command people like him. Who would fall apart at the first real crisis. But the 'Yards were telling him that the lieutenant had gone down in the hole. Alone. He was either very stupid or very brave. Bobby would have bet the former.

Finn cursed when Bobby told him. "That boy's trying real hard to be a hero. Too damned hard. Elmo, you want to go down there and find out what's going on? Be careful. Asshole's likely to be a little trigger-happy."

Chapter 7

Bucky Epstein drew in a deep breath, let half of it out, and settled the crosshairs of the scope on some vegetation whence he had seen a telltale spurt of fire. He was aiming at a point some 325 to 350 meters away. He knew this because of the range cards he had so laboriously prepared over the last six months, in which he had noted specific landmarks and physically walked the distances to each.

Each heartbeat caused the scope to jump, ever so slightly Such a jump, at this distance, would move the strike of the bullet as much as three inches, enough to miss something as small as a man's head.

He timed his heartbeats, making sure the scope was exactly where he wanted it in the tiny interval in between each beat. Everything else was zoned out. He did not hear the chatter of the Montagnards in the trench below his sandbagged position. The red dust that blew across the camp with a sudden gust of wind affected him not at all. There was nothing except the slowly tightening tension of his trigger finger.

The recoil of the weapon came as a surprise, as it should

have. Quickly he settled the scope back on the target, was rewarded with the sight of a body flipped over by the impact of the bullet, his uncamouflaged face clear in the excellent optics of the Leatherman.

In the long watches of the night, when you and the other American on duty had nothing to do but try to keep awake long enough to make the periodic checks of the perimeter, he was sometimes asked how he felt about such things as this. People back in the States, he knew, regarded the Green Berets as hardened killers, incapable of feeling. That was anything but true. No man killed another without feeling something, even if it was only a momentary sadness.

But, he'd had to admit to his questioners, there was far less feeling at killing at a distance. It became a matter of trajectories, effect of wind and humidity, downhill versus uphill shots, control of the body. Almost an intellectual exercise, although one with all-important consequences.

The dead sniper on the hillside above would have felt about the same thing, if it had gone differently. Theirs was an almost gentlemanly war, fought at a distance, with none of the blood and shit and terror of the up close and personal.

"*Trung Si* Bucky," his Montagnard spotter said. "Another one right two finger, up five finger."

Epstein traversed his scope to the spot described. Early on, when he had been training his spotters, he had despaired of them ever learning distance measurement. The concept of feet, yards, meters, kilometers, or any other Western-oriented measurement systems was as foreign as would have been quantum mechanics. Yet among themselves they picked out spots to which other 'Yards were referring, quickly and accurately. Believing that it was far easier to use something they knew rather than try to drill them in something they didn't, he began to use the same method of reference. He hadn't been disappointed.

There! A piece of vegetation that was swaying slightly, even though the surrounding leaves were still. The NVA, and the Viet Cong before them, tended to interlace fresh vegetation on a wicker frame carried on the back. It was a good method of camouflage if you stayed perfectly still. On windy days you could get away with moving around a bit, since the surrounding vegetation was also moving.

But on a day like today, when the wind came only in gusts if it came at all, the slightest movement caused the leaves and branches to sway unnaturally, becoming a beacon to the trained eye.

His own position was deep within a bunker on the corner of the camp. He kept well back from the firing slots, not willing to expose himself by telltale muzzle flash or powder smoke. Unless someone was looking directly down the barrel when he fired, he was well nigh invisible. Still, he knew that to stay in the same spot for too long was suicide. He would engage one or two more targets, then move to another bunker.

It wouldn't be as if he didn't have anything to shoot at, no matter where he set up. It was, as they say, a target-rich environment.

He centered his scope on the spot.

"Captain, sir?"

McCulloden whirled to see Lieutenant Sloane, looking tired but triumphant. "How the hell . . ."

"You've got to come see this," Sloane said. "You won't believe it."

McCulloden followed the lieutenant to a low building, most of which was underground. The sides were shielded with several layers of sandbags, and across the top was the standard sandbag/psp/tin roof. Trash littered the trench outside. Across the door was a painted plywood sign, warning in Vietnamese of the dire consequences that would follow, should any unauthorized person enter.

"LLDB supply room," Sloane explained. "They wanted one of their own, said the ones we had the 'Yards could come and go at will. Steal everything."

"And it never occurred to anyone that all the supplies came from us, that if we wanted to let the 'Yards steal things, we could?"

It was a long-standing tradition in the A camps that a little "leakage" was an acceptable thing. If the family of a Civilian Irregular Defense Group soldier suddenly had new blankets to keep themselves warm against the highlands chill, was that a bad thing? After all, they didn't get paid much, there were few sources of supply in the jungle, and they'd been moved out of their longhouses long ago. So who cared?

Sloane looked almost shamefaced. "Captain Koslov didn't see the harm in it," he said, his voice defensive. "I didn't either, until now."

McCulloden pushed his way through the opened door, was met by the sight of shelf after shelf of equipment and clothing. There must have been two hundred sets of tiger-stripe fatigues, cases of Bata boots, new-looking radios, crates of mosquito repellent, bag after bag of rice, the latter showing the handshake symbol of the United States Agency for International Development. Finn had seen many such bags in the caches he and his teams had raided over the years, finding it ironic that the rice farmers of Arkansas and Louisiana were helping feed the Viet Cong.

"Running a big-time black market operation out of here," he surmised. "No wonder they didn't want to let anyone inside."

"Easy for them to do," Sloane said. "Look at this."

He led McCulloden to the back of the bunker, opened the door of a big teakwood cabinet. The steps leading down into the tunnel below showed Finn everything he needed to know.

"Sly bastards," Finn said, almost in admiration. "Not only did they dig a goddamned freeway under the camp, they used our own electricity to light it." He pointed out the wires leading from the lighting system to the outside, where he was sure they would be hooked into the camp generator.

"And we never knew," Sloane marveled.

"One thing we do know. The LLDB didn't do this by themselves. It had to come from the outside. I think we need to pay a little visit to their team house, don't you?"

Olchak had just delivered the wounded sapper to the LLDB. The senior NCO, in charge now that the LLDB lieutenant had fled the camp, smiled and thanked him and offered him tea, or perhaps the *Trung Si* would like a beer?

He'd refused, of course. He took an instant dislike to the oleaginous little man, seeing in him the same characteristics as he had in so many of his countrymen. Smile at you to your face and slip the knife through your ribs when you turned your back.

Slats Olchak had little use for the Vietnamese, even less for the Laotians with whom he'd had to serve on his first tour in Indochina, on the old White Star teams. Someone had once asked him, if he'd had his way, how he would have fought the war.

I'd take all the good Vietnamese and put them in a boat, he'd said. Wouldn't have to be a very big boat. Then I'd go back and nuke the country until it was a fused-glass parking lot.

Then I'd go out and sink that damned boat.

"Slats!" he heard Captain McCulloden call, just as there was the report of a pistol from within the LLDB bunker.

Cursing, he drew his own pistol, slammed through the door of the bunker just in front of the captain.

The LLDB sergeant was standing over the now dead prisoner, a wisp of smoke still coming from his pistol barrel.

"He try to escape," the Vietnamese stammered. "Had to shoot!"

"Drop the gun!" McCulloden commanded. Behind him, Sloane slipped through the door, flattening himself against the wall and covering two of the LLDB, who looked as though they might want to go for the rifles hanging on the wall.

The Vietnamese sergeant was smiling again, the very picture of cooperation. "I tell you, he try to escape," he said again. "Very bad man."

Olchak paid no attention at all to his words, looking instead at the eyes. Somewhere in the depths he saw movement swimming, just as the sergeant twitched the gun toward him. Olchak fired, the trigger finger working before conscious thought could tell it to. The heavy slug caught the sergeant high in the chest, the thump of the bullet loud even in the aftermath of the report.

Suddenly there was a roar as Sloane's pistol went off, hitting a Vietnamese who had pulled his own pistol from beneath the bunk he was sitting on. After that Olchak couldn't really have told who shot whom, knowing that the battle was over only when his slide locked back.

The room was heavy with powder smoke and the stench of death. Six Vietnamese lay in sprawled disarray, one of them still moaning.

Calmly, Olchak extracted another magazine from his pouch, reloaded the .45, and shot the man in the head.

"I'm hit," Sloane said, suddenly slumping against the bunker wall. He'd felt a hammer blow to the side of his head, so hard it crossed his eyes. He reached up to feel blood streaming down the side of his face. My God, he thought, I've been shot in the head. He felt dizzy, wanted to sit down. Perhaps to wait for the end to come.

McCulloden crossed over to him, closely inspected the wound, took a field dressing from Sloane's own pouch, and quickly covered the wound. He pressed down hard, sending a shot of pain right through the lieutenant's head.

"Scalp wound," he said. "They bleed a lot. Don't think it was close enough to the skull to do any internal damage. You're going to have a hell of a headache for a while, though. Here, hold this while I tie it off."

Sloane did as he was told, pressing the bandage as hard as he could against the streaming wound. He didn't care about the pain. He wasn't going to die!

McCulloden tied the ends of the bandage securely

around the lieutenant's skull, then took an Ace bandage from his own kit and wrapped it around and around until Sloane looked as if he were doing tryouts for a mummy movie. After a few moments the blood stopped flowing, leaking only slightly through the combined bandages. Sloane was lucky in that the bullet had missed the temporal artery, otherwise, McCulloden thought, he'd have to be rummaging around in the wound with a set of forceps, trying to pinch it off. This way elevation, pressure, and Sloane's own clotting process would soon stop even the seepage.

Olchak had busied himself by searching the team house. He drug several cases of fragmentation grenades from beneath one of the bunks. "What do you reckon they were going to use these for?" he asked.

McCulloden looked up from where he was working on Sloane. "My guess would be they were going to go around and toss them into the bunkers. I expect that the ones with Americans inside would get first priority. Classic VC strategy, get someone on the inside, take out the critical points, confuse and disorient the defenders. The guys coming through the wire do a walkover."

"And it would have worked," Olchak said.

"It would have worked," Finn agreed. "Had the same thing happen to me down at Vinh Thanh, in '66. First Cav sent a convoy up our road, resupplying us with artillery ammo. Since we'd stolen our 105 from them, it only seemed fair they'd have to give us ammo for it." Finn grinned, relishing the thought. There was nothing a Special Forces man liked better than to put something over on his peers in conventional units.

"Anyway, one of the officers left his camera in a jeep while he walked around; it got stolen of course. We closed the camp down, searched everywhere. Found the camera. Also found all sorts of caches like this, and detailed plans for attacking the camp. That night."

"Lucky."

"Yeah," Finn said. "Lucky."

Sometimes when he couldn't sleep—and that was all too often these days—he would think about just how lucky he'd been. He wasn't a particularly religious man, but sometimes had to wonder if something or someone truly was watching over him.

Or was fate just the result of some cosmic crapshooter, and so far he had been coming up sevens? In which case snake eyes was bound someday to follow.

"They shot the sapper because they were afraid we'd find out about the big tunnel," Olchak said. "Didn't know the LT here had already found it."

"That'd be my guess. Think you can walk, Lieutenant? We'll get you over to the dispensary. Take a few aspirin and lie down for a while. Andy Inger will want to look at that wound, anyway, fill out a casualty tag."

What he didn't say was that Inger would also want to observe the lieutenant, make sure there was no brain swelling from the tremondous concussion such a wound could cause. He'd been watching Sloane's eyes while bandaging him, satisfied to see that pupil size remained the same on both sides. But the body was a strange mechanism. He'd seen men take a half dozen rounds, any one of which should have been fatal, and spend no more than a month in the hospital. And others with no visible wounds at all, die for no apparent reason.

You tried to take no chances.

"Gonna get a Purple Heart, Lieutenant," he said. "This your first one?"

This is getting interesting, Bucky Epstein thought. He had, according to his own estimation, killed or wounded six enemy snipers so far. But it hadn't seemed to slow down the volume of fire coming into the camp. It seemed that when he took out one, they replaced him with at least one and possibly two more.

Sooner or later, he knew, they were going to figure out where he was. Probably time to move.

Almost in confirmation of the thought, a round came through the embrasure and struck the sandbags on the far wall. Damn, he thought, they're getting better.

"Where did it come from?" he demanded of the spotter.

"No see, *Trung Si*," the Montagnard said.

"Goddamnit, how could you not see? Close as he came, you should have been looking right down his barrel." He launched into a tirade, the gist of which was that if the 'Yard couldn't do a better job than that, he was going to send his ass back down to the trenches.

Snap! The crack of the bullet passing by his ear, breaking the sound barrier as it did so, was enough to draw his sudden and alert attention back to the matter at hand. There! Branches and leaves moving in a way they shouldn't, the sniper undoubtedly trying to get a slightly better angle.

Too bad, asshole, he murmured as he settled the scope on the spot, took up the slack on the trigger, felt the satisfying shove of recoil. He settled the scope back, only to see that the branches were still moving in the same rhythmic way.

The realization that he had been taken in came at almost the same time as the bullet. Only the fact that involuntary muscles had jerked his head up, off the scope, saved him from taking it somewhere around the cheekbone. As it was, it clipped off a chunk of his ear. He dropped to the floor of the bunker, pulling the rifle down with him.

"Time to get the hell out of here," he told the spotter.

There was no response. He turned to see the Montagnard slumped on the floor, watching with dull eyes as the last of the blood from a severed carotid artery washed down the front of his shirt.

"Son of a bitch!" he swore.

He'd been outfoxed. Taken advantage of because of his overweening self-confidence. That someone out there was at least as good as he was came as a terrible shock.

And it had caused a man's death.

Think about that later! Now get out of here. Get the bastard who did it.

Sergeant Stankow was having problems of his own. The snipers were making it extremely difficult to work the 4.2-inch mortar. One of his ammunition bearers had been killed, and the others were unwilling to stand up and expose themselves to the fire. That reduced them to crawling back and forth to the bunker, pushing the heavy shells in front of them as they went.

It would get worse if they couldn't shoot at all. At least now he was able to keep harassing and interdictory fire on the likely assembly points, keeping their heads down if not killing them. Once you stopped that, they wouldn't have to use snipers. The regular riflemen would be pouring it on, and with the volume of fire that would be coming into the camp, disaster would be inevitable.

He instructed the Montagnard mortar sergeant to keep firing and, crouching and sometimes crawling, made his way to the nearest 81mm mortar pit. The 81 had a much smaller bursting radius, but was far easier to use. Best of all, the ammunition was considerably lighter.

He found that crew cowering at the bottom of a trench, not daring to raise their heads up for fear of getting them taken off by sniper bullets.

"You would make the fire chief ashamed," he told them, in passable Jarai. The fire chief was a holy man in their tribe and was primarily responsible for their recruitment by the Americans. Stankow had seen him once, at a rice-wine ceremony, the wizened 'Yard looking as if he were at least a hundred years old. Although, given the stresses and strains of living in the jungle, hunted by both sides, subsisting off monkey meat and grubs, he could as well have been no older than Stankow.

It worked. One of the 'Yards, not the sergeant, who obviously wanted to remain under cover, spoke sharply to them. They crawled over to the gun, started handing Stankow the high-explosive rounds.

He cranked the elevating mechanism up, sighted on the aiming sticks, pulled the safety wire from the warhead, and dropped the round down the tube. *Whomp!* and it was on its way, the arc of the slow-moving round clearly visible. For a moment Stankow thought he might have elevated the tube too far—the round was being pushed by a gust of wind and looked to be coming right back down on them.

It was, he knew, an optical illusion. The round drilled its way back down, the slight wobble creating a ululating whisper. A whisper that someone below would hear only at the last second.

When it was far too late to do any good.

The explosion came just outside the outer perimeter wire. Right where he would be massing his troops, were he the enemy commander.

"More!" he said.

Finn McCulloden, having sent Lieutenant Sloane, assisted by Olchak, to the dispensary, quickly made his way back to the command bunker. He too was concerned about the increasing amount of small-arms fire coming into the camp.

"We still have commo?" he asked Becker.

"Voice and CW," the sergeant replied. "Which do you want?"

"Voice," Finn replied. Becker tuned the big Collins transceiver, handed him the handset.

"Charlie Six, this is Cowboy Six, over."

Came the welcome voice of Sam Gutierrez. "Good to hear from you, Six. How's it going?"

"Better than we have any reason to hope, not as good as I'd like." Finn thought about telling Gutierrez about the tunnels, decided to send that particular information over the CW, coded by Becker on his onetime pad. No use in letting the enemy radio intercept get more information than he was ready to allow.

"What can I do to help?"

"Get us some support in here. Air, artillery, gunships—I don't care. They're wearing our asses out with sniper fire, and I'd like a little relief."

"Stand by."

Finn waited by the radio, its crackle the only noise in the bunker. Outside the steady thump of small-arms fire seemed to be increasing.

"Cowboy, this is Charlie Six, over."

"What took you so long? I was getting lonely."

It had only been a few seconds, and he knew Gutierrez would take it in the spirit of the joke it was, but there was a certain amount of truth to the plea. Camp Boun Tlak was getting to be a lonely place. It felt, he thought, as if you were standing on the absolute edge of the world, and someone was steadily trying to saw it off.

"Guns on the way," Gutierrez said. He gave Finn the frequency of the helicopter gunships, coded by a simple transposition code they'd agreed upon during mission planning. You took a word of ten letters, none of which could be the same, and assigned a number from one to zero to each letter. A trained cryptologist could, of course, break the code through analysis of often-recurring letter combinations, but one hoped that the NVA didn't have any cryptologists handy down at the regimental level.

"He has your call sign," Gutierrez continued. "Be on-station within fifteen. You got a way to mark targets?"

"Do I ever," Finn replied, thinking of the piles of white phosphorous shells, called by the soldiers Willy Peter, he'd seen stacked in the mortar bunkers. Willy Peter was originally designed for laying down smoke screens, the incendiary mixture inside starting to burn fiercely upon contact with the air. It produced a choking cloud of white smoke that could hide a battalion in the attack, if the wind was right and you used enough of it. A WP strike would be clearly visible even in the heavy jungle. Perfect for marking a target.

It had the ancillary benefit of being a great antipersonnel round. The mortar casing itself fragmented, creating some damage. But far more was caused by the particles of burning white phosphorus, which hit the skin and continued to burn until smothered by lack of oxygen. If it wasn't smothered it would burn its way completely through the body.

"Sending a FAC back over," Gutierrez continued. "He'll spot for the one-seven-fives. They can fill in the gaps while the guns rearm and refuel."

The information eased Finn's mind at least a little. Between helicopter gunships and artillery they could keep the fire from outside the camp to a minimum. Likelihood was that the NVA had dug in so deep they wouldn't be taking too many casualties from it.

You did what you could. The real test wouldn't be today, anyway.

He looked at his watch, once again amazed that it was still so early. Hours to go before dark. Not that he minded. He wished that somehow the earth could be forced to stand still, the sun never go down.

As well wish for God to send lightning, he thought.

"Those one-seven-fives, do they have any TD fuses?" he asked. TD, time delay, would allow the big shells to bury themselves in the earth before detonating. Hopefully, to collapse some NVA bunkers and tunnels.

"TD it is," Gutierrez replied. "I'll relay the request."

"No other arty?"

"Afraid not."

"Getting to be redheaded stepchildren out here, aren't we?"

"Haven't we always been?"

"Hell, why change things now?" Finn said, reflecting upon the fact that Gutierrez was right. Since its inception, the Special Forces effort in Vietnam had been predicated upon the fact that it was more acceptable back home to lose a very few American soldiers and a whole lot of indigenous ones. Looked far better on the casualty figures.

"How's the battalion doing?"

"Still no major resistance. Ahead of schedule," Gutierrez replied.

"That won't last."

"Don't worry. They're not taking any chances."

Wouldn't mind if they did, just a little bit, Finn thought. It would certainly have made him feel more secure to have the other two Mike Force companies here now. Even a North Vietnamese regiment would hesitate to take on such a force in entrenched positions.

Not to be. Even if the battalion met no resistance at all, they could not physically move that far in less than two days.

This was as good as it was going to get. He tried to tell himself that it wasn't so bad, that he'd been in far worse positions and had survived.

But that was like trying to lie to yourself. Every time before there had been an out. No matter how bad it had got, you could fight your way through, break up and escape and evade, if necessary. Lose yourself in the jungle. The VC didn't track all that well, and the North Vietnamese were worse. Not hard to shake off pursuers, particularly if you left them the occasional surprise.

There would be no E and E here. It was stand and fight. And die.

For just a second he allowed himself the luxury of wondering, yet again, what the hell he was doing here. At any time over the last few years he could have resigned his commission, as so many had, and returned to the States. Where his only contact with the war would have been on television and in the newspapers.

And where you would have died, slowly, inside. Suicide, the weapon of choice being alcohol, or drugs, or just despair and guilt.

He signed off, told Becker to mind the radio, that he was going to go out and get ready for the helicopter gunships that had been promised. He quickly scribbled a report on the tunnels, told the commo man to encode it and send it by CW.

Becker looked at his face —and for the first time became afraid.

The captain looked—what was it? Sad. That was it. Sad and resigned.

Oh, shit, the commo man thought. We're in more trouble than I thought.

Andy Inger looked up from where he was treating a strike force trooper for a sucking chest wound to see Olchak bring in the lieutenant. He noted the blood-soaked bandage on the officer's head, quickly determined that the bleeding was only seepage at the moment.

"Take a number," he said, his voice cheerful. "Be with you in a moment."

For a second it looked as if Lieutenant Sloane was going to protest. Inger turned his back to the officer, grabbed a set of angle scissors, cut away the striker's fatigue jacket to reveal the black-rimmed hole where the bullet had gone in. A light pink froth bubbled from the hole with each breath the soldier exhaled, was sucked back in on inhalation.

He turned the man over, sharply sucking his breath at the sight. The bullet had obviously tumbled, tearing out a great chunk of rib and the flesh surrounding it. Still, there was no sign of either arterial bleeding, which would have been bright red, or the dark red flow of a major vein.

The man's breathing was becoming steadily more labored, indicating to Inger that the affected lung had probably collapsed. He ripped the cover off a petrolatum-impregnated bandage, pressed first the bandage, then the waterproof cover it had come in, over the wound. The surface quickly dimpled, showing him that he had a good seal. He did the same to the front wound, then wrapped a big Ace bandage around the man's chest to keep the bandages in place. He then had the striker lie down on the affected side, the better to allow the unaffected lung to expand into the space that the damaged lung had opened.

The effect was immediate. The striker started breathing far more easily, and within seconds the slight blue tinge left his lips.

There was one final step. Inger asked one of the Montagnard medics for a thoracentesis pack. From it he took a long needle, a three-way valve, and a huge syringe. He swabbed a spot just over the striker's floating rib with Betadine solution, then inserted the long needle between the ribs. The striker's face screwed up with the pain, but he endured it stoically. It never ceased to amaze Andy Inger how much the Montagnards trusted them to do the right thing. Stick my hand in the fire? I really don't want to, but the American must know what he's doing. Okay.

Blood immediately started flowing from the needle. Andy slipped the three-way valve on it, then affixed the syringe. Turned one way, the valve allowed him to aspirate blood through the needle by pulling back the plunger on the syringe. When the syringe was full, he turned the valve the other way, pushing the plunger back down and squirting the blood and other liquids into an emesis tray.

He pulled out, he estimated, a full 500 ccs of liquid before the needle started coming up dry. Now that the entry of outside air into the closed system was blocked, the other lung would be expanding. As a sign of this, the striker was now breathing almost normally.

He left the needle in place, instructing one of the 'Yard medics to watch the man, let him know if there was any sign of respiratory difficulty. The 'Yard wanted to know if he should give the striker some morphine. Now that the shock of wounding was lessening, the man was showing clear signs of pain.

"No can do," Inger said. "Morphine depresses the breathing. He's just going to have to grin and bear it."

He turned his attention to the lieutenant, who had slumped on one of the few empty cots and was now watching his every move in fascinated silence.

"So, LT," he said. "Let's take a look at your little boo-boo."

He cut away the bandage, noting approvingly that Captain McCulloden had placed it very professionally. Once a medic, always a medic, he thought.

It started bleeding again. Some venous flow, which could be stopped by pressure, but one bright little arterial spurt. He opened a surgical pack, took from it a pair of hemostats and a set of tweezers. He grasped the flesh next to the artery, pulled it away from the flow, ignoring the sharply drawn breath indicating just how painful the process might be. With the hemostat he dug in the wound, finally exposing the end of the small artery. He clamped down on it, was rewarded with the immediate cessation of bleeding.

He rummaged through the pack, found the catgut sutures, pulled the artery out even farther, and quickly tied it off above the hemostat, drawing the catgut as tight as possible. When the wound was closed, the catgut would slowly be absorbed into the body, eliminating the need to go back in and take it out.

He unclamped the hemostat, checked for bleeding, saw that there was none, then performed the same procedure for the larger veins.

"I'm gonna close this up," he told Sloane. "We leave it open, the scalp has a tendency to retract. Makes it a hell of a lot harder to close it up later. Besides, this'll keep most of the dirt out. I'll give you enough antibiotics, should keep any infection down. That okay with you?"

There had been no mention of evacuation, Sloane thought as the medic scrubbed out the wound with a pHisoHex solution. And, he surmised, there would not be. The real reason Inger was closing up the wound was that it would enable Sloane to go back out and fight.

The headache that had been pounding behind his eyes suddenly grew much worse.

Chapter 8

"Cowboy Six, this is Red Leg Two Zero, over."

Finn pulled the handset from its perch on the left shoulder of his web gear, pressed the push-to-talk switch, and acknowledged the call of the artillery forward observer, flying overhead in a little single-engine Birddog.

"Understand you need a little help down there, Six," the forward observer said.

"Anything you can do would be appreciated, my friend."

"One-seven-fives are standing by. Where do you want 'em?"

Finn had come up with a plan, which he quickly described to the FO.

"Might just work," Red Leg Two Zero replied. Finn could almost read the amusement in his voice. "Wait one."

Finn listened to him relay coordinates to the faraway cannon, then heard the word "Shot." That was his acknowledgment of the battery's notification that the first shell was on the way.

Moments later, though to Finn it seemed an eternity, he

heard the FO report, "Splash." Bullshit, Finn thought. Either they missed the whole damned area, or the shell had been a dud. Certainly there was no sign of an explosion.

Then the ground shook beneath his feet, the tremor stronger than that he remembered coming from the only earthquake he'd ever been in. A huge cloud of dust mixed with explosives smoke spurted from the ground like a dirty geyser, two hundred yards outside the wire.

The time-delay fuse had allowed the big shell to burrow itself deep into the ground before exploding. The soft ground had transmitted the shock, almost like ripples through water and, Finn hoped, collapsed any trenches or tunnels within range.

"How's that, Six?" the FO inquired.

"Fire for effect," Finn replied.

"Fire for effect, roger." The forward observer transmitted the command to the faraway battery, who would be standing by with shells in the tube, waiting. All the tubes would fire at the same time, upon the same coordinates, depending upon slight differences in powder weight, heat of the cannon, wind, humidity, and a dozen other factors to keep the shells from falling upon exactly the same spot. Something like two tons of explosives, Finn knew, were now on their way.

He heard "Shot" again, counting the seconds this time. There was a slight rushing noise, growing louder by the instant, then a series of dull thunks. This time when the explosions came, you could actually see the ground move. Dirt filled the air, and from somewhere outside the wire he could hear a faint scream.

"Right one hundred, up one hundred," he commanded.

"Fire for effect." No time to feel any sympathy for the poor bastards who were now waiting for the next onslaught. No time to worry about the shells perhaps bursting in the wrong place. No time for anything but killing.

And the killing was just getting started.

The next shells came in, most of them on target but one errant projectile landing just outside the wire, where the resulting crater swallowed up a section of the outer defenses. "Shit!" Finn swore. That was why you didn't call 175s on danger-close. If he had, the errant shell would have landed just about atop the bunker in which he was standing.

But you used what you had, and it was proving effective. From his vantage point he could see signs of movement in the formerly empty enemy trenches. Their bunkers were taking a beating—it only made sense for them to abandon those being subjected to fire and regroup somewhere else.

Which was exactly what Finn was waiting for.

"Right two hundred, up one hundred," he commanded the forward observer, moving the next barrage farther away from the wire. No sense in making it easier for the attackers. "Then check fire and bring in the birds."

"Roger, copy."

Once again Finn heard the relayed commands, the indication that the rounds were on the way, the "Splash" signal. Once again the ground erupted, this time the rounds so freakishly close together it looked like a volcano erupting. The wind shifted, bringing the acrid smell of high explosives mixed with pulverized dirt so strongly to him he fell into a fit of sneezing.

His nasal explosions almost drowned out the steady beat

of incoming blades as the first choppers of the aerial rocket-artillery (ARA) battalion swept in from the south. Through teared-up eyes he watched the puffs of smoke and fire spurt from the rocket pods slung next to the skids, each ripple of fire loosing forty-eight 2.75-inch rockets at the hapless targets beneath.

The first birds peeled off just as the second wave came in, Finn hearing a clear "Wooo-ha!" from one of the pilots. Seldom did they get targets like these. Mostly they fired their ordnance into the jungle, guided by the troops on the ground against targets they couldn't see, depending upon reports to tell them how well or how badly they'd done.

Now the impact of the rockets on the troops in the trenches was quite clear. Many of the missiles, it was true, impacted harmlessly outside the slits in the ground, but enough found their way into the trenches to cause absolute carnage.

After the first strike the forward observer gave them free gun, which allowed the birds to seek targets on their own. And there were plenty, as the troops not in the artillery strike area, having been given the command from their superiors to abandon the close-in bunkers anyway, streamed toward the relative safety of the jungle hundreds of meters away.

American troops, at least those he had trained, would be taking stock of their situations, would be receiving orders from squad leaders, platoon sergeants, platoon leaders there with them, to hold fast, to go back to the bunkers. To avoid the withering fire from the helicopters, many of which had now expended all their rockets and were now raking the trenches with on-board 7.62mm miniguns. You tried to drill it into the junior leaders—take the initiative! Those who did generally survived and, more important, insured the survival of most of their men. Those who didn't—well, Darwin had been right.

The North Vietnamese command structure didn't generally allow for such flexibility. An order was passed down from on high, and it was followed regardless of the consequences. Some people, and Finn included here those who had little actual field experience in the matter, said that it was because of the relatively primitive state of the troops the NVA commanded. How could you expect an uneducated peasant to take the initiative?

Finn knew that to be nonsense. Few people came from a more primitive state than his Montagnards, but they readily adapted to small-unit, independent action. Over the years he'd been in Vietnam he'd personally seen dozens of incidents wherein the American adviser had been killed or wounded or simply wasn't in the right place at the right time, whereupon a 'Yard who had only last year been surviving by slash-and-burn agriculture, supplemented by the occasional crossbow shot at a monkey, would assert leadership that would have done a West Pointer proud.

He'd counted on the NVA reaction when he'd planned the strike. They'd keep streaming out of the bunkers until someone managed to countermand the order to do so, and their communication was slow and poor.

For a full half hour the helicopters pounded the fleeing men, until the supply of targets finally started to dry up. Which was, conveniently, at about the same time that the gunships ran out of both ammunition and fuel.

Finn was again talking to the forward observer when the latter broke off his transmission to yell a warning to the commander of the ARA battalion, who was now overflying the battle zone on a personal damage assessment. Finn saw the cause of the warning, a sudden spurt of fire from somewhere in the tree line, then a streak almost too fast for the eye to follow.

Jesus, Finn thought, that's a goddamn missile.

He'd heard intelligence reports about the possible arming of the NVA with SA-7 ground-to-air missiles, somewhat analogous to the American Redeye, though more crude in function. Shoulder-fired, heat-seeking, it probably wouldn't be as effective as the Redeye was against fast-movers. But it could obviously do a job on a chopper.

The pilot only had time to break right slightly as the missile sped toward his exhaust pipe, which caused it to impact upon the tail rotor rather than flying right up into the engine before detonating with disastrous results.

Bad enough. The explosion destroyed the tail rotor, taking away a large part of the boom. Inasmuch as the tail rotor stabilized the centrifugal forces produced by the main rotor and was the only method of keeping the chopper from spinning at exactly the same rate as the main rotor, the bird became instantly unflyable.

And it looked like it was going to come down right on top of him.

Sloane woke from a drugged sleep to find dirt falling in his face. The entire underground room was shaking so hard he had to hold on to the sides of the cot to keep from being thrown out. Around him the other patients were crying in terror.

Andy Inger came lurching down the corridor, the tremors bouncing him from one side to the other. "It's okay!" he said. "Arty strike right outside the wire. Givin' Charlie hell!"

He moved around the tiny room checking IVs, replacing bandages where they had bled through, taking the vital signs of the ones who remained oblivious to the chaos. When he got to Sloane, he took out a flashlight and closely examined the lieutenant's pupils.

Sloane sat passively as the light shone in his eyes. He was still groggy from the codeine tablets Inger had given him earlier, something to combat the intense headache. Which, he noticed, seemed to be almost bearable at the moment.

"Lookin' good, LT," the medic said. Sloane knew from his limited cross-training this meant that his pupils were the same size and reacted normally to the bright light. If they had not been, or if one had narrowed more slowly than the other, it would have meant brain damage. Swelling from the trauma. Worse, a broken blood vessel somewhere inside that was slowly, insidiously filling the limited space in the cranium with blood and fluid, destroying the brain.

He'd heard Sergeant Matthesen, whose lifeless body now reposed in another room, talk about treating such an injury. He'd described a field trephining operation, wherein he'd bored a hole into the skull of a patient, luckily picking just the right spot. The blood had flowed out the hole, relieving the pressure, saving the man's life.

Sloane shuddered at the thought. You could only hope

you'd be deeply unconscious during the procedure. The medic wouldn't be able to use much, if anything, in the line of painkillers. The breathing would already be depressed—morphine or Pentothal would only depress it more. Matthesen had performed the procedure by first cutting through the scalp, exposing the skull, then boring through the bone with an ordinary brace-and-bit taken from the team carpenter kit. Sloane could just imagine the grinding, scraping progress of the drill bit as it slowly chewed its way through the bone.

"I need to get back out there," he said, attempting to stand and immediately falling back onto the cot.

"I'd give it a few more minutes, I was you." Inger gently pushed the lieutenant's shoulders back down, settling his head on the bloody pillow. There had been some seepage through the bandage, he noted, but nothing to worry about. Natural clotting factors should take care of it, as long as it wasn't reopened.

Sloane didn't protest. At the moment the hard cot seemed as welcoming as a mother's womb. He knew that his duty lay elsewhere, that his father would even now be calling him a weakling for lying there while there was fighting to be done!

But he didn't care. Let someone else handle it for a while. He'd done a good job so far, that he knew. No longer was there the tinge of contempt in the eyes of the other Americans. Captain McCulloden had almost, if not quite, praised him for his support in the LLDB bunker. And Olchak, helping to support him on the way to the dispensary, had been almost chatty.

He felt a surprising warmness in the soul he had deliberately hardened against these men. Good men. Far better than the political hacks, the martinets who didn't know any other way of commanding troops, the washed-up, old time-servers who had been in his father's circle of acquaintances.

To be one of them seemed almost preferable to winning the Medal of Honor.

But not quite, he thought, his cynicism returning to save him from what he thought would be turning into a puddle of mush, as he drifted back off to sleep.

The chopper pilot managed to get the engine killed before the aircraft hit the ground. Which meant that the main rotor, instead of smashing into the ground under power, where it would have chewed up the fuselage and anything inside it as it broke into pieces, was stopped after only a couple of turns.

Still, the impact was enough to smash the thin metal of the helicopter like an egg, throwing the bodies of the crew chief and gunner out the open doors. Finn smelled the sudden stench of aviation fuel, realized that he had only seconds to help any survivors before they were consumed in a pyre of gas, exploding ammunition, and the magnesium alloy of which many parts of the chopper were made.

He was already up and running before the twisted metal came to a complete stop, grabbing the unconscious crew chief by the shoulders and pulling him quickly into a nearby trench. From the way the man's head flopped, Finn suspected he had been on a fool's mission.

Sergeant Washington was already at the downed bird by the time Finn came back up from the trench. Washington had acquired an ax from somewhere and was trying to chop through the Perspex windshield. Finn went over to the other body lying on the ground, that of the gunner, and saw that he could give no help. The man's head had cracked like a melon, probably from the impact of what had been left of the main rotor. He dragged him away from the fuselage anyway. Some mother would want to know what had happened to her son, and leaving him there to be consumed by the flames would be the height of cruelty.

Finn returned to the fuselage, seeing that Washington had managed to cut a hole through the tough plastic and was trying to release the catches from the inside. Through the bloodied window Finn could see the face of the pilot, obviously still alive.

He wouldn't be for long, if they didn't get this thing open.

Olchak came running up, carrying a long crowbar he'd found somewhere. He thrust it into the hole Washington had cut, and with all three of them on the end, they managed to prop away the window.

"Copilot!" the man inside managed to gasp. "Hurt."

Finn grabbed the K-bar knife from its sheath on his harness, quickly cut away the pilot's harness, and with Washington's help pulled him out the window. The young man looked relatively unscathed—obviously the blood that had spattered the inside of the cockpit had come from someone else.

Finn leaned far into the hole, seeing that the copilot was unconscious, but obviously still breathing. He cut away the harness, attempted to pull the man out, couldn't budge him. The man, a captain, Finn saw, was pinned by his legs deep under what was left of the front fuselage. The chopper had finally come to rest on that side, and the thin metal had collapsed on him.

The inside of the cockpit looked as inviting as an open grave. The smell of gas was almost overpowering. One spark, or vapors reaching the still-hot exhaust, and the thing would go up like a gasoline-soaked bonfire.

"Shit," he said, and crawled inside.

He first checked the neck pulse on the unconscious man. Strong and steady. He was almost sorry. While he was willing to risk his life to save a man, he was far from willing to recover a dead one.

He tried to see what was holding the man inside the wreckage, but couldn't contort his body inside the tiny space well enough to see. With a sigh of exasperation and another muttered "Shit!" he pulled himself out the window, turned around, and reentered headfirst. Almost immediately the blood started pooling in his head. Gonna have a hell of a headache after this, he thought.

I don't hurry up, he then thought, I won't have a head to worry about. The smell of gas was getting stronger and stronger. It didn't take too much of an imagination to visualize it dripping somewhere, pooling on the red dirt, slowly making its inexorable way to a sparking electrical connection.

The desire to get out of there, get the hell away from this death trap, was almost overwhelming. Nobody would blame him. Hell, they didn't even have to know that the man inside was still alive. He could say that he'd checked the pulse, found nothing, and had gotten out. Who was to know?

You are, asshole, he told himself.

He squirmed to a position where he could see the trapped man's legs. As he had feared, they were quite firmly pinned in the wreckage. He thought he might be able to tear away enough debris to get the one closest to him free, but saw that the other one was not only trapped, but had a chunk of the fuselage embedded in it just below the knee. Blood was dripping out on the ground, just as he had imagined the avgas would be.

Freeing the unconscious captain would take moving the fuselage, turning it over, then prying the wreckage loose with a crowbar. And there simply wasn't time for that.

He pried the nearest leg loose, pulled it to the side to expose the wounded limb. "Shit!" he said one last time.

"I'd give a goddamn Yankee dollar for some more room in this son of a bitch," he swore as he twisted around, first taking a cravat bandage from one of his belt pouches. He tore the plastic cover off, left the green cloth folded, tied it loosely around the leg just above where it was pinned, grabbed a piece of metal that had once been part of the controls of the chopper, inserted it beneath the bandage, and started twisting. It took only a few turns before the bleeding stopped. He secured the makeshift tourniquet by tying the end of the metal rod with the loose ends of the bandage.

Next he removed two morphine Syrettes from the five-pack he carried, injected the unconscious man with them. He wanted him to stay unconscious. What he was getting ready to do was going to hurt a lot, and pain had a way of bringing people back up from unimaginable depths. The last thing he needed was to have the patient flailing around as he cut off his leg.

Because that was what he had to do, as much as he hated the idea. He'd done an amputation only once before, and that had been on a hapless mutt back during Special Forces Advanced Medical Training, commonly called the Dog Lab.

The principles are the same, he told himself. Just more meat to get through.

Damn good thing I sharpened my K-bar, he thought. Once more he pulled it from its sheath, gritted his teeth so tight his headache suddenly achieved a new level of ferocity, and made the first cut.

The skin parted nicely, exposing the muscle beneath. He cut as closely as possible to the piece of metal that was pinning the limb down, still regretted that he was going to have to remove so much. The pilot, if he lived, would have a hard time getting a prosthesis attached. More than likely some doctor down the line was going to do the job again and was going to take it off at the knee.

But not me, he thought. Such a thing was so far alien to his training that the thought never really made an impression on his mind.

Next through the muscle, separating each layer as he went. Natural tension retracted it as it was cut, making his job easier. The only bleeding was a little seepage, indicating the efficiency of his tourniquet.

A few more careful cuts, and he was down to the bone. It gleamed pinkish white in the light coming through the Perspex.

Okay, wise guy, what do you do now? When he'd operated on the heavily sedated dog, he'd had a nice clean table, with sharp scalpels and retractors and hemostats and most important, a bone saw.

Then he remembered a little item he'd tucked away in a belt pouch, along with a signal mirror, pen flares, mini-smoke-grenades, and some line and fishhooks. One never knew when it might be necessary to escape and evade, and if you didn't make it back to friendly lines within days, you were going to have to somehow survive. A piece of cable that could be rigged into an animal trap, which could, if equipped with handles made from branches, serve admirably as a garrote, why, such a thing would be invaluable.

And if it could also cut down trees, so much the better.

The survival saw was nothing more than a piece of wire with teeth. And it would serve the purpose admirably.

The grinding and grating of the saw against bone was nearly unbearable to him. He couldn't even imagine what it would be like to be on the receiving end. But within seconds he had sawed through both the tibia and the fibula, and the leg was free. Now backing out, he was able to pull the pilot with him. How much time do I have? he wondered. Seemed like he'd been in there forever.

The fuselage was rocked by an explosion, then another. From somewhere outside he heard the telltale rush of incoming artillery. The 157s from across the border, he surmised. Getting even.

He squirmed harder, wriggling like a snake that had something far too large for it in its mouth. Every snag, every outcrop, every jagged piece of Perspex grabbed at him. Clutching as if it wanted to hold him there.

Forever.

Let him go! his reptilian hindbrain screamed. Save yourself. You've done all that could be expected of anyone. You'll do no one any good by dying here.

He felt something grab him by the ankles, and suddenly he was being hauled out of the fuselage so fast the snags that had held him up now took their revenge at his escape by chewing out large chunks of flesh.

He didn't care. Get me out, get me out, get me out!

His head cleared the window, and he saw Sergeant Washington still pulling at his legs, his face purple with the strain.

"I got him, sir," Becker, who had run from the commo bunker upon seeing the chopper go down, said. Gratefully, Finn released his hold on the still-unconscious aviator. Washington helped Becker pull him the rest of the way out of the cockpit, and together they slung his arms over their shoulders and hurried for the nearest trench.

Finn heard the rush of the next incoming and decided he might like to find a little cover too.

When Lieutenant Sloane woke again, he knew the explosions were no longer those of friendly artillery outside the wire. Dirt rained down; rats scurried from the broken sandbags and scattered, chittering down the corridor. Don't want to be buried alive, do you? he asked them.

Smart guys. Neither do I.

He staggered to his feet, almost fell back onto the cot. Got to get out of here, he thought. If I have to crawl.

He made it as far as the makeshift operating room before running into Washington and Becker, carrying a much-the-worse-for-wear man in aviator Nomex.

"Put him down here!" Inger commanded, indicating a

relatively clean operating table. The medic paid no attention at all to the artillery, which seemed to be coming closer and closer. Neither, Sloane noticed, did the two NCOs who had brought in the casualty.

Inger checked the stump, saw that there was no bleeding, slapped a blood pressure cuff on the aviator's arm, and pumped it up. After a moment he shook his head, felt for the pulse in the neck.

"BP's down," he said. "Pulse weak and thready. Shock, I expect. Better get him stabilized. Cap'n McCulloden'd be real pissed off, he does all that good work and I let him die."

Inger got an IV going, having to do a cut-down on the man's collapsed vein to get a piece of polyethelene tubing inside after trying without success to do it with a needle. As Inger worked, Washington gave a running commentary about what had happened, how the captain had worked himself up inside the chopper, cussing all the while, cut the man's leg off right there! Thought he'd be a goner for sure.

Sloane listened and raged. That should have been me out there! I'm the one they should be talking about with such obvious admiration. I could have done it.

Well, maybe not the amputation, he thought, looking at the stump of a leg and feeling distinctly queasy.

But all the rest of it!

The NVA obviously had their own forward observer some where out there in the hills. The artillery barrages were being adjusted as precisely as the inherent inaccuracy of the Russian-supplied weapons allowed, marching from one critical point to another.

The FO had apparently decided that the chances of nailing someone on the helicopter rescue were too good to pass up. After a false start, when the shells fell a hundred meters short, they were now pounding the wreckage into tiny pieces.

Finn knew he owed his life to pure chance. Perhaps the enemy forward observer had misread his map. Or had incorrectly estimated distances. Or maybe it was that the battery across the border hadn't properly placed their aiming stakes, or it could be that the fire-direction-center people were slightly inexperienced.

Whatever it was, it meant that while he was cutting the aviator, whose name the pilot had told him but he'd already forgotten, free from the wreckage the shells were falling somewhere else. And by the time they'd corrected their mistake, he was gone. Otherwise they'd have had to pick him up with a broom and dustpan.

Of just such chances of fate he'd survived thus far. People like him often ascribed it to luck. I'm just a naturally lucky person, they'd say. Sonsabitches can't get me, I'm too lucky!

Others attributed it to God. They were protected by their special relationship with the deity, no matter what that deity might be.

And still others subscribed to the notion that everything was preordained. It didn't really matter what you did. You were either going to live or die depending upon how it had already been written in the book of fate. Just not my time to die, they would say after coming out of a situation wherein they, by all logic, should not have.

And finally, there were those who thought they were indestructible. That the world couldn't possibly do without them, and thus couldn't imagine their own demise. Ten foot tall and bulletproof.

Finn had gone through all those stages at one time or another. Thinking himself bulletproof had departed immediately upon his receiving his first wound. The bullet hit you, and of course the shock and pain were there. But worse was the realization that you could really die. That the round that entered your leg, the shrapnel that tore up your arm, the mine fragments that peppered you without really doing any serious or long-term damage, could very well have had an entirely different outcome.

Generally, the thought of being lucky departed at about the same time. The really self-deluded, however, told themselves that this was merely one more sign of their good luck. That had they not moved this way or that, the bullet that had hit them in the arm would have impacted directly in the middle of their chest.

Or was God guiding the aim of the enemy? The Montagnards certainly thought so. Few of them would go into combat without their Buddha amulets, generally clutched in their teeth. Buddha will protect you, *Dai Uy,* a long-ago Rhade sergeant had told him upon presenting him with an exquisitely carved jade Buddha on a gold chain. You must wear this, he had said. Always.

And Finn still did, although the man who had presented it to him was long-since dead, perishing in an ambush in the first burst of fire.

His own intellect would not let him believe that his fate was preordained. That no matter what he did, he would die or not depending upon how it was written. If so, he told himself, it doesn't really matter. Attack or retreat, assault or hide in a bunker, it makes no difference. Death will find you. Or not. What was the purpose of it all, if this was true?

He'd had plenty of time to think it over. In his three combat tours. In the long, sweaty nights back in the United States, waking from tortured sleep. Trying to bury yourself in this or that bit of warm flesh, all the time knowing that as soon as it was over, the moment you dropped off, the dreams would again come. And alcohol did not the least bit of good, nor would, he suspected, any other sort of drug. Might put it off for a while, if you got drunk enough. But sobriety would again come, and so would the thoughts.

With hard-won understanding came resignation. It was nothing more than chance, pure and simple. A slight wind shift that moved the impact of a bullet. The involuntary flinch of a shooter. The fact that you were at the back of a column instead of at your usual point position when the claymore went off.

And with that came the realization that, sooner or later, chance would go against you. You improved your survival possibility by not taking foolish chances, by good tactical choices, by training those with you to use their weapons and brains and courage toward the success of the mission.

But you couldn't beat chance, not forever. The more you were out there, the more likely it was that chance was going to go against you.

That realization had moved brave men to seek jobs in the rear, where chance had less of an opportunity to affect them. Had ruined soldiers he'd admired. Had sent heroes into gibbering insanity.

And, like all those who had served as he had, he held nothing against those who couldn't anymore. Sooner or later, it affected you. If you lived that long. He hadn't reached that point yet, but couldn't be sure when he wouldn't be able to go on.

And it might just come right now, he thought as the barrage shifted.

There is little that affects an infantryman more than being trapped under artillery. You feel absolute impotence. Nothing you can do except hunker down, hope that the next shell doesn't come right in on top of you, that the impossible noise of the explosions and the shrieking of shrapnel and the cries of the wounded don't drive you right over the edge.

You make yourself into as tight a ball as possible, rock with the explosions, pray, curse God and the people who caused you to be here in the first place, and forget about patriotism and mom and apple pie and all those damned John Wayne movies that made it all seem so simple.

And if you had a part of a mind that was not reduced to chasing itself around like a rat in a cage, you counted the shells. Thanked whatever powers that were that the NVA seemed to have run out of shells equipped with time-delay fuses. That the Seabees who had built the camp in the first place had spared no time and expense in burrowing so far into the ground that even direct hits did nothing more than loose showers of dirt down on you.

And you hoped that sooner or later they would run out of shells. Or would see that it wasn't doing much good and decide to save the ones they had for support during the actual assault.

Although that would be a mixed blessing. It would mean that instead of huddling down here in relative safety, you would have to be outside, firing into the masses of men who would be coming through the wire.

But at the moment that didn't seem to matter.

He just wanted it to be over.

Chapter 9

Staff Sergeant Van Alexander of Recon Team Texas heard the booming of artillery and judged it not too far from his position. RT Texas was out of the Studies and Observations Group (SOG) base in Kon Tum called Command and Control Central. Two days ago they'd walked across the border into Laos to conduct a road watch mission. He'd chosen the walk rather than helicopter insertion because increasingly the recon teams were being shot out of the mission immediately upon hitting the ground.

Many, all too many, were never heard from again. The enemy was becoming adept at counterrecon operations, had all the likely landing zones covered, and upon seeing the telltale approach of a chopper could quickly summon up sufficient forces to wipe out the teams, which generally consisted of two to three Americans and four to six Montagnard Special Commando Unit (SCU) troopers.

SOG had begun to try parachute and HALO missions, but these too were being compromised. The parachute missions, of a necessity, would have been familiar to the

Forestry Service back in the United States—in fact the jumps were made using the padded uniforms and helmets with mesh faceplates used by smoke jumpers. You couldn't count on a cleared drop zone. Hell, if you had a cleared area big enough for a jump, the likelihood of its being compromised was even greater, therefore you had to plan on landing in the trees. And that could be a very unpleasant experience. The branches tore at you as you ripped through them, all too often creating more injuries than a hard landing on the open ground would have. These jumps, despite the danger, might have worked if the Viets, hearing the drone of the low-flying drop aircraft, hadn't soon vectored in on the area where you'd landed—and the chase was on.

So, HALO—High Altitude, Low Opening. Fall out of the airplane way above the normal drop altitude, free-fall down to two or three thousand feet, open the chute, and still make a tree landing. The technique had been perfected as a method of infiltration behind the Iron Curtain—fly along trying to mimic an airliner, get out, and hope their radar wasn't good enough to pick up the tiny signature of a human body falling through the night.

But even the HALO missions had been compromised. Too many people lost. Way too many.

Some thought there was a traitor somewhere in the chain of command, and there had already been a shutdown of operations while everyone who might have knowledge of where the teams were being inserted and a means for passing it on to the enemy had undergone lie detector tests.

And they had found exactly nothing. Since there was a pressing need for timely intelligence on the massive North

Vietnamese reinforcement effort, and since air assets and sensors weren't providing it, the recon teams had to go back in.

Alexander had not only chosen to infiltrate his area of operations by walking in, but had deliberately falsified the check and rally points he had sent back to Kon Tum. As a result, he had managed thus far to remain undetected. The only one who really knew his position was Covey.

Covey consisted of an Air Force lieutenant piloting a double-engine 0-2 Skymaster, with a SOG soldier, called the Covey rider, in the back. The rider was generally someone who had been wounded, wasn't yet recuperated enough to go back into the field, but who knew firsthand what the teams had to face down on the ground. Thus he could be trusted.

He'd reached his overwatch position, a small hill at the base of the limestone cliffs, called karst, that characterized this part of Laos. The last part of the trip had been made literally inch by inch, the team moving with painful slowness, the knowledge that even the slightest noise might bring overwhelming force down upon them guiding their feet.

The information he had already passed to Covey should have alerted the brass down in Saigon to the depth of the problem. Not only were trucks stacked nearly nose to tail on the many offshoots of the Ho Chi Minh Trail, he had seen the tracks of some sort of armored vehicle. PT-76 amphibious tanks, he suspected, though he had not yet managed to glimpse one. Until he did, he wasn't going to report them. Saigon tended to dismiss as the effects of vivid imagination the reports of tanks on the trail. In one incident, infamous in the ranks of SOG, a team leader had actually taken a plaster cast of the track marks of one such vehicle. The analysts in

Saigon had dismissed it as probably the track of a bulldozer.

That was shortly before PT-76 tanks had broken through the wire of the Special Forces camp at Lang Vei, overrunning the camp and killing a hell of a lot of good men. Did the analysts in Saigon suffer for their mistake? Of course not. The blame had been laid back on SOG. Should have gotten photographs of the tanks, they had been told. Then we would have known for sure.

Now, Alexander suspected, some camp was in deep shit again. There would be only one reason for artillery to be firing over on this side. There were no other recon teams within the area, so it wouldn't be directed at them. There were no CIA-sponsored Hmong guerrillas in the area. They'd been chased away from the trail a long time ago. No, the artillery had to be pounding some poor bastards hunkered down in ratty holes in the ground, somewhere across the border.

"Covey, this is One Zero," he said.

"This is Covey. Go."

"You see where those guns are? Over."

"That's a negative. We're holding orbit at checkpoint Bravo Zulu, can't see anything. Hearing traffic on air-to-ground from Boun Tlak. Getting the piss pounded out of them."

Knew it, Alexander thought. There was little triumph in the thought, however. If Covey couldn't see them, it was likely no one else could from the air, either.

"Roger. I can hear them. Sound pretty close. Request permission to go find 'em, call in a strike, over."

There was silence for a few moments as Covey passed on the request to the forward operating base. Alexander occupied himself by trying to identify unit patches on the men below, who were now up and moving again after a delay caused by an air strike somewhere farther down the trail. Look like goddamn ants down there, he thought.

"One Zero, this is Covey, over."

"This is One Zero. Go."

"That's a negative on your request. You are instructed to continue mission, over."

Alexander had expected this response. Some asshole officer in Kon Tum would be too afraid to contact Saigon and request a change of mission, so he wouldn't even have passed the request along. So Team Texas would have to stay here, hope that no one stumbled on their overwatch position, and count trucks until their food ran out.

Stupid, but he was used to stupid decisions.

"Roger, understand," he said. "But we're gonna have to change position. Can't see very much from here. We'll be heading out on an azimuth of zero two seven, over."

"Roger," Covey said. "I copy zero two seven. *Bonne chance,* over."

Within seconds the team was up and moving, this time away from the trail below. An azimuth of 027, Alexander surmised, should put them somewhere in the area of where they could still hear the big guns booming. Covey would know that. Perhaps even the launch officer back in Kon Tum would know that. But it covered everyone's ass.

Everyone, that is, except his.

Mixed blessing, Bucky Epstein thought as the big shell impacted just twenty meters short of the bunker in which he was huddling. At least the snipers aren't shooting, so I don't have to raise my head to shoot back at them. I can just sit here, stare at the 'Yards—who stared back at his deliberately impassive face. Ain't no big thing, he wanted to tell them. We're deep, the bunker walls seem to be holding, all we got to do is sit it out.

He wished he believed it. If Charlie got his act together, dropped a few in the same spot instead of trying to waltz them all over camp, they'd soon start blowing away the overhead cover, burrowing ever deeper until inevitably one came through, or the tons of dirt atop them collapsed, or you just couldn't stand it anymore and went bug-shit crazy and ran the hell out of there.

Bucky thought the latter was most likely. For himself as well as the 'Yards. He took small consolation that the 175s were still falling outside the wire, keeping the assault force down as well. If they were to come through the wire right now, there probably wouldn't be anyone even to see them, far less open up with a machine gun.

Right after the shrapnel from each explosion stopped whining, he would pop his head up and take a quick glance out the firing ports, just to make sure. Not that he could see much. Between black explosives smoke and the thrown-up red dirt, the air looked alive. Swirling, malevolent, seeking out every nook and cranny, coating the lungs, crusting the eyes. If your imagination worked just a little bit overtime, you could see huge animals, creatures out of nightmares, lurking in the haze.

He tried to keep his imagination under control.

The next explosion was right on top of the bunker. One

'Yard screamed in fear, the others huddled even closer to one another. A very human reaction—seeking comfort in the closeness of another human body. Tactically very unsound. What they should have been doing was scattering themselves as far away from one another as possible. That way there would be at least some chance of a few surviving if a shell came through the overhead.

He didn't feel up to scolding them right now. Actually, it was only with some effort that he didn't crawl over and get right in the middle of the pack.

Clods of dirt came raining down. A scorpion landed on his leg, stood there alert and obviously angry at being disturbed from its cozy lair. Its tail arced above its back, the stinger quivering. Bucky casually flicked it away, watching as it ran back into the dirt, frantically burrowing.

That's what I'd like to be doing right now, he told the insect. Couple more of those like the last one, and we won't have any choice.

The noise of the big guns was muffled by the jungle, but was getting ever closer. Alexander halted the team, listened, motioned with his hand to alter the direction of march of the point man, and then they set off again. He'd stopped communicating with Covey fifteen minutes before. Right now they would be inside the security zone of whatever troops would be protecting the guns. There would be no more noise until it was absolutely essential.

The point man raised his right foot high in the air, his eyes scanning the brush around them, the ground beneath his feet, the small space his leg would be moving, always alert to the slightest sign of danger. Was that bush up ahead in fact a camouflaged NVA machine gunner? As you move your leg forward, are you going to brush up against a trip wire? The spot where you've chosen to put down your foot, is it relatively clear of twigs, dried leaves? The little piece of foliage sticking up, is it in fact a sprout, or is it the characteristic three-prong probe of a mine?

The lifted foot is slowly brought down, outside edge of the sole first. Slowly and ever so carefully the foot rakes the ground, moving leaves and twigs out of the way. The foot is put down into the cleared space, and weight is then shifted from the rear foot to the front. The rear foot is lifted, and the whole painstaking process is repeated.

And they were moving with what, to Van Alexander, was extreme rapidity. At least some of the noise of their passing was masked by the booming of the artillery, now almost constant.

Move another hundred yards, it taking almost a half hour, halt again. Another slight shift in direction. Sounds among the trees can be deceptive, the waves being deflected by the heavy vegetation. What seems directly ahead can be off to one side or the other, and the only way you are going to know it is to get ever closer. Triangulate with the ears, watch for the shock waves of overpressure moving the trees. Listen for the shouts of the battery commander as he directs the firing.

Not too far now, Alexander thought as he heard that very sound, faint yet and considerably muffled by the jungle. He looked up through a slight gap in the canopy, saw one of the limestone cliffs looming not too far away.

He thought he might have figured out why none of the airplanes flying overhead had spotted the battery. But he'd have to get closer to be sure.

Ahead again, now moving even slower.

The point man froze, one foot still in the air. Slowly and carefully he brought his foot back to the spot it had just left. He pointed to a spot just off to the side.

Alexander focused his eyes on the spot, trying to see the pattern emerging from the foliage. It was like staring at a painting, trying to gather the tiny bit of information the artist had hidden somewhere there, a slight curlicue of the brush that told you what you were seeing wasn't really what you thought you were seeing.

Then he saw it. A slight movement, something only the sharp eyes of the point man would have picked out. An arm, being brought up, and when it stopped, you could see that it had reached a face. Slight shine of sweat. Rhythmic movement of the jaw.

A sentry, eating something. As yet totally oblivious of their presence.

Alexander didn't have to look at them to tell that the remainder of his team was standing exactly as stock-still as was he. The sentry was absorbed in what he was doing and wouldn't be expecting trouble this far over the border, but all it would take would be the smallest careless movement and the situation would change. He'd get off at least a warning shot before they could kill him, and within seconds others would swarm the position. Then it would be immediate action drills and break contact and a hell of a run, calling Prairie Fire emergency the entire way, and hoping like hell you could get enough air to keep them off your ass until finally somebody could come in and whisk you away.

Team Texas had been in that situation a number of times before. And it wasn't pleasant. Alexander had no intention of doing it again, if he could avoid it.

Besides, it would make it absolutely impossible to find the guns. And some poor bastard across the border, maybe even someone he knew, would die.

Not acceptable.

He slowly drew the sound-suppressed High Standard .22 pistol from its holster on his survival vest, pulled the slide back slightly to confirm a round was in place in the chamber, let it slide back into battery. Thumbed off the safety. Rested the barrel on his free hand and took a sight picture right about where he judged the bridge of the nose to be.

The report was only slightly louder than the noise made by the slide as it ejected the spent shell and chambered another. He fired again, knowing as he did so that he was merely gilding the lily. The sentry had slumped with barely a grunt, now lay exposed beneath his camouflage canopy. The second round hit him in the top of the head.

Van Alexander didn't like to take chances. The .22 round, slowed by the sound suppressor, was a notoriously unreliable man-stopper. The first time he'd used it, against an enemy point man, he'd shot for center of mass. The surprised victim had slapped at the wound as if at a pesky mosquito. He'd had to shoot the man twice more in the face before he'd finally died.

The point man, who had stood as still as a statue the entire time, being dangerously exposed and subject at any moment to discovery, now began his slow movement forward again. They passed by the sentry, the jungle ants already swarming at the tiny trickle of blood that seeped from the hole next to his left eye.

Within minutes they were, Alexander judged, inside the security perimeter. Able to move faster now, any worries about noise eliminated by the steady booming of the guns, the shouted orders of the crews, now the only worry the chance encounter.

Then the point man once again stopped, looking quizzically upward. Alexander moved forward to join him, like him surprised at the sight of a sheer limestone cliff rising at least three hundred feet straight up.

They had been fooled, he judged, by the echos of the guns, bouncing off the cliffs. Now it was quite clear that the howitzers were somewhere off to the right.

Once again on the move, getting a little distance away from the cliffs. Far too easy for someone to channelize them, hem them up with the unscalable rock on one side, many guns on the other.

As they moved, Alexander cursed himself. What on earth had caused him to think this was going to be easy? At any moment they could stumble across any number of North Vietnamese, far more than could be quickly and silently removed, as he had the sentry. And it would be expected that they would have good communications here within a base area. Good enough to notify every reaction force around, good enough to get them surrounded, with the only choice then being to surrender or die.

Van Alexander had seen firsthand, on Bright Light missions sent in to recover what might have been left of recon teams, the results of surrender. That, he vowed, would never happen to him. Not as long as he had at least one round left in any weapon.

Sweat was pouring off him, even though it was quite cool here in the shade of the cliff. His heart was pounding; his fingers felt as if they were emitting liquid fire. He had an almost overwhelming urge to piss, finally said screw it, and let it run warm down his leg. The ammonia smell, with a sweet underlay of pure filtered adrenaline, came sharp to his nose.

Time to get out of here, he thought. Call in a general location, guns can't be that far away, let the zoomies take care of it. Only reasonable course of action. Won't do anyone any good, we die here.

But the team kept going, linked perhaps more closely to the mission than they were even to one another.

Alexander shook his head, glanced back at the assistant team leader, Sergeant Leroy Billings, gave him a wry smile. Billings smiled back, his expression understanding. Yep, it said, this is pretty goddamn stupid.

But they didn't stop.

"Covey, this is One Zero," came the whisper over the radio, so soft the Covey rider had to strain his ears to hear it.

"Go, One Zero," he said, shifting in the tiny seat to ease the pressure on his right leg. It still ached fiercely where the doctors had taken a fist-size chunk of muscle out, the flesh pulverized from the AK-47 bullet that had tumbled through like a crazed somersaultist.

Had it not been for that wound, he would have been on

the ground on a mission like this one, so he was particularly attentive to the team leader below.

"When we moved, I think we ended up next to those guns we were talking about," Alexander said. "Purely by accident, of course."

The Covey rider looked up to see the Air Force pilot smiling back at him in his rearview mirror. "Of course," the rider said. Their conversations would be monitored by signals intercept and recorded for further analysis by the technical and tactical boffins down in Saigon.

"Check out grid Uniform Tango five seven zero six, eight five four seven," Alexander continued.

An eight-digit coordinate! RT Texas's One Zero must have stumbled very close to the guns, indeed, the rider thought. A four-digit grid, in the military grid-reference system, meant you had placed something within a thousand-meter square and was often about as good as you could get in the jungle. A six-digit coordinate located you to within a hundred meters. Good enough for government work, unless you were calling in a danger-close.

An eight-digit coordinate meant you had located the spot to within ten meters.

The Covey rider might have scoffed at such a claim coming from someone else. But he knew Alexander, had in fact been the young sergeant's first one-zero. Fresh out of an accelerated Special Forces qualification course, not yet twenty years old, Alexander had been typical of the young men they were now receiving. Expecting them to survive the most dangerous and difficult missions being run in Southeast Asia.

Most, if not all, the older sergeants, those who had multiple tours, who had run recon practically from the beginning, either had been killed, had been so severely wounded they were medically discharged, or had simply given it up. The realization came, sooner or later, that if you kept doing this stuff, you were going to die. It was that simple.

So kids like Alexander came, were given a little bit more training down at the Combat Orientation Course in Nha Trang, and were sent to the various Command and Control units to become assistant patrol leaders. If they showed any promise at all, they were then sent to the Recon Team Leader course at Long Thanh and became one-zeros.

From the beginning, Alexander had shown such promise. As loud and boisterous as the others in the club, in the field he became a quiet, competent professional. No matter what situation they got themselves into, and there had been more than a few, he never lost his head. And he had an almost uncanny sense of direction, able to read terrain features as a lover might the face of his sweetheart.

A much better map reader, the Covey rider was happy to admit, than he was. And he thought himself pretty good. So if Van Alexander said it was at those coordinates, it damned well was.

The rider already had the acetate-covered map spread out on his knees, quickly locating the indicated spot. Right to grid five seven, up to grid eight five. Five seven zero meant that the spot was close to the grid line itself. If it had been a hundred meters to the right, it would have been five seven one something. Eight five four meant that it was something over four hundred meters up inside the grid.

For the last numbers he took out his protractor, which

contained boxes marked with tick marks. He quickly put a pencil mark 60 meters to the right of the five-seven grid line, and 470 meters up from the eight-five grid line.

The map showed the spot to be right up next to a sheer limestone cliff. He selected two prominent terrain features, one a particularly noticeable piece of karst they'd flown over earlier, and the other a characteristic bend in the river, drew lines between each and the indicated spot on the map, and used the protractor again to measure the angles.

He keyed the intercom. "From Parrot Head peak, azimuth one seven five, and Minton loop, azimuth zero two five," he said. "Mark."

The pilot would now be able to fly over and, when he reached the intersection between the two known points, be right on top of the guns. More important, he would be able to put a white phosphorous marking rocket right on top of them, showing the way for the air strikes he was already calling on the air-to-air frequency.

The Coveys had their own names for prominent terrain features, which served as a sort of rough-and-ready code. And also sometimes recognized what had gone on down there in the jungle.

Minton loop, for instance, was named for a one-zero who had allowed his team to get backed up against the river when it was in full flood. The ones who hadn't died from the North Vietnamese assault had drowned when they'd tried to escape across the raging water.

Now it was possible that this particular cliff of limestone could become Alexander's wall. He hoped not. They had lost way too many good men already.

• • •

"Trucker Five, this is Covey, over."

"This is Five, go."

"Got a hot one for you. Interested?"

The pilot of the A1E, bored with flying circles in the sky, was instantly alert. The old prop-driven plane he piloted, left over from the Korean War, jumped a little bit as he corrected the stick. About time, he thought.

"Roger," he said. "Gimme something to shoot at, over."

"You know those guns the FAC was talking about earlier? Well, I think we got 'em."

"Yee-haw!" the pilot shouted, thoroughly startling his wingman, who was so bored he had almost been asleep, driving the other plane with what he liked to call autopilot. Except, of course, the old birds had nothing like an autopilot.

Quickly the Covey gave the location to the lead pilot, who used the call sign Trucker because the A1Es carried so much ordnance they were referred to as the dump trucks of the sky, and also because he had the most truck kills of any pilot in Southeast Asia. He winged over, pushed the throttle to the fire wall, and bored a hole in the sky on the way to the spot only twenty or so miles south of his current position. Within just a few moments he picked up Covey, flying an imprudent five hundred meters above the jungle canopy.

"Got you, Covey," he said. "What do you want?"

"Got a team on the ground," Covey replied. "They say the guns are butted right back against that limestone cliff you see at about your seven o'clock. Slight overhang right above them, damn near makes it like they're shooting out of a cave. Probably why we couldn't spot 'em from the air earlier. Target run is going to have to be parallel to the cliff, north-south or south-north, your choice. Suggest five-hundreds on the first run, blow some of the canopy away, then CBUs, over."

As Trucker toggled the right switches to pick ordnance, he considered the problem. They were going to have to make a fairly shallow angle of attack to make sure the big five-hundred-pound bombs went exactly where they were supposed to. A fraction too far to one side and they would hit the cliff, detonating dangerously early and perhaps blowing the plane out of the sky. Too far to the other side, and the team, whose location he had now been given, would be in the impact zone. Besides, it wouldn't do much to silence the guns, and that was what they were there after, wasn't it?

Of course, that was going to put them into a run that Charlie would undoubtedly be covering with every bit of antiaircraft artillery he had.

Nobody ever said it was easy, Captain, he told himself.

"Roger," he said. "South to north it is. You ready to mark?"

"Stand by for mark," Covey said, lining up the tiny airplane, aiming the nose downward, centering the homemade crosshairs on the Perspex windshield on the target area. He punched the firing button, was rewarded by the *swoosh!* of the marking rocket as it left the pod beneath his wing. Straight and true it flew, erupting in a burst of white-hot particles as it impacted the jungle canopy just short of the limestone cliff. A gout of white smoke quickly formed, bright against the dull green of the jungle.

His course took him right over the white cloud. He was

just getting ready to confirm target to the strike aircraft when
with a great *whoosh!* the next salvo of 157 rounds erupted
from the foliage below. One came so close the plane was
rocked like a toy boat in a hurricane.

"B'lieve you got the right spot, Cap'n," came the dry
voice from the Covey rider in the backseat.

"You could be right," the pilot said, his hands shaking on
the stick, adrenaline pumping through his system like fire. It
was for such a moment that you lived, he thought.

"Got a mark, Covey," Trucker Five said.

"Roger, Trucker. Have fun."

"Oh, yeah," Trucker said. "We will."

Recon Team Texas hunkered down in a bomb crater so old it
was overgrown by vines and brush that were able for the first
time to gain a foothold as a benefit of the sunlight blasting
down through the blown-away canopy. Their tiger-stripe
fatigues blended well with the foliage, and Alexander had
passed around a camouflage stick to replenish the face paint
that had eroded through three days of sweat. They moved
with the deliberate slowness of men who knew that quick
motions would be picked out by the eye, but that impercep-
tible movement would be ascribed to visual trickery.

Alexander focused his binoculars, shielded against glare
from the late-afternoon sun by a homemade shade of C-ration
cardboard, on the one howitzer he could see, some two hundred meters away. It was firing steadily, the gun rocking back
on its cradle as each shell left, then being pushed back forward
by the on-board hydraulic cylinders. By the time it had
reached its forward position, the gunner had opened the

breech, let the expended shell casing fall free, and the two loaders, struggling under the weight of the heavy shells, had fitted another in place. A few seconds for the gun commander to twirl elevation and windage dials in response to the faint commands heard from the fire direction center, then he steps away. A quick pull of the lanyard and yet another shell is on its way to wreak havoc on the unseen target.

The clouds of smoke expelled from the muzzle are caught by the canopy overhead, swirling in lazy patterns through the leaves. Sergeant Alexander had to give the enemy credit—the guns were in an outstanding position. And the swarming little men, bodies sheened with sweat, were working as fast and as efficiently as would have any gun crew back at Fort Sill. Perhaps it took a few more of them to hoist the shells—that was all.

He could, he thought, easily have picked them off at this range, several of them dying before anyone could get a fix on the far-off reports. But get a fix they would, sooner or later. And gun crews could be replaced. All he would accomplish would be to get the team compromised, possibly killed.

Let the zoomies do their stuff, he thought. Then we'll see what happens.

He heard the growl of aircraft engines at about the same time as did the enemy. The gun commander signaled a stop, and the crew looked fearfully up into the sky.

The growl turned into a high-pitched howl as the plane dropped into a dive. Signal enough for the Vietnamese to drop down into their dug-in protective bunkers. Time for us to get our heads down too, Alexander thought, scuttling back down the rim of the crater and tucking himself into a ball.

The first bomb always took you by surprise. No matter how many times you'd been in the vicinity of a five-hundred-pounder, your mind never seemed to maintain the memories of the shock. The noise was impossible, drilling through the head even when your hands were clapped firmly over your ears. The earth beneath you rippled like a live thing, as if a giant snake somehow lived beneath and was now twisting in its death throes. The hum, rather than whine, of flying shrapnel told you just how big were the pieces of bomb cutting through the trees, slicing through the thick trunks with no more difficulty than a chain saw through balsa. Clouds of dirt filled the air, combining with explosives smoke to make breathing more like chewing.

Alexander knew better than to raise his head. More than one overeager spotter had forgotten, in the heat of the moment, that this would be only the first of three, as the flight overhead followed the leader.

The next bomb landed somewhere close to the first, and the final one came uncomfortably close. Close enough to collapse part of the crater wall, half-covering him in dirt. Another little wind shift and that one would have landed right on top of us, Alexander thought. Team Texas would simply have ceased to exist. Listed in the rolls as missing, as so many others had been. Made into mincemeat, legs and arms and guts blown into the trees, there to be feasted upon by the flies and whatever jungle scroungers finally got up enough courage to overcome the fear of approaching the site of the cataclysm.

He shook off the thought and crawled back up the rim of the crater, once again focusing on the battery position. Shit!

The bombs had fallen short by at least a hundred meters, the smoking craters marking their impact point doing nothing more than clearing out empty jungle. The howitzer he could see had been shifted, but looked otherwise unhurt.

He crawled back down into the crater, accepted the handset of the radio from the assistant patrol leader.

"Gonna have to do better than that, Covey," he said.

Trucker considered the information he had just been given by Covey. The problem with his approach pattern had been that the cliff made a slight curve just before the pickling point for the bombs. The A1E, as maneuverable as it was, had had trouble adjusting to the curve that had been necessary in midrun. A slight mistake and the wingtip would have brushed the rock, with obviously disastrous consequences. It was drop slightly early and hope the bombs cruised in, or take the chance of vastly overshooting, and with the team on the ground being so close, that wouldn't have been a good idea. They'd already come close to that, with the third man in the flight hitting the release button just a fraction later than had he and his wingman.

There had been a scattering of antiaircraft fire as they'd rolled in, more so for the last man than the first, but still less than he had expected. Mostly small arms, though he had seen the telltale puffs of something larger exploding just off his right wingtip as he circled—37mm, obviously, from the size of it. Not radar-guided, otherwise that puff of smoke might have been right under his engine.

He considered the next approach. Angling more toward the cliff and coming in from that direction wouldn't work—

by the time he got to a release point he would be far too close to the looming rock. No way of jamming the throttle to the fire wall and leaping up over the cliff.

He could come in from the other direction, but dreaded the thought. The approach from that angle would necessitate his flying down the narrow valley that fed into the slight opening. A flak trap if ever there was one. For at least part of the run he would have to be so low they could shoot down on him.

He shrugged, then touched for luck the left pocket of his survival vest. Inside it he carried a Saint Christopher medal. It had been given to him by his father, a pilot like himself, who had survived air combat throughout the Pacific, and another stint at trying to get himself killed in Korea. Don't know if it does any good or not, his dad had said. But what the hell. Can't hurt.

He keyed the mike on the command frequency. "Follow my lead," he said. He winged over and headed for the mouth of the valley.

Chapter 10

The barrage had been going on so long that when it stopped, Finn McCulloden didn't at first realize it. His ears rang with a tinnitus that went bone deep. His head pounded, each beat of the heart seeming as if it would squirt blood out his ears. The air was so thick he could barely breathe it.

And he was in a deep bunker shielded from the worst of it. He remembered pictures he had seen of the trenches in World War I, the landscape looking like something shipped down from the moon. How could they have stood it, day after day? It must have seemed a relief to finally get the command to go over the top—better to face the machine guns than huddle under the incessant shelling.

Periodic radio messages from the other members of the team had told him just how much the camp was suffering. Bunkers collapsed, burying everyone inside. Ammo dumps exploded. Guns knocked out. Enough explosions in the wire to blast great paths, paths through which the sappers would soon come.

And there wasn't a hell of a lot he could do about it.

That, he supposed, was the worst part. Always before he could influence the action, attack or retreat, break contact and run like hell if necessary.

There was no place to run. Nothing to do except huddle here and hope the next one didn't finally collapse the overhead cover. He'd already been buried alive once today and had been lucky. He didn't want to go through that again. There might not be anybody around to dig him out the next time.

Now sounds were filtering through the ringing. Cries for help, in both Montagnard and English, and some even in French. The crackling of a big fire somewhere. Shouts.

He didn't know what had caused the lull, or how long it would last. What he did know was that he had damned well better take advantage of it.

Reluctantly, he grabbed his gun and went outside.

Hell, he thought, couldn't have looked any worse. There was little recognizable from the camp he had earlier seen from the air. Chunks of wadded-up tin from the aboveground barracks littered the ground; pieces of sandbags fluttered in the slight breeze. Over all was the miasma of smoke, of blood, of shit. Some of it was fresh. He saw that the half-barrel latrine nearest his bunker had been blown to bits.

Some of the debris was the torn-apart intestines of a Montagnard who'd made the mistake of coming out of his bunker—perhaps driven mad—only to catch a huge chunk of shrapnel across his stomach.

The 'Yard's dark eyes watched him as he approached, the knowledge of his impending death absorbed into a wisdom as old as the dirt upon which he lay. He breathed in short, panting gasps, blood flowing from between the fingers that tried to hold his intestines in.

Finn saw the gray of death settle in, the soldier now breathing easier, longer, more shallow. And then he breathed no more.

"Dai Uy!" he heard someone call. "Over here."

Sergeant Washington was digging frantically at a caved-in bunker, having freed only a pair of tiger-striped legs. The jungle boots, as opposed to the rubber Bata boots worn by most of the Montagnard strike force, told Finn that the man buried beneath was an American.

"Think it's Driver," Washington said, as Finn helped him lift one of the heavy beams. "Told him that goddamn bunker was too shallow! Son of a bitch wouldn't listen, as usual." Tears were streaming down the black man's face as he continued to call Driver every name in the book—"stupid goddamn honky" being only one epithet.

Driver and Washington had been together ever since training group back at Fort Bragg. Driver had been an unregenerate redneck, and Washington was from a middle-class black family from Alexandria, Virginia. Against all stereotypes, they had become fast friends.

And now, as they lifted the last bit of debris from Driver, it was apparent that Washington had lost his friend. One of the eight-by-eight mahogany beams supporting the ceiling of the bunker had been blown in two by the force of a direct hit. That beam had crushed Driver's chest, driving his ribs all the way into his backbone.

Washington gently wiped the dirt from his friend's face,

then covered it with a cravat bandage. He stood staring for a moment, looking into the surrounding hills.

His look was of stony implacability. Like some Zulu prince, staring down at the British column, clutching his spear and vowing death. Finn, who had faced down death so many times it had become a habit, shivered slightly.

Glad he's on my side.

"C'mon," Finn said. "This ain't gonna last forever. Lots of other people out here need help."

Washington shook himself, much as a horse might shake off a good sweat. "Gonna be some motherfuckers die here tonight," he said.

That there are, Finn thought. Only problem is, some more of 'em are likely to be us.

"Well, y'all, here's the drill," Trucker drawled. Despite his being from upstate New York, he liked to affect a slight Southern accent. Something about the slow, measured, hell-this-don't-mean-anything-anyway cadences of the South soothed nervous subordinates, made even the most hairy of missions seem like nothing to worry about.

"Gotta come in from the north. Fly our asses right up that little draw you see off your left wing, drop on the mark, and break left. Snuffy down there says we dropped a hundred or so meters short last time. We got one bomb apiece left. Let's make 'em count."

He got rogers from the other two, the pilot flying the last bird sounding perhaps a little less sure of it. Trucker didn't blame him. Hell, he wasn't sure of it himself.

He stood the plane on its wing, dropped altitude in a

screaming dive, pulled up just below the head of the valley, jinked right to avoid an outcropping that had been invisible from up above but now seemed to want to reach out and grab him.

"Damn," he muttered to himself. "This is about more fun than I need."

He didn't dare give the bird full power. It was a toss-up. Any faster and he would likely become a greasy spot on the rocks on either side; any slower and he was a fat target for any chump with enough sense to apply enough lead.

A stream of green dots rose to meet him, seeming slow until they came close, then whipping by the canopy and cracking into his right wing. Pieces of the aircraft's skin spun away, the formerly smooth surface replaced by ugly blackened holes.

Glad that son of a bitch didn't aim a little more to the left, he thought. Those rounds would have been bouncing off the armor under my ass. They had enough sense to use armor-piercing, I'd have gotten a lead enema.

Now more tracer came up to greet him. And, to his horror, he saw yet other streams coming, it seemed, from the cliff faces.

So much of it that to fly through was simply an exercise in stupidity. While he had long ago become resigned to the fact that he was likely to kill himself in one of these runs, he'd be damned if his suicide included the murder of his friends.

He jammed the throttle forward, pulled the stick back. The old bird leaped like a hawk coming out of a power dive, clearing the edges of the cliffs just ahead of most of the tracer. He heard several thunks in the rear, hoped that they hadn't hit anything vital.

He twisted his head, saw that the others had followed him. His wingman flew underneath, looking at the damage, came up to the side, and gave him a thumbs-up.

The old Spads took a hell of a beating and kept on flying. Not like the jets that so many of his classmates were so proud of. Good thing.

"Waal, that didn't work worth a shit," he drawled. "Anybody got any bright ideas?"

Alexander saw the planes pull up, the tracers reaching after them like spectral green fingers. Pieces of the tail of the first one flew off, spinning in the sky and catching the light like aluminum pinwheels.

Word had obviously gotten to the gun crews. He focused his binoculars on the nearest howitzer, saw a number of khaki-clad figures swarming over it, leveling the carriage, twisting the traverse mechanism, replacing the aiming stakes.

Once again he considered taking them out with small-arms fire, and once again he rejected the idea. While he had confidence in his team and its ability to get away—coming up against it was like kissing a buzz saw—it would simply do no good. They would have replacements for the men he killed, and the barrage would go on with scarcely any interruptions.

"Covey, this is One Zero," he said.

"This is Covey. As you can see, we've got some problems down there."

"Clear. Your guys willing to do some south-north gun runs, over?"

The channel was filled only with the crackling of the ether as Covey talked to the A1E pilots on the other band. Van Alexander considered the situation. What he was planning to do was little better than assisted suicide. But it might just work.

"Gimme all the thermite grenades," he ordered. Leroy Billings looked at him quizzically, then, as understanding hit, started to protest.

Alexander stopped him short. "I got a new plan, Sundance."

"Aw, shit," Billings said. During the last stand-down they'd watched a new—to them—movie, *Butch Cassidy and the Sundance Kid,* on a homemade screen back in Da Nang. You had to be careful watching action movies with the Montagnards. Every once in a while one of them would get inspired and put a burst of six into the bad guy, often ripping the screen to shreds. But this one kept them enthralled. And Butch had said the same thing, just before the duo had tried to assault the entire Bolivian army.

Billings gathered the thermites from the team members, six of them. These grenades contained a powder that, once initiated, burned so hot it melted armor plate. They carried them to sabotage any trucks they might come across, placing the grenade on the engine block, pulling the pin, and allowing the white-hot material to burn its way down through head and cylinders, quite thoroughly destroying the engine.

And, Billings remembered from his training, they were quite useful for spiking cannon. Open the breechblock, toss the grenade inside the chamber, close the block, and the grenade would fuse it to the cannon. Never to be opened again, even with a cutting torch.

"Aw, shit," he said again, but this time only to himself.

That's one brave little son of a bitch down there, Trucker Five thought as he held orbit high enough to avoid any but the most long-range of AA fire. But he expected little else.

On his second tour in Vietnam he had determined to see just what it was like down on the ground among the troops he supported. He couched the request to headquarters carefully—we're always getting complaints that we don't respond fast enough, don't listen to ground control, drop our ordnance too far away or too damned close. Maybe if I go out with one of the units, I can come up with some new tactics.

To his surprise, his commander had approved the request. This individual, a jet jock, a Korean War ace, pissed at being relegated to command a squadron whose main mission was not the air-to-air combat that defined fighter pilots, probably did it out of boredom, Trucker had thought.

But get a little training, so you don't embarrass us, he had been told. Trucker had then pulled a few strings through some Special Forces officers he had met in the club in Bien Hoa and had been given a slot in the Combat Orientation Course run for new guys by the Recon School in Nha Trang. A week's worth of that, and he was deemed ready.

Just how unready he was, he found out on his first patrol with the III Corps Mike Force. He'd always thought himself a good map reader, but now saw that if he wasn't flying over the terrain, able to pick out distinctive features, he couldn't tell where the hell he was at any given moment. The jungle had a monotonous sameness to it. One stream was indistinguishable from another that might run a couple of hundred meters away. One hill looked just like another. He couldn't tell a saddle from a ridge, a valley from a blind draw.

Worse, he felt terribly exposed. Out there with only a fatigue jacket between you and the bullet you were sure was coming your way. And firepower? You had an M16 with its puny 5.56mm bullets instead of bombs and rockets and the lovely .50-caliber machine guns ready to spit out ounce-and-a-half slugs at a range of thousands of meters. How could you protect yourself with an M16?

And the noise! He knew he must have sounded like a herd of clumsy elephants. Periodically one of the snake-eaters would stop, scowl at him, adjust this strap or that, admonish him to fill his canteen as often as possible so it wouldn't slop half-full, duct-tape a snap that kept clicking against its keeper.

But by the second patrol, the first one luckily having made no enemy contact, he felt a bit more confident. He'd shed his insignia of rank—Wanna be a target, Captain? one of the Mike Force troopers had asked. You do, just keep wearing those railroad tracks. He'd lost ten pounds of Officers' Club–induced fat. The immediate-action drills they'd conducted on the short stand-down period increased his confidence in his ability to hit something with the M16, and the demonstration of the seemingly puny 5.56mm ammunition on a fifty-five-gallon drum filled with water had definitely revised his opinion of the weapon. The drum had simply exploded.

All that confidence fled with the first contact.

The company had been choppered in to the Special Forces camp at Loc Ninh, near the Cambodian border. It was supposed to have been a simple body recovery mission—the Loc Ninh Strike Force had been ambushed some ten klicks outside the camp, losing ten Cambodian strikers and one American. Since then the jungle around the ambush site had been thoroughly worked over by air assets of all types, including a B-52 strike. The NVA, the briefer at Bien Hoa had said, have pulled back across the border to lick their wounds. Should be a walk in the woods.

And it had been, at least for the first day. Loc Ninh was surrounded by rubber plantations, long since abandoned to the encroachment of the jungle. Still, visibility was good; they could move fairly swiftly and easily made the first day's objective, just a kilometer short of the ambush point. There the rubber ended, and second-growth forest took its place. None of the triple canopy you ran into higher in the country. Here the trees were short enough to let light down to the floor, which of course meant that undergrowth of all types flourished. Wait-a-minute vines with barbed thorns curled their tendrils over bushes oozing sap that burned exposed skin. Here and there elephant grass, with its razor-sharp leaves, sprouted higher than your head. There were trails, of course, but they were likely to be mined and booby-trapped. From here on said the Mike Force commander, a grizzled captain with three tours under his belt, it would be machete time.

Trucker had slung his jungle hammock between two rubber trees, slathered himself with bug juice, and wrapped his body in a poncho liner. Such attempts to sleep on the first patrol had been met with body aches, startled wakefulness at the slightest sound, mosquitoes as big as dragonflies sucking the life out of you even through the layers of uniform cloth.

Now it took only moments to fall into a sleep interrupted only by someone shaking him at one o'clock and whispering that it was his time to go on watch. You went out with the Mike Force, you did what the Mike Force did. And that included taking your place on the perimeter, straining your eyes in the darkness to try to determine if that really was a bush you were seeing, or a North Vietnamese with a knife in his mouth.

Wisely, the Americans on the Mike Force left control of the claymore clackers in the hands of the Cambodes, who could tell the difference between the sound a man makes and that of the animals that roamed the underbrush. Otherwise the toll on wild pigs, monkeys, and tigers would have been frightful.

The next morning, after a quick breakfast of instant coffee in water heated in canteen cups suspended over fiercely burning pieces of C-4 plastic explosive and, in Trucker's case, a Milky Way candy bar, they were once again on the move. Two Cambode machete men, guarded by four other Cambodes armed with M16s, cutoff M-79 grenade launchers, and a Mossberg shotgun, sliced their way through the undergrowth in two parallel paths. The Cambodes cut only enough of the vegetation away to slip through, which was the cause of much muttered cursing on the part of the Americans. Much taller than their counterparts, they had to constantly stoop and sometimes get on their knees to get through the growth.

It was slow going, and everyone was glad to finally get to a cleared spot. Here some tribe had practiced slash-and-burn agriculture before being pushed out by the war, and the growth had not yet had a chance to make its mark. A tumbledown bamboo hut was in the middle, and a stream flowed near the tree line on the other side. Trucker was often struck by the sheer beauty of the country, never more so than now. He could imagine a family living here, their needs met by the fertility of the soil, their only concerns how to find husbands for their three daughters. Why he gave them three daughters he could not rightly have said. Possibly because he had three of his own.

They rested for a moment, Trucker drinking heavily from his canteen in anticipation of filling it up when they crossed the stream. He wondered if he could chance drinking it straight, without the chemical taste of halazone tablets that supposedly killed all the pathogens that waited for the unwary.

Probably not. He wiped his face with the sweat rag tied around his neck, shifted his rucksack so that the new sore spots would get a chance to heal while the old ones got broken in again.

The point men were halfway across the clearing when one of those chance occurrences changed everything. Of such chances, he thought later, were wars often decided.

A feral pig burst from the jungle, running straight across their front. The point man's reaction was instantaneous. You didn't pass up fresh meat. He gave it a burst of three rounds, forgetting to apply lead and watching the dust kick up behind the fleeing hog. His security man, only a few steps behind, took up the slack, firing a full magazine and neatly knocking down the porker.

The point man didn't have a chance to say a word before the jungle in front of him erupted. Some of the stray rounds had snapped by the head of a young Viet Cong soldier, and he, thinking he was being shot at, returned fire. The VC to either side opened up as well, and the firing spread within seconds to every member of the Viet Cong battalion entrenched just inside the tree line.

The point and security men were cut to pieces. So would the rest of the company have been, Trucker later thought, if they'd been out in the open. The VC would have waited until they stopped to get water, then would have triggered the ambush.

As it was, the fire that got to them was unaimed, most of it going over their heads. The Mike Force commander was quick to deploy a base of fire, using his machine guns to keep Victor Charlie's heads down while the two handheld 60mm mortars started pounding the tree line. Within minutes the FAC flying overhead had diverted two flights of F-4 Phantom jets out of Tan Son Nhut, whose ordnance that day was heavily weighted with napalm.

It was the longest fifteen minutes of Trucker's life, lying there on the ground, wishing he had an entrenching tool, trying to take shelter behind bushes so pitifully small they wouldn't have stopped a BB, much less an AK-47 round. The Cambodes all around him, on the other hand, were laughing and chatting as if on a picnic, all the while returning fire with a practiced ease. The Americans with the patrol were moving here and there, calling in fire, redistributing ammo, reassuring the troopers even when they didn't need to be reassured.

The lone medic was treating a Cambode with a gunshot wound to the chest, paying not the least bit of attention to the rounds that snapped by.

So, yes, Trucker didn't think it strange that the American down below was going to risk his ass, probably die unnoticed—but not unsung—in the jungle. Trying to help people he probably didn't know.

That's the way they did it, these guys in the funny green hats.

And he was damned sure going to do everything he could to help.

"You ready?" Sergeant Billings asked.

Alexander glanced over at his one-one, seeing him getting braced to go over the lip of the crater.

"You're not going," he said.

"The hell I'm not."

"Need you with the team," Alexander said. "I don't come back, you're gonna have to get 'em out of here."

"Bullshit!" Billings said. "They're perfectly capable of getting themselves out. You know that. You, on the other hand, need somebody to cover your ass. You carryin' all those grenades, how is it you expect to protect yourself if somebody decides to pop up out of one of those holes?

"Besides," Billings said after a moment, when Alexander didn't answer, "can't have you getting all those medals by yourself. Your melon head's too goddamn big as it is."

They both chuckled at the thought. If people came to

SOG for the medals, they were to be sorely disappointed. The recon teams did the extraordinary so often that missions that might have won everyone on the team Silver Stars or better were chalked up as just one more walk in the woods.

After a moment Alexander nodded. Billings had a point. And while he accepted that he might be killed doing what he was going to do, there wasn't any sense in getting killed before it was accomplished.

Billings handed him the handset. "Covey, this is One Zero," he said.

"This is Covey. Go."

"Bring it on. Out."

Billings handed the radio to Ksor Tlang, the senior SCU. In rapid-fire French he instructed the Montagnard to take the team east four hundred meters, wait at a designated rally point for two hours, and if the Americans didn't join them by then, make their way back across the border. The 'Yard, ten years older than either of the Americans, looked distressed. But he would do as he was told.

At least as far as taking the team to the rally point. And if the Americans didn't show up, he vowed, he would come looking for them. If they were alive, he would get them out. If they were dead, he would make sure a prayer was said over their remains.

And then he would kill as many of the Vietnamese bastards as he could.

Alexander was looking through the binoculars again. The gun crews had almost finished relaying the howitzers. Then, as the far-off growl of engines grew louder, they hesitated, looking toward their commander for instructions.

That individual cocked his head, realized that the planes were coming in from another direction—this time east to west—and shouted a command. The khaki-clad figures disappeared almost as if by magic, going into prepared positions that, Alexander knew, would stand up to almost anything but a direct hit by a fairly large bomb.

And that put them exactly where he wanted them. He braced his legs for the leap as the first plane opened up with its .50-caliber machine guns, the roar even at this distance deafening. The ground erupted all around the gun, the heavy slugs tearing through trees, snapping off branches, sending up great gouts of dirt. The few that actually hit the gun spanged off crazily doing, unfortunately, little actual damage.

As the plane flashed overhead, the engine noises increased to a scream as the pilot pulled the stick back into his stomach, desperately climbing over the limestone cliff just ahead. He cleared it with only inches to spare.

"Damn!" Billings swore, rubbing his head where one of the expended shell casings had hit it.

The next plane came in, and then the final one, which instead of making a gun run dropped a canister of cluster bomb units. Like giant firecrackers they exploded in the treetops, shrapnel whining like angry hornets. But, as with the .50 calibers, doing little actual damage to the guns.

Didn't matter. Alexander was up and running almost before his mind could register the fact, heading straight for the nearest howitzer. The hundred meters was covered in record time, even with the heavy bag of thermite grenades banging against him, even though the chewed-up ground seemed to be sucking at his feet, even though his lungs felt as if they were on fire.

He reached the first gun, saw that the breech was still open, pulled the pin on the grenade he was carrying, and shoved it inside the chamber. The safety spoon clinked against metal as it flew off, but he was already closing the breech, locking it tightly down.

Next gun! He could see it off to the right, set at an angle. As he ran toward it, he could hear the heavy footfalls of Billings running right behind him. At that moment he was glad the younger sergeant had insisted upon coming along. He felt very alone out here as it was.

The airplane noises that had receded into the distance suddenly became loud again. This time they were coming in from the south, and the chattering of the guns was once again in the distance.

As he reached the second gun, the ground erupted just off to his right, the planes deliberately flying at such an angle as to miss them. But the people under their feet wouldn't know that. At least not yet.

He twisted the breechblock open, dropped in another thermite, closed it up. Two down, one to go.

Shit! Where was it? He stood stock-still for a moment, listening to the receding growl of aircraft engines and the heavy breathing of Sergeant Billings. No sign of it. Had to be there somewhere. He'd clearly heard the outgoing of three guns.

His hearing was shattered by the report of Billing's CAR-15 going off right beside his ear. A figure that had popped up just beside a rock outcropping to their front dissolved in a spray of blood.

"Gonna be all over us in a minute," Billings shouted.

Alexander ran toward the outcropping, passing the body of a North Vietnamese lieutenant on the way. A gun commander! Now where the hell was the gun?

He felt a hand grab him by the load harness, pull him back behind the rock he was getting ready to go around. He had caught a glimpse, just before taking cover, of at least three Vietnamese coming up from an underground bunker. And also the other gun, just beyond them.

Billings fired three bursts, felling the soldiers as he would have targets on a range. He ducked back down, changed magazines, popped back up, killed yet another man who had just made the mistake of looking out of a bunker to see what was happening.

"Cover me from here?" Alexander asked.

"Aw, hell," Billings replied. "G'wan. I know you're going to, anyway."

Alexander was already up and running. He was pulling the pin on the thermite as he reached the gun, then holding the spoon down as he tried to twist the breechblock open. Shit! Jammed, possibly by the impact of one of the .50-caliber slugs. But the NVA would be able to repair it.

He balanced the grenade on the traversing mechanism, let the spoon fly. Within seconds the white-hot material had melted its way down through the gears, fusing them into a muddled mass.

Billings, who had killed two more NVA by this time, watched as his team leader stopped, considering the situation, it seemed. Come on! he wanted to scream. There would be NVA swarming all over the place within seconds, and he damned sure wasn't going to be able to fight them all off.

Then Alexander was shinning his way up the barrel of the gun! Goddamn it, he was going to get them both killed!

Another Vietnamese came out of a bunker somewhat farther away, looking up in wonder at the sight of a tiger-clad figure clinging to the barrel of the gun, ducked back down, came up with a rifle, and was just sighting in as Billings took the top of his head off.

Alexander was halfway up the barrel by now, and moving more slowly. As Billings watched, he rid himself of the heavy bag of grenades, holding only one as he continued to climb.

Billings heard a noise behind him, whirled just in time to shoot an NVA soldier who had been clawing at his holstered pistol. Another officer, this time a major. Christ, what had they gotten themselves into?

He once again turned to cover Alexander, saw that the sergeant had finally reached the muzzle of the gun. He pulled the pin on the grenade and, with the aplomb of a champion basketball player, dunked the cylinder down the tube. Instead of attempting to climb back down, he dropped the ten feet or so to the ground with an audible grunt and thump, rolled, and was back on his feet, running toward the sheltering jungle.

Billings took the time to spray the area from which most of the enemy soldiers had appeared, grabbed a white phosphorous grenade, pulled the pin, and hurled it. It burst, showering the area with glowing particles of heat, creating almost in an instant a choking cloud of white smoke.

Then he was up and running, following Alexander into the jungle. As he burst into the trees, he could hear rounds snapping behind him, then the blinding flash of a CAR-15 as Alexander returned fire, covering Billings until he could himself get a good firing spot.

Came the growl of aircraft engines again. He grabbed his URC-10 survival radio, keyed the mike, and gasped, "On the smoke!"

Up above, the lead aircraft swerved, sighted on the billowing cloud of white smoke, opened up with all his machine guns.

"Shall we get the hell out of here?" said Alexander, as seemingly cool as if he'd just finished a training exercise.

Billings grunted. "Y'know, we get out of this alive, I might just kill you myself."

Sergeant Van Alexander just grinned. Billings said the same thing almost every time.

Trucker, pulling up from the gun run, thought he might try something different next time. By now the Americans below would be clear of the target area. He'd always wanted to practice a maneuver he'd learned back flying the old F-104 jets, a maneuver designed with nuclear weapons in mind. The problem had been that if you just flew over the target on an ordinary bomb run, a nuke would knock you out of the sky. Therefore you went into a run, pulled up in a power climb at a predesignated point, and pickled the bomb as you were on your upward arc. Too soon and the bomb would go too far beyond the target, too late and it would follow you up on your arc. It took a sure hand, and he thought he'd developed it on the many practice runs back at Nellis Air Force Base in Nevada.

And while he didn't have a nuke now, though he would have loved to, he did have a remaining five-hundred-pounder. It would have to do.

His best angle, he figured, would again be north to south. It would carry him back over the flak trap, but he would be high enough to avoid most of the small arms, and the heavier stuff would find him a lot harder to hit. He informed the others about what he was going to do by saying simply, "Watch this trick!"

He ignored the tracer that followed him from the moment he started the run. Most of it was well behind, as he was coming in at full speed. Only a few bursts somewhere off his right wing told him that someone down there with a 37mm was getting pretty good at his job.

The old bird was vibrating like a ramshackle Mexican bus. You could damn near reach the speed of sound with an A1E in a power dive. Of course, if you did, the wings would fly off.

Now pull up! Gravity fights you, the bird is sluggish in responding, but the power of the engine is sufficient to overcome all the forces working against you. One hiccup, one slight bit of carbon in the fuel, and it is all over. Not for the first time Trucker blessed the dedicated young men who maintained the aircraft.

At an angle now, just before flying straight up. He didn't have the indicators with which the F-104s were equipped, would have to just do this one by the seat of his pants. When he thought it was at the right point, he punched the button, felt the aircraft respond quickly as the heavy weight fell away, just had time to see it arcing above him in the opposite direction as he twisted the stick, rolled the aircraft, and sped away.

"SAM, Jesus, SAM," he heard his wingman scream. Still fighting against the g forces that shoved his head back against the seat, he twisted to see in his rearview a telltale stream of smoke emerging from the valley. As he watched in helpless fascination, it grew into a dot, and he knew at that moment he was going to die.

He desperately fought at the controls, intending to dive, to jink and turn and do anything to avoid the deadly little heat-seeking dart.

It flashed past, missing him by at least two hundred yards. It was on a dead course to where he would have been, had he been making an ordinary bomb run. His little "trick" had damn near gotten him killed by exposing him to the SAM-7 in the first place, then saved his ass by fooling the gunner.

Time to get the hell out of there. He fire-walled the airplane, dropped down to just above the trees, and sped for the safety of the beckoning border.

Shitheads had SAMs, it wasn't a place he wanted to hang around.

He was never to know that the bomb arced down directly upon the assembly point for the North Vietnamese company forming to chase down the recon team.

Recon Team Texas made it safely back across the border. Upon arrival at the launch site, Staff Sergeant Van Alexander was told to report immediately to the launch officer, a relatively new guy to the business.

Alexander slouched into the Tactical Operations Center, stood loosely in front of the field table the captain was using for a desk. The young officer stared hard at him, Alexander finally divining that the captain wanted him to assume the position of attention. He rearranged himself as best he could, given that he was dog-tired and wanted nothing more than to lay his head down for just a few moments. Couldn't this have waited?

"I assume you know your rights under Article 31 of the UCMJ," the captain said.

Alexander stiffened even more. Article 31 was the military equivalent of the civilian warning of the right to remain silent, that anything you said could and probably would be held against you.

"I'm bringing you up on charges," the captain continued when Alexander remained silent. "Disobeying a direct order. Endangering the mission and the lives of everyone on the team. If you have anything to say for yourself, you'd better spit it out right now."

Alexander felt the flush crawl up his neck, suffuse his cheeks. What right did this silly bastard have to talk to him like that? The story going around was that he was only a launch officer because he'd screwed up the first mission he'd been on, a fairly simple bomb-damage assessment. Alexander's mouth opened just a crack.

Don't be stupid, Van. All he needs is for you to shoot off your mouth, call him the asshole he is. Then you get insubordination piled on top of all the rest of it.

"Nothing to say, eh? Thought not. You know as well as I do how badly you screwed up. Consider yourself restricted to quarters. Formal charges will be filed as soon as we get back to Kon Tum. Dismissed!"

Staff Sergeant Alexander turned to go, was stopped by the captain, who said, "Aren't you forgetting something?"

It finally penetrated his fatigue-addled brain that the captain was actually expecting him to salute.

The gesture, when it finally came, was suspiciously sloppy—three fingers drooping as if it were just too much effort to straighten them, only the middle finger stiff and erect.

He got out of there before the officer could respond, and before he threw it all to the wind and crawled over the desk to strangle the silly son of a bitch.

Upon their return to the Command and Control Central base in Kontum, no more was said about charges. The captain who had tried to bring them up was abruptly reassigned, some said to a leg unit down in the Delta. The commander of CCC instead declared a lengthy stand-down for the team as they rested, refitted, and retrained. The stand-down was calculated to last just long enough for the Americans on the team to finish their tour and return to the United States. It fit with his intention of recommending Alexander for the Medal of Honor and Billings the Distinguished Service Cross. You couldn't have heroes back out there risking their asses again, possibly getting themselves killed. Army public relations people didn't like such things.

Much to his surprise, the recommendations came back approved. The new executive officer in SOG headquarters down in Saigon recognized the value of awards and decorations, thought that his men were being terribly shortchanged by the current attitude. After all, when the war ended, they would be in competition with their peers for promotions. And those peers would inevitably be highly decorated for far less than the teams were doing daily.

The whole process did nothing but piss Van Alexander off. His tour was cut short, and he was shipped back to the States. Never to return to Vietnam, he was told. Policy.

Screw policy, he often thought as he got word of this or that friend being killed while he sat back in a cushy job at Fort Bragg.

But there was nothing he could do about it.

Chapter 11

It had been almost an hour, and there had been no more artillery. McCulloden and Washington wrapped Elmo Driver in a body bag and left him in the dispensary. Along with a growing number of others. They were being whittled down, slowly. And they could afford to lose no one. Each rifle lost was one more spot that would not be covered, or one man less for their already pitifully small reserve.

Becker restrung his antennas, and soon notified Captain McCulloden that he once again had communications with the C team commander.

"You can thank SOG for the break," Gutierrez said.

"Saved our bacon," Finn replied. "Another hour or so of that, they wouldn't have had much trouble walking in here tonight."

"That's the good news," Gutierrez said. "The bad news is Charlie Secord's got himself into a real shit-storm. Battalion-sized ambush. We've got air helping them, and ARA, but we need arty. Can you do without the one-seven-fives for a little while?"

Finn considered the request. On the one hand, he would

need all the help he could get, and if the artillery took out even a few of the attackers, he would be that much better off.

On the other hand, the enemy was well dug in, and it was only by chance that one of the shells would find a bunker. His trick of driving them out into the open where the ARA could pot them would work only once. He wished they were stupid enough to fall for it again, but knew they were not. They'd hunker down, stick tight, just as he had when the 157s had been falling.

The guns would have a lot more success against the troops in the open who were facing Secord and the rest of the Mike Force. Finn hadn't really had much hope that they would make the camp in time to make any difference, but they damned sure wouldn't even come close if they were chopped up.

"Go ahead," he said. "But make sure they're ready to divert if we call for it."

"Roger. Understood. How are you guys holding out?"

"Lost Elmo Driver," Finn said.

There was silence for a moment. Gutierrez had known Driver for years, ever since he'd joined Special Forces, in fact. Often the then-captain had despaired of ever making a soldier out of the tough little trooper. Way too fond of "Combat Alloy" down in Fayetteville, and the inevitable fights that broke out between the SF guys and the paratroopers of the Eighty-second Airborne. Generally it started when one of the paratroopers would ask, in as loud a voice as possible, "You know who wears green beanies?"

And the response would come "Why, hell, everybody knows that. Girl Scouts!"

And the fight was on.

Driver's inevitable response, when he was standing in front of the company commander's desk, eyes bloused, face cut, wincing from at least one broken rib, was "You should see the other guy!"

Driver had the distinction of being the only man who'd graduated qualification course with the highest score seen in two years, and having the most delinquency reports (DRs) of any man in Special Forces.

"Others?" Gutierrez managed to ask.

"Four strike-force KIA, twelve wounded," Finn said. "Two Mike Force KIA, one wounded. Out of that, probably seven in all will be able to go back on the wire. Others need evac. No chance of that before nightfall, is there?" He already knew the answer. It would be perhaps an hour before the sun set behind the jungle to the west, and another thirty minutes of twilight. Given that they'd already lost one chopper, it was doubtful that the Fourth Infantry Division was willing to risk another. Particularly when it was only to evacuate indigenous troops, he could almost hear the division commander saying.

"I'll try," Gutierrez said.

"Roger. In the meantime, we're gonna get ready. Artillery blew the wire to shit, probably took out some claymores. Got people out taking care of that now. You're sure there's no more heavy stuff coming our way?"

"Not unless they've got more hidden that we don't know about. Which is always possible. But I think they'd be dropping it on you right now, if they did."

"Agreed. Well, guess I'll get back to work, unless you've got anything else."

"*Vaya con Dios, mi amigo,*" Gutierrez said.

"*Sí. Y con frijoles también,*" Finn replied, finishing the old, old joke.

Gutierrez stared at the dead handset, resisted the urge to pound it against the field table, passed it instead back to the commo man.

He would, of course, try to get an evac chopper out to the camp, but knew there was little chance of its happening. And if, by some miracle, he did get the chopper, he would have to resist the almost overwhelming urge to get on it, to join the men in the camp. He would, he told himself, be far better here scaring up whatever support he could get for the beleaguered men. In the camp he would simply be one more rifle.

But sometimes all you wanted to be was one more rifle.

"How you doin', Lieutenant?" Finn asked.

"Just fine, sir," Sloane replied, his voice stiff. Was the captain accusing him of malingering?

"I think we can do without the *sir* shit by now, don't you? Most people call me Finn."

I've noticed that, Sloane thought. Entirely too familiar. But then what can you expect out of a former enlisted man?

Somewhere in the back of his mind there was a nagging voice that said, Yeah. But have you noticed how much more respect they put into his first name than they do in your rank?

That, of course, made him hate the captain the more.

"You up to going out and helping put the perimeter back together?"

Sloane stiffened. Was that an appropriate job for an officer? Stringing wire, driving stakes? Shouldn't he at least be helping to plan for the final defense of the camp?

"Sure," he said. "Where do you want me?"

"Olchak could use some help on the south side. You sure you're up to this? Andy, what do you think?"

"No sign of intracranial swelling," the medic said. "He's past the bad point. Wouldn't recommend pounding in any stakes with your head though, LT."

Finn smiled. "Be careful out there," he said. "Most of the snipers, ones Bucky hasn't killed in any case, are keeping their heads down. Could take a pop any moment, though. You've been shot once today. Next time you might not be so lucky."

Sloane pulled on his shirt, gingerly touched the bandage on his head, decided against putting the hat on. He ached to go back to his tiny bunker and grab the steel pot that waited there. No matter how much it might hurt. The shock of the bullet smacking against his skull had shown him just how vulnerable he was. Now everything was a threat.

He grabbed his rifle and headed toward the door of the bunker. Back stiff, legs working as if he were on a parade ground back at the academy. Ignore it all, he told himself. The fear, the looks he knew must be directed against his back, the snickers that would follow as soon as he left the bunker.

"Ben?" he heard.

To his horror tears started to his eyes. The last person to call him Ben had been his mother. Who had, according to the death certificate, succumbed to a nameless disease, etiology unknown, while he was a plebe at West Point.

Sloane knew better. All those years she had taken his father's abuse, protecting her son when she could, consoling him when she couldn't. Herself suffering his drunken rages. His endless philandering. His denial of anything that might have confirmed that she was of any use at all, much less a human being worthy of love, of respect.

And when her son hadn't needed her anymore, she had simply given up. Stopped eating. Stopped responding. And within months she had died.

To his own everlasting shame, he had found himself agreeing with his father, who told anyone who would listen that his late wife was simply too weak, too delicate for this world. That she was proof positive that only the strong survive.

For the most part, Bentley Sloane was able to keep up that facade. Only in the long watches of the night, when he questioned his own worth, his own strength, did he miss her quiet patience, the inner strength that had allowed her to go on for so long.

He kept his back turned so that McCulloden could not see his face, would not laugh as he expected him to at the sight of tears running down his cheeks. "Yes?" he said.

"Watch your ass out there," Finn said.

"It's them that better be watching their asses," Sloane replied, affecting a bravado he did not feel. In truth, he would much rather have stayed in the dispensary, kept out of the open where death waited, coming from sources he could not even imagine. And he had a vivid imagination.

Finn shook his head as the lieutenant exited the bunker. A prickly one, that. Getting shot in the head hadn't taken all the piss and vinegar out of him. He might just grow up to be a good soldier, if he survived.

Finn turned to Inger, who was deeply involved in debriding a shrapnel wound in the buttock of one of the strikers. The medic worked quickly and steadily, cutting away the discolored dead flesh, clamping bleeders, probing deeper into the wound and finding the pieces of metal that had gone every which way. The striker bore it stoically, chewing on a great wad of betel nut, wincing only when Inger probed particularly deep.

Couldn't do it better myself, Finn thought. And even though he had been one himself, he was once again amazed at the capabilities of the Special Forces medics. This operation should have been done in a sterile operating theater, by a highly skilled surgeon backed up by an anesthesiologist and a team of surgical assistants. Inger was working by the light of a hissing gas lantern, the camp generators having been turned off during the artillery barrage and not yet restarted. His surgical instruments had been sterilized by placing them on a tray just above the boiling water in a pressure cooker. His one assistant was a Montagnard medic who, a couple of years ago, would have been wearing a loincloth and hunting monkeys for sustenance.

Inger pulled the last piece of metal from the wound, dropped it in an emesis tray to join the half dozen other pieces there, flushed the wound with sterile saline, dabbed it dry, and inspected it. He grunted his satisfaction in seeing only a little capillary oozing. He snipped away one more tiny piece of flesh, then packed the wound with sterile gauze, leaving the Montagnard medic to finish the bandaging. He would not close the wound, at least not now. Better to allow it to drain. God knew what pathogens had been carried into it, and despite one's best efforts, you couldn't get rid of all of them. Close it up and they would fester and spread. Leave it open and you could inspect it at each bandage change, look for the telltale signs of infection. Debride that, keep filling him up with antibiotics, and wait for the flesh to granulate. Worse came to worst, the wound would someday close itself, although it would leave a hell of a scar.

They wouldn't have to worry about that, Finn thought. Either they would hold out, in which case sooner or later the siege would be lifted and the striker would be evacuated back to a proper hospital, or they wouldn't. And if they didn't, the Montagnard would have a much worse problem than the wound in his ass.

"How are you holding up, Andy?" Finn asked as the medic stripped off his gloves and gauze mask.

Inger grinned. "Tired. So what else is new?"

"Anything I can do?"

"Yeah. Get us the hell out of here."

"Sure. Business class okay, or do you want up front with the rich guys?"

"Right now I'd settle for economy. Hell, I'd even take a seat in the smoking section."

"Your standards *have* fallen. Tomorrow be okay?"

"Can't get a ticket for the red-eye?"

"All booked up."

"Well, in that case, screw it. Might as well stay here and keep you guys out of trouble. Any chance of getting a resupply before dark?"

"Slim," Finn admitted. "Won't be a chopper, of that I'm fairly sure. Seems our fearless aviators ain't too fond of being shot out of the sky. Can't say I blame them. What is it you need?"

"Serum albumin, antibiotics of all kinds—penicillin, streptomycin, most of all chloramphenicol. Got two guys in the back, wounded before we got here, having to give them massive doses. Probably get gas gangrene, we don't. Whatever bug is in them laughs at procaine."

"Anything else?"

"How about a nice field hospital, complete with good-looking nurses?"

"Probably have to wait for a couple of days on that one. But I'll see what I can do about the rest. You might think about grabbing a couple of hours of sleep in the meantime. Gonna be a hot time in the old town tonight."

"Might just do that. Think I ought to set the alarm?"

Finn laughed. "Got a feeling you won't need to."

Sloane found Sergeant Olchak and a group of Mike Force soldiers, stripped to the waist and sweating profusely, replacing wire as best they could where the artillery had wadded it up. Without a word he pitched in, and soon he was sweating as copiously as they. The late-afternoon sun was still brutally hot, and worse, there had been a sudden increase in humidity. Olchak mentioned as they worked that it looked like the long-delayed monsoon would soon be upon them.

After the second time Sloane ripped the skin from his fingers, tugging on the recalcitrant wire, he reluctantly accepted a set of heavy work gloves from the sergeant. It didn't help his simmering resentment at having to work like a damned prisoner. Endlessly he recited a litany of complaints, wisely keeping them inside his mind. Olchak, like all the other Americans in the Mike Force, spoke only admiringly about their commander. Sloane didn't think that his opinion, which was that Captain Finn McCulloden didn't know the difference between enlisted men and officers, among other things, would be greeted with any enthusiasm.

Well, by God he did! Though his jacket was sweated quite thoroughly through, he was not going to pull it off and sweat like a stevedore. He glanced down, appalled to see that the neat crease he insisted the house girls iron in his pants had completely disappeared, and that his usually well-shined boots were covered with dirt and wearing several scars where the barbed wire had dragged across them. And he'd just replaced those boots! It was all very well for the NCOs to wear their footgear until the cleats were nearly worn off, but he'd be damned if he'd do it

One had to maintain standards, after all. Even if you were here in the middle of the jungle, about to be overrun by thousands of screaming fanatics.

Those outside the wire—yes. They'd soon find out what they'd gotten themselves into. For a moment he was swept away by his dreams of glory. Parades, perhaps. He completely ignored that the war was so unpopular back home that even Medal of Honor winners were sneaked in and out of the White House, as if they were poor relatives you had to acknowledge, but didn't have to talk about.

But even without the parade, there would be glory

enough. He savored the thought of going to the Fort Myers Officers' Club on a Friday night, when General Sloane (retired) and a bunch of his cronies met for poker and heavy drinking, and walking up to the table. Completely unannounced, of course. He wouldn't even be wearing the neck medal. Too ostentatious, too speaking of premeditation. No, the little blue ribbon with stars, worn atop all the other medals and decorations—now including the Purple Heart! he reminded himself—that would be enough.

They'd jump up to congratulate him, these old men who had laughed so often at the jokes and insults his father had heaped upon him. And their words would be tinged with bitter envy.

His father would just sit there and smile his crooked little smile and say nothing. But he would know. Oh, yes, he would know.

Even if he didn't get to do that, if he died in the attempt, it would still be good. Maybe even better. Let the old bastard choke on it. I hope it kills him!

He swayed, suddenly dizzy. Olchak saw him, thought it was from the heat and exertion, insisted that he get out of the sun, rest a little while. He was surprised at the concern he heard in the sergeant's voice. Yes, he said, maybe I'll do that. I'll be back out to help in a few minutes.

"Ah, bullshit," Olchak said. "We're just jacking off here, anyway. Charlie wants to come through this wire, he's gonna come through. All we can do is slow him down a little bit. Get some rest. You get a thump like that on your noggin, you gotta be careful. We've already lost enough people today."

You're not going to lose me, Sergeant, he said silently. At least not yet.

Stankow was working with Bucky Epstein on the other side of the camp. There too the wire was wadded up, and worse, several of the claymores had been destroyed through sympathetic detonation. Stankow had his 'Yards fetch more from one of the bunkers, replacing each as he came across a bare, scorched spot. The ones still in place he signaled Bucky to run a continuity check on. This consisted of inserting a tester in between the wire and the firing device, called a clacker because it resembled a kid's toy popular back in the fifties. Squeeze the clacker, which would ordinarily have sent a shot of electricity down the wire, detonating the mine, and it was shunted into the tester, which lit up if the firing circuit was complete. Their decision to bury the firing wires as deep as possible was obviously paying off. If the wire hadn't been clipped at the mine itself, the circuits were inevitably good.

For the most part, Stankow was able to hook the new claymores up to the old wires, thus securing the circuit. Several of the mines he booby-trapped, carefully burying a zero-delay grenade under the body of it, holding down the spoon by the weight of the mine itself. Charlie had a habit of sneaking sappers into the wire and turning the mines around, or stealing them for later use. Pick one of these up, and the resulting explosion of not only the grenade but the mine itself would shred the body so that it bore little resemblance to anything human.

As they finished with each area, Stankow had the 'Yards carefully rake the ground, smoothing out their footprints, removing any debris. Any marks that appeared there now would stand out like, as Stankow delicately put it, a whore in church.

His flame fougasse mines were, he was glad to see, intact. Next he installed a number of trip flares. Ordinarily the flares weren't a part of the defenses—wind and the occasional small animal making its way through the wires set them off all too often. Everybody would jump to alert, see that there was no reason for it, stand down, and jump to alert again. After a while they would get so used to it that they would no longer pay any attention.

Which was, of course, the point at which Charlie would be coming through the wire.

Didn't matter now. They'd all be awake tonight anyway.

Very occasionally a round would snap by, but they were from far off, the NVA obviously not yet willing to chance the 175s by coming in closer. He simply ignored it. Unaimed as it was, the chances of one of the rounds hitting him were small. And if one did? Obviously it was just his time to go.

Fatalism had been a part of his makeup ever since as a young man he'd joined the partisans. No one expected to live through that war, anyway. If you didn't get killed in combat, you were going to get tracked down by the Nazi special troops combing the forests. And if they didn't get you, perhaps your own side would find you of insufficient reliability and kill you themselves.

Which the communists would have done, if he'd stayed there after the defeat of the Germans. First they rounded up the noncommunist fighters, trumped up charges of collaboration, and had them shot. The communist fighters went next. After all, if you were to control a country, you couldn't very well have people running around who already had a history of fighting against anything they saw as oppression. No matter what the ideology.

Stankow wondered how many of the Viet Cong realized what was going to happen after the war. They should already have seen the writing on the wall. Tet '68 should have shown them that. The NVA had allowed them to bear the brunt of the fighting, exposing themselves in an offensive that bore absolutely no chance of military success. They'd been told they would be welcomed with open arms by the residents of Saigon, Da Nang, Nha Trang, and all the lesser cities, that the people would rise up in general revolution once they achieved their goals.

Only to find out that they had been lied to. That the people, instead of supporting them, gladly turned them in. That the second wave of North Vietnamese regular forces they had been told to expect had not been forthcoming. And the Viet Cong had died by the thousands. Even now, in areas that during his first two tours had been regarded as VC sanctuaries, you could go with scarcely any chance of encountering the enemy.

Unless the NVA had moved their main-force units in. Which was the case all along the border. Slowly nibbling away at the forces that opposed them, then disappearing back into their sanctuaries.

And the people back in Washington? Stupid! Trying to negotiate a peace, arguing about the shape of the conference table in Paris. When everyone knew the only way you could negotiate with a communist was to utterly defeat him.

And of course you couldn't defeat him if you let him

retreat and lick his wounds, reorganize, reequip, retrain, and be back at you.

At least Nixon had let them cross the border into Cambodia, destroying in the process hundreds of tons of ammunition, countless caches of food, and ripping up bunker complexes it must have taken them years to build. But that incursion had been limited to twenty miles, and of course the NVA had known that—it had been no secret. Their main-force units had merely pulled back behind the twenty-mile limit, bided their time, and when the Americans had left, come back. Their supplies were quickly replaced, their bunkers rebuilt. And it was business as usual.

Stankow didn't regard himself as a great military thinker. He'd leave that up to the generals. But damn! Didn't they have anyone with the sense and, more important, the balls to stand up to the politicians?

He realized his face was growing red, the blood pounding in his ears. Calm down, he told himself. All you can do is the best you can.

He looked back over his handiwork. The ground was flat and smooth, the claymores were well-concealed and properly aimed, the trip flares were fixed to the posts that supported the wire. The razor wire gleamed in the late-afternoon sun. To a professional soldier, it was as beautiful a sight as was the latest centerfold.

"I need a beer," he said to Bucky Epstein.

"Thought you'd never ask," Bucky said. "Generators are running again. Should be some cold ones in the team house."

"Any luck on those choppers?" Finn asked.

"None at all," Gutierrez replied. "Cozart volunteered, got told he tried it, they'd bring him up on charges."

Finn's laugh had no humor in it. "Wouldn't be the first time that happened."

"Nah. But this time they mean it. You saw what the SAM-7s, handheld antiaircraft missiles, did to that chopper."

"I know what a SAM-7 is," Finn replied, his voice short.

"Yeah. Guess you do," Gutierrez said, belatedly remembering that it had been Finn McCulloden's team that had found the first cache of the deadly little missiles, the weapons that the intel people in Saigon had sworn would not be in-country, being far too valuable for the Soviets to give them away.

"Guess I understand," Finn said. "Wouldn't want Wes to get one of those up his tailpipe, anyway. I've got another idea. You got any way of getting hold of the Spads down in III corps?"

Gutierrez instantly knew what Finn was proposing. "Leave it to me. Have Becker send a list of what you need. We'll get it done. Out."

Finn sat staring at the dead mike for a moment. Then he roused himself, passed Becker the list of items they'd need.

"You get through with that, come over to the team house," Finn said. "I want to talk to everyone."

Oh, shit, Becker thought. Here comes the pep talk. God damn it, I hate it when that happens.

Means we're in even deeper shit than I thought.

"Beer, *Dai Uy?*" Olchak asked.

"Don't mind if I do." Olchak tossed Finn the rusted, blessedly cold can, and he ran it over his forehead. Schlitz, he noted with disgust. He thought drinking Schlitz beer was only slightly better than drinking horse piss, and that would only be because it was cold.

The REMFs in Da Nang got to the beer supplies long before anyone else could, skimming off the Budweiser and sometimes even the Pabst Blue Ribbon. Generally the only things you could get out here in the A camps were Schlitz and Hamms.

Better than Ba Moui Ba, "33," which had been all they could get on his first tour. He had been told that, in France, 33 was quite a good beer. Obviously it had lost something in the translation to Vietnamese breweries. It tasted exactly as you would expect formaldehyde to taste, that ingredient being added, he had been told, to preserve it against the tropical heat.

One way to get embalmed before your time, he supposed. The other choice had been a raw Algerian wine, Marengo. He'd felt quite the cosmopolite, drinking Algerian red wine in the outdoor café at the Continental Hotel in Saigon.

That was, of course, before they'd thrown grenades into the Continental. Now the café was surrounded by chain-link fence, and the only people who drank there were USAID civilians and contractors from RMK. The VC didn't even bother with them.

He snatched a church key from the bar, popped a hole in the can, another for ventilation, and drank it off in one thirsty gulp. Best to do it that way, he'd found. All you had to contend with was the aftertaste. Something like you'd expect from wringing out dirty socks.

"Encore?" Olchak asked.

Finn shook his head. "About as much of that fun as I can stand. Everybody here?"

"All 'cept the LT," Olchak said, just as Lieutenant Sloane

came in. His bandage was sweated through, and beneath the dirt there was a tinge of blood.

"Best get Andy to look at that bandage," Finn said. "Ain't gonna be much time later."

"I'm fine," Sloane said.

Finn shrugged. "Suit yourself."

"I guess we're all wondering why you got us together, Cap'n," Bucky Epstein said.

Finn groaned. "Old joke."

"Figured you'd recognize it, that way," Epstein replied. Captain Finn McCulloden was all of twenty-eight years old. Which made him an old man in Epstein's eyes.

"Yeah. Well. Glad you recognize superior wisdom. Sergeant Olchak, you want to give out the assignments?"

"Got it. Stankow, mortars. Epstein, recoilless. Inger, dispensary. Becker, commo. I've got north wall, Sergeant Young with me. Lieutenant Sloane, south, take Noonan. Washington, east, with Curtis. DiUlio, you and Wren get the west wall. Redmon, you're the recon platoon adviser, right?"

Staff Sergeant Dennis Redmon, one of the members of the original A team, confirmed that he was.

"You're the reserve. Bartlett's with you. You're the junior medic, right, Bartlett?"

Bartlett, barely out of training group before being thrown into this cauldron and feeling very, very unlucky, said that he was.

"Be ready to help Andy Inger, if he needs it. Any questions?"

"Only one," Redmon said. He directed the question at Captain McCulloden. "Gonna happen tonight, isn't it?"

"I'd be the most surprised son of a bitch in the world if it didn't," Finn replied. "We've hurt 'em today, but not enough. Whoever it is out there in command, he's got to be thinking, 'I don't want any more of this shit. Let's get it done, get the hell out of here. Before these crazy mother-fuckers think of something else to throw at us.' "

"And what else have we got to throw at them?" Curtis, the junior weapons man from the team, asked.

"Not much," Finn admitted. "We can call Sky Spot, drop some heavy shit, but you know as well as I do how much good that does. Especially if they're in the wire."

"So how much chance do we have?" asked Sergeant First Class Wren, who, since he was a full-blood Chicka-saw Indian, had been forced to endure the affectionate name of Blanket-Ass for his entire career with the Special Forces.

This is where I'm supposed to be delivering a speech so inspiring, it's going to cause these guys to go out there and kick the ass of an entire goddamn NVA division, Finn thought. Alternatively, draw a line in the sand and say that it is your choice to stay or go, realizing that those who stayed faced almost certain annihilation.

Problem was, he wasn't a speechmaker. And even if he had been, he couldn't have forced himself to deliver it.

And as for the go or stay? Not a hell of a lot of choice there. The time for going was long gone.

So he ignored the question, choosing instead to deliver the rest of the operations plan. They knew it wasn't a question that could be answered, anyway.

"We're gonna get a quick resupply in here at last light," he said. "Spads, dropping nape canisters. Most of it will be for you, Andy. The drugs you requested. Couple of other things may make life outside the wire more interesting. There'll be no choppers. Charlie has SAMs, along with all the other shit he's managed to move in here. We grab it, stow it away, and then I suggest you try to get as much rest as you can. We'll keep a skeleton watch on, but I don't think the NVA are gonna try anything before full nightfall. They never do.

"We hit 'em hard in the wire. They get as far as the final protective line, the machine guns stay to their zones, should cut a lot of them down. Past that, we start retreating to the inner perimeter. It gets bad enough, we'll get in the central bunker, wait them out. Just like at Lang Vei. Hold out long enough, there'll be people here to help."

"And if we can't make it back to the bunker?" Wren asked.

Damn, Finn thought. Wish he hadn't asked that.

"Then you try to go the other way," Finn said. "Get the hell outside the camp, E and E. Head south. Rest of the battalion is that way. Get with them, you're okay."

Wish I was as confident as I sound, he thought.

"Great plan," Master Sergeant Olchak said. "You know, for that, I think we should sing the captain a hymn."

And from every throat came the rousing chorus.

"Hymnnn,"

"Hymnnn."

"Fuck himnnn!"

"Go in peace, my children," Finn said.

Chapter 12

At dusk the Spads, A1E prop-driven aircraft from a different squadron than the Sandys, came roaring in. Just at the edge of camp the first one dropped the napalm canister; it tumbled end over end before smacking into the ground near the flagpole. The NVA must have been wondering what the Americans were doing, bombing themselves. Ordinarily when the silver canister hit, it would release jellied gasoline, immolating anything in its path.

This time there was no fire, no explosion. Only a swarm of Montagnards, grabbing the canister and pulling it into a bunker before the next plane came in.

The North Vietnamese gunners recovered from their surprise quickly enough, pursuing the third plane with green tracer as it sped over the camp. The pilot dropped his canister, pulled up in a power climb, cranked the plane over, and dove, opening up with his machine guns on the peskiest of the antiaircraft fire. He swooped back toward the south, then came back, this time doing a snap roll over the camp.

Wonder how that boy gets those big old balls in that little old cockpit? Finn thought.

Another power climb and he had disappeared in the clouds that were beginning to form to the east. Clouds that were moving in far too fast to suit Finn McCulloden.

A burst of automatic weapons fire sprayed across the ground, driving him inside the bunker. Charlie's moved back in, Finn thought. Didn't think he'd stay away long.

Sam Gutierrez had just informed him that Charlie Secord and the rest of the battalion had managed to break contact with the ambushing force, and that they had suffered only a few casualties. They were going to try another route in, backing off sufficiently to come at the camp from an entirely different angle.

But they'd lost at least a day. That the NVA hadn't really pursued them in any coherent fashion meant to Finn that this result was exactly what the enemy wanted. Keep any relief forces far enough away that even if some of the defenders did manage to escape an overrun camp, they would have little chance of reaching safety.

They intend to kill or capture every last one of us, Finn surmised. Now I know what Travis felt, when he heard the sounds of the *Dugello* played by the Mexican military band outside the Alamo.

"Looks like we got a present here, Cap'n," Olchak said, holding up a fiberglass weapons case. Three others were still in the canister.

Finn popped open the case, relieved to see that it seemed to have survived the ride with no damage. Inside was an M16 rifle, atop which was a bulky starlight scope. Instead of a flash hider at the muzzle, there was mounted a long black tube—a Sionics sound suppressor.

"Want to have some fun?" he asked the sergeant.

"More'n you know," Olchak answered.

• • •

Private Duong Van Trinh was a careful man these days.

If he'd made a habit of being careful before, he would still have been Sergeant Duong Van Trinh, and he would not now be making his way beneath the barbed wire. His mistake had come when he'd been forced to attend yet another indoctrination session, conducted by the division political officer. He'd resented it, thinking that it seemed to be casting doubt on his reliability. And he'd been fighting this war far longer than the political officer, who had come down from Hanoi only the month before. That in itself should have testified to his reliability.

The PO went on and on about the poor, oppressed people of the South, how they were being crushed under the heels of the imperialist Americans and their running-dog South Vietnamese lackeys. How they were starved into submission, the fruits of their toil confiscated by the criminal Thieu government, and how the glorious North Vietnamese army had a duty to save them, a duty put forward by Ho Chi Minh himself, he of glorious memory.

Trinh, who had seen firsthand the conditions in the South, had obviously let his disbelief at this nonsense being spouted by the officer show on his face. Suddenly the captain had stopped his speech, looked directly at him, and asked him if he did not believe in the ultimate victory.

Trinh didn't know why he'd said it. Perhaps it was because he had been there so long, had lost so many friends, had suffered wounds for which there was seldom enough medicine. All he knew was that suddenly he was fed up.

"I believe in the ultimate victory," he had said. "But it

won't be because the people of the South rise up. It won't be because of the glorious efforts of our comrades the Viet Cong. It will be only because of men like these"—he swung his arm to indicate the soldiers sitting there—"who will go on fighting, no matter what. Sometimes because of our leadership. And sometimes in spite of it."

There was complete silence, his comrades-in-arms turning away from him, pretending perhaps that he didn't exist. Or if he did, that they didn't know him. Dropped from the sky in their midst, perhaps.

The political officer had been apoplectic. He had demanded that the sergeant be seized and taken out and shot—*pour l'encouragement des autres.*

That Trinh hadn't been executed was due only to the fact that he had been such a good soldier, recognized as such by his company and battalion commanders. However, he obviously could not go unpunished. And he could not stay in the same unit, for fear of infecting the others with what the political officer called his defeatism.

He'd been publicly stripped of his rank and reassigned to a sapper battalion.

And now he was one of the twenty-two sappers whose job it was to make their way through the defenses of the camp, carrying satchel charges that they were to throw into the machine gun positions, command bunkers, communications center, and ammunition dumps. More here to be careful of than just your unguarded mouth, he told himself.

He lay on his back, using only shoulders and hips to wriggle his way forward. His right hand was extended to the front, feeling for trip wires, the prongs of buried mines, the wire itself. Each strand was carefully raised and placed atop the bamboo pole he carried in his left hand. By pushing up slightly on the pole he made space enough to move forward, inches at a time.

It was slow, painstaking work. He had been at it for an hour and was only now almost through the first barrier. No trip wires, no mines, no tin cans with pebbles inside. The enemy would, he knew, be saving that for the closer-in defensive belts.

Behind him would come the next group of sappers, these pushing bamboo poles filled with explosives before them. The poles would be joined together and, when the time came, detonated. Bangalore torpedoes, he had heard them called, though the Vietnamese name was different.

The bangalores would blow great gaps in the wire, detonate any mines within a few feet, create paths through which the assault troops could come screaming in. It was a time-tested technique, having worked again and again in camps and outposts throughout the country. But much depended upon him and others like him. If the machine guns weren't taken out, they would with their interlocking fire simply mow down the assault troops. Few if any of the first wave would get through. The commanders would not stop, of course. They would assault again and again until the enemy guns got so hot they couldn't fire or ran out of ammunition or were hit by lucky shots from RPG-7 launchers.

But in the meantime, hundreds would die. Many of them would be his former friends. And although they now shunned him, he did not want to see them dead.

He passed the last bit of concertina wire, now working

his way into the tanglefoot. Here he would be far more likely to run into trip-wired flares. Push on the wire, and the flare would go off. Cut the wire, and the spring-loaded trigger would fire the flare from the other direction. In either case, he would be caught in the light like a bug on a wall.

Almost as soon as he thought it, he felt the telltale resistance of a tiny piece of wire, much smaller than the barbed wire he was going through. He ran his fingers one way, finding only its anchor point, and then the other. There was the trigger. He reached down into the bag on his chest, pulled out a roll of tape. It had, he knew, come from one of the American supply depots, purloined by a greedy sergeant and sold on the black market. Duct tape, they called it, or hundred-mile-an-hour tape. Trinh had no idea what either meant, but did know it was wonderful stuff. He tore off a strip and wrapped it around trigger and flare, securing the trigger quite well. He then felt safe enough to cut the wire, using a set of cutters he had also secreted in the bag.

He did not allow himself to feel satisfied. There would be, he knew, many more. And he had to be very good, or very lucky, each and every time.

He did not allow himself to think about anything else—not his wife, left behind two years ago when he marched South. Not his two sons, neither of whom really knew their father. Not his perpetually grumbling stomach. There was seldom enough food, and the fare was so monotonous that the soldiers often took to the jungle to scrounge lizards, insects, the occasional edible root. Of course, when this many soldiers were in one place, the jungle was soon stripped of edibles, the forest floor resembling what it would look like after a swarm of army ants had marched over it.

Concentrate! Was that just the slightest brush of another wire?

He never felt the bullet that took his life. It smacked into the top of his head, the energy dump from the high-speed round creating so much overpressure in the skull it blew both his eyes out of their sockets.

Behind him a sapper dragging a bangalore torpedo died too.

Finn handed the weapon to Olchak, who sighted through the starlight scope to see the two dead men, glowing eerily in the green enhanced light.

"Looks to me to be zeroed about right," Finn said, his voice flat.

"Good enough," Olchak grunted.

"Let's get one of these on each side," Finn instructed. "If we can take out the sappers, we can slow things down a bit."

Olchak left to do Finn's bidding. Finn put the rubber grommet of the scope to his eye again, swept the perimeter. Nothing was moving at the moment. They would, he knew, re-group and try to come in again. Wondering what had happened. The heavy sound-suppressor would have made it difficult for them to hear the shots, much less tell where they came from. More important, the suppressor completely hid the muzzle flash. The still-burning gases that created both the report and flash were redirected into swirl chambers within the metal tube, slowing them and allowing the burn to complete. The round, still supersonic, would still crack in the night air, thus the tube was called a suppressor, rather than a silencer.

The only way you could tell where the round was coming from was to be looking exactly down the barrel at the moment the round was fired. And if you were, you weren't going to be in any shape to tell anyone where it came from.

They'd figure it out sooner or later. They weren't stupid, after all. Then they'd try to suppress the fire by means of their own weapons while the next wave of sappers came through. It was always a measure of this or that, one measure being met by a countermeasure, like a giant game of chess.

Only difference was, here, if you got checkmated, you didn't fold up the board, put your pieces in their holders, and walk away.

"You ever used one of these before?" he asked Sergeant Young, who was standing beside him, obviously eager to take his turn.

"Back at Bragg, sir."

"You a good shot?"

"Better'n most."

"That's what I like. Modesty."

Sergeant Young grinned, his teeth gleaming in the little bit of light coming in through the bunker embrasure. "Farm boy, sir."

Finn smiled back. The sergeant didn't have to say anything more. He was of that type that flocked to the Special Forces, kids raised on farms in Mississippi, Iowa, New York, and every other state in the Union. Kids with no prospects, other than backbreaking labor for little reward. Kids who were smarter than the rest, who knew there was something besides getting up before the chickens, repairing equipment that should have been replaced years before, waiting for crops that died from insects or drought or too much rain or just plain bad luck.

Kids who would have been shooting the family rifle since they were big enough to pick it up, using it to supplement the commodity beans and rice and cheese passed out by bureaucrats left over from the New Deal. The one thing you didn't do, when you might have ten or twelve .22 bullets to your name, was waste one of them.

Finn handed him the weapon, noted approvingly that the sergeant first checked to see if it was on safe, then retracted the bolt slightly to make sure a round was in the chamber. In the early days the M16 had had a distressing tendency to jam, and no soldier took it for granted even now that the problems seemed largely solved.

Young stood slightly back from the embrasure and scanned the perimeter. By staying to the shadows deep in the bunker he lessened his chances of being seen by the alert NVA spotter, who would be looking through binoculars to see the flash of glass, the movement of a barrel, the shape resolving itself into a body.

Satisfied, Finn left the bunker. He drew his pistol, hunched down, and traversed the connecting trench. While he didn't think any of the sappers had yet managed to get through the wire, there was no use in taking any chances. Each twist of the trench was negotiated carefully, pistol held close to the body to make sure someone on the other side of the next turn couldn't grab it and twist it away.

The only people in the trench were Montagnard sentries, who were satisfyingly alert. Two men covered each stretch of the trench. They flashed gold-toothed grins at him as he passed. The Montagnards counted their wealth by how many gold teeth they could accumulate, many of them with fancy inlays of hearts and stars of semiprecious metal. Some said the North Vietnamese rear-area troops carried around pliers, specifically to deal with the teeth of the 'Yards killed by the assault troops.

He felt a wave of affection for these men. Recruited from their longhouses by Special Forces troops, pulled from their families, facing little but the likelihood of their own death, they served with little complaint. They adapted to modern weaponry, after having used only bamboo crossbows all their early lives, like a duck would to water. One of Finn's favorite Mike Force troopers carried a Browning automatic rifle (BAR) that was longer than he was tall. He'd stripped the weapon of bipod, carrying handle, or anything else that added weight but could be done without. His favorite trick was to fire the massive .30-06 cartridges one at a time, with appalling accuracy. Almost inevitably after a battle a number of the enemy soldiers would be found to have one .30-caliber-size hole right between their eyes. When the Mike Force had been issued M16s, replacing the underpowered carbines with which they'd previously been armed, this soldier had been offered one of the new weapons. He had refused to take it, vehemently voicing his preference for the BAR.

He still carried it.

Finn made the rounds of the bunkers as well, finding that each had alert soldiers at the guns. The camp was built in the shape of a star, with machine gun bunkers at each point and at the vee where the legs of the star met. There were three machine guns in each, sometimes the newer M60s and sometimes the old 1919A6 in .30-06 caliber. Personally, Finn had no preference between the two, but wished that they fired the same bullet. Trying to keep two different kinds of ammunition, especially when you were trying to resupply one of the bunkers while under fire, was a nightmare.

The guns in the left and right embrasures had their zones of fire at approximately forty-five degrees off-center, the one in the center embrasure with a zone that overlapped the other two. While the enemy was still at a distance, they would engage with point fire. Only when the assaulting force got too close would someone call for final protective fires. At that point the guns would be locked in on a fixed azimuth, each one overlapping the fire from the machine guns on the bunker to either side. The guns in the vee would fire directly down the legs of the star, covering the point bunkers and laying down a curtain of lead that no one could get through.

At least in theory. The problem was that if you lost one bunker, you lost the ability to cover the other bunkers to either side. And if you lost two?

Well, you just hoped the enemy wouldn't be smart enough to exploit a sector that would be covered only by the rifle fire from the men in the trenches.

Unfortunately, Charlie was never that stupid.

That was why they had the claymores. Charlie would rush as many men through the breached defenses as he could, and if the claymores were tripped at just the right time, they would slaughter some of the best troops the enemy had. One hoped that such a debacle would give the enemy pause, perhaps even cause him to break off the attack.

Of course, if it didn't, the second wave was going to come right into the camp, with only individual defenders to stop them. Past that, it was every man for himself. Finn had the utmost confidence in the fighting abilities of his troops. Problem was, you could be the best fighter in the world, but when you were outnumbered by ten or twenty to one, the outcome was pretty much ordained.

He could only hope it wouldn't come to that.

He reached the command bunker for the west wall to find DiUlio and Wren arguing over who would get the starlight-scope-equipped weapon. It seemed that DiUlio had missed a shot, and Wren hadn't, therefore Wren obviously needed to be the sniper. Armando DiUlio swore that he wouldn't have missed if Wren hadn't picked exactly that moment to cough loudly, thus throwing off his aim.

"Didn't do it on purpose," Wren said.

"Bullshit!"

"I think you guys have been together too long," Finn said. "Person didn't know better, he'd think you were married."

Wren grunted. "His tits ain't big enough for that."

DiUlio, who took such pride in his conditioning regimen that to maintain it he had fabricated an entire free-weight system out of steel pipes and tin cans filled with concrete, puffed up his chest. "Lots bigger'n yours," he said.

Finn left them there to continue their good-natured bickering, having decided between themselves to alternate turns with the weapon. In truth there was such a closeness between the men in the Special Forces that wives did often accuse them of loving their teammates more than they did their spouses. It often manifested itself in arguments like those endlessly engaged in by DiUlio and Wren, who had served back-to-back tours in the same camp.

Sometimes the affection was overt, particularly when the men were around outsiders. An SF trooper, seeing a buddy enter the room, would jump up, grab him, and kiss him squarely in the ear, sometimes with so much tongue you felt as if it were going to come out the other side. The kiss would be accompanied by "You sweet motherfucker! Don't you ever die! Don't you even catch a cold."

Or the closeness could lead to fistfights that looked as if they were going to result in the death or the maiming of both participants. Followed by heavy drinking and the swearing of eternal friendship.

The friendship was what kept them here, volunteering for tour after tour, when they could safely have returned to the States, gotten a job in a basic-training outfit somewhere. The primary worry then being how to avoid trying to beat some sense into a stupid-ass trainee.

No one would have questioned the decision. No one would have looked down on them, talked about their losing their nerve, scoffed at the cushy life they'd be leading back in the world.

A man had only to answer to himself. And for most, the fact that his friends were still there, fighting the good fight, was enough. How could you not be there too?

Finn continued his rounds, ending up back on the north wall, where Olchak had rejoined Sergeant Young. "Got three more," Young said. "Now nothing for the last thirty minutes."

That meant one of two things. Either the NVA had gotten wise, stopped sending men to certain death, and would wait until the main assault to take out the bunkers, or they didn't know what was happening at all. Finn would have bet on the latter. The North Vietnamese were perpetually short on means of communication—the men in the wire would have had no way of telling the ones outside what was happening.

Instead of depending upon radios, as the Americans and now the South Vietnamese did, the men would have been given their orders and expected to carry them out. They should have been in position by now, ready to throw the satchel charges, blow the bangalores. The first that the platoon and company commanders outside would know they had failed was when the signal for the attack was given and nothing happened.

He'd have liked to have seen their faces.

Shut up, he told himself. You will, soon enough.

In the command bunker on the south side, Lieutenant Sloane ignored Specialist Fourth Class Theodore "Teddy Bear" Noonan, who was so intent upon spotting for targets through his own starlight that he ignored being ignored. Teddy Bear—he hated that nickname, but since he was named Theodore and was big and soft-looking, he didn't think he'd ever get rid of it—had already killed four sappers and was now drawing a bead on a fifth. He pulled the trigger and the weapon chuffed, the bullet on its way to a rendezvous with death.

Maybe someday I'll write a poem about it, he thought as he settled the scope back on the target, seeing a brighter green where the blood was flowing from the top of the sapper's head. *Bright blossom of death*—what rhymed with *death?* Better free verse.

He did not, of course, let anyone know he wrote poetry. He couldn't even have imagined what his nickname would have been, if he had.

After the war he would perhaps send some of it to one of the literary magazines. He allowed himself a bit of fantasy. Would they regard him as the Graves, the Sassoon, the Wilfred Owen of the Vietnam War?

Probably not, he admitted. No one cared. About the war. Or about poetry.

It was enough that he did. It had to be.

He scanned the perimeter again, seeing only the bodies now. No other targets. At least not at the moment. He decided he could relax for just a few minutes, stretch as much as he could in the cramped bunker.

Lieutenant Sloane was busying himself by stacking up ammunition at one of the M60 machine guns. Noonan frowned. The LT was being all too helpful. Not like before, when all he'd do was watch—and sometimes sneer—when the enlisted men were doing physical labor. Maybe that bullet had knocked some sense into him, Teddy Bear thought. Realizes how much he needs us. Wants to stay on our good side now. Too damned late, LT.

He went back to the scope, once again focused on the outside world.

Maybe, *Death's bright blossom.*

But what rhymed with *blossom? Possum?*

Nah. That won't get me an anthology.

Unnoticed by Noonan, Sloane left the bunker. He was carrying two ammo cans of linked 7.62mm ammunition, each can containing two hundred rounds. He stashed them in one of the shell craters from the earlier barrage, then went back and got two more. These he stashed in yet another crater.

Defense in depth, isn't that what they called it at West Point? Though I hardly think they had this in mind. Two up, one in reserve, the mantra went. Look for the military crest. Reverse slope defense. Retrograde. The now meaningless words ran through his head, somehow soothing the thoughts that gathered in his tortured mind.

How come they never taught us anything about this? Did they think it would all be just like it had been in the "Big One," as the older officers called it? Did they never consider that we'd be down here with no place to retrograde to, the only military crest the one the enemy is occupying, the only defense in depth the distance you could run before they cut you down? Reserve? We've got a thirty-man recon platoon.

He wanted to laugh, avoiding it only because he didn't want to draw attention to himself. The Americans would think he'd gone nuts probably because of the head wound. The Montagnards would think he'd gone nuts, too, but probably because the night creatures from the forest had sneaked into him.

Maybe they had. What he planned was certainly crazy.

But who cared? They were all crazy. Otherwise they wouldn't be here.

He stashed yet more cans of ammunition. Now for the grenades.

"How long you been in the army, Curtis?" SFC Washington asked.

"Four years," Sergeant (E-5) Leonard Curtis replied.

"You re-up?"

"Extended. I was with the Ninth Division, down in the Delta. Wanted to get the hell out of there."

"And they sent you to Group?" Washington was amazed. It was a sign of the times, and not a good one, that people were being assigned to the Special Forces without having been trained for it. Good troops, most of them in any case, but they should at least have been sent back to the States for a stint in Training Group.

"Needed the bodies, I guess," Curtis replied. Once again he felt the acute sense of inferiority that had plagued him ever since he had been assigned to the camp. While he thought himself a good soldier and had proved his bravery in actions throughout the watery Delta, he more than anyone else realized just how much a fish out of water he was here among the seasoned Special Forces troops.

They had assigned him as a light weapons specialist, and while he knew enough about the M16s, M60 machine guns, and M-79 grenade launchers with which his platoon in the Ninth had been armed, he was brought up short the first time he ever saw an M-2 carbine, brought to him by a Montagnard who expected him to fix it. And as for the 1919A6 machine guns and the BARs and the M-1 rifles, forget about it. Much less the cast-off weapons from at least three armies—the Kar-98 Mausers, MAT-49 submachine guns, MAS-36 rifles, Swedish-K submachine guns, among others—that the Regional Force Popular Force (RF PF) outposts guarding the villages were armed with.

Sergeant Stankow had tried to give him a crash course in weaponry, but there had been so little time!

"Where you from?" Washington asked, seeing the young sergeant's discomfort and deciding to change the subject.

"L.A.," Curtis replied.

Washington looked at him in clear disbelief. "With an accent like that?"

"Lower Alabama," Curtis replied, grinning.

"Thought so." Washington smiled back, his teeth gleaming like a beacon in his black face. "Lots of good folks come out of Alabama."

"And some not so good ones too. You ever go down there?"

"Went through there once. As fast as I could."

Curtis understood. People like he used to be, and his family still was, wouldn't have made it pleasant for a man like Sergeant Washington.

He'd seen just how far his own attitudes had changed while home on extension leave. His two brothers and father kept going on and on about nigger this and nigger that, wondering how he managed to keep from shooting the black bastards himself while in combat—be a pretty good time for it, wouldn't it, everybody thinking the Veet Cong did it?

He'd wanted to protest that it wasn't like that. That the black guys in his platoon were his buddies, that they shared the same hardships, the same dangers, and when you did that, you found out they were people just like you. With their own fears, their own attitudes, and, yoo, their own prejudices. Which you found were just as strong, and as ill-founded, as yours.

But he hadn't. He'd just nodded his head and kept his mouth shut. And was ashamed at being such a damned coward.

It hadn't made it any better when his father had dragged him down to the local VFW, insisting that he wear his uniform with the Bronze Star with V Device prominently displayed on his chest.

First of all, the middle-aged World War II vets who inhabited the hall had let him know in no uncertain terms that theirs was a *real* war, with real enemies. Not like those pissant Veetnamese—and how come they were having so much trouble with a little bunch of gooks, anyway?

And, of course, the subject of race had quickly reared its ugly head. Maybe the problem, one of the vets—now a sheriff's deputy—had said, was that they had so goddamn many niggers. Not like in his day, by God. Niggers then had their own place, and they kept to it. Truck drivers, cooks, maintenance men. Not down in the goddamn combat battalions. Cowards, all of them. Couldn't be trusted. Hell, you'd have more trouble keeping them on the front line than you would keeping the enemy out of it.

From the lack of a combat infantryman's badge on the VFW cap the deputy wore, as well as no sign of a Purple Heart, Leonard Curtis suspected the vet had never come close to the front lines himself.

But still he'd said nothing, nursing his beer and listening to the stories that got more wild with each telling. And silently vowing he'd never set foot in the place again.

Nor would he return to Alabama. If the army had taught him one thing, it was that he didn't belong among people like these.

The personnel officer in Nha Trang had promised him that after his extension was up, he would be reassigned to

Fort Bragg, there to get the training he needed. Then he'd be slotted in one of the Groups—the First in Okinawa, Tenth in Germany, Eighth in Panama perhaps. Or the Seventh right there at Bragg.

But first he had to get through this. And people like Sergeant Washington made it slightly more likely that he would. The big man moved with practiced ease, checking the guns, tweaking this or that sight, sending 'Yard assistant gunners outside to move the limit stakes slightly to ensure overlapping fire with the next bunker. He talked as he worked, an ongoing rap about what to expect, how he wanted Curtis to react to this or that, what to do in the eventuality that one thing or another happened.

"You got all that, my cracker friend?" Washington finally asked.

"Got it, Sarge," Curtis answered. "Only one thing?"

"And what's that?"

"How come they call you Spearchucker?"

Washington grinned. " 'Cause they know I'd kick their lily-white asses, they called me a nigger."

Outside the wire, in a bunker dug so deep even the 175 delay shells hadn't touched it, the North Vietnamese colonel checked his watch. The timepiece, taken from a dead Legionnaire at Dien Bien Phu, ticked steadily on.

Time seemed to be passing so slowly!

But it would not be long.

Chapter 13

The waiting was the hardest part. He checked his watch: only ten minutes later than when he had checked it before. His palms were wet, and his mouth was dry. He wiped his hands on his fatigues and took a swig from the canteen propped up next to the radio.

Becker was sitting in a corner, reading a dog-eared paperback—a Travis McGee novel, Finn noticed. One he'd already read. For a moment he toyed with the idea of telling Becker the ending, but realized the young sergeant probably already knew it. Out in the camps you read, and reread, anything you could get your hands on. Finn had read this particular book three times.

Come on! He silently told the men outside the wire. Get it over with. Anything but this infernal waiting.

In a few minutes he'd go out and make his rounds again. Make sure no one was sleeping, though in the last couple of rounds no one had been. He suspected he was being regarded as a pain in the ass, but couldn't help it. He was tired—it had been a *very* long day—and had tried to grab a couple of minutes of sleep himself earlier. And had realized that he was simply wasting his time. Thoughts chased one another through his head—have I done everything I needed to do? What have I forgotten? What if this, or that, or the other?

So he had gotten up, brewed a quick cup of C-ration coffee on the little camp stove Becker had set up in a corner of the commo bunker, cursed as always when he burned his lip on the canteen cup. The bitter liquid coursed through him, but not nearly as fast as did the adrenaline when this or that report came in, telling about the movement of figures—just out of range—seen through the starlight scopes.

He felt a sudden chill, hoped it wasn't the malaria coming back to visit. That's all I need right now, he thought. He tried to remember if he'd taken his chloroquine/primaquine tablet that day. Don't know. Take another one now? He popped one out of the little blister pack he carried in his personal first-aid kit, swallowed it without water. He didn't take the dapsone that the medical establishment insisted upon. While it might supplement the effects of the chlor/prime, as they said it would, it also gave him the screaming shits. Not exactly a condition to be in when expecting a full-scale attack.

He'd come down with a full-blown case of falciparum malaria on his second tour, had spent a month in the malaria ward in the hospital in Cam Ranh Bay. Alternately burning up as the sporozites invaded his red blood cells and reproduced therein, and shaking with chills so violent he sometimes fell off his cot when the cells burst and the new spores went out to find new hosts.

They'd pronounced him cured, but he knew that the disease still lurked in the bloodstream, waiting for the defenses to go down so they could once again raid his body like the NVA were getting ready to raid the camp. It happened when he came down with some other disease, or when he drank too much and left his body defenseless, or when under great stress.

Like now.

Not gonna happen, he told himself, willing the chills to go away. Think of something else. Last R&R in Sydney. The redhead with the incredible green eyes, who'd been very willing to help him forget the war for just a little while. He closed his eyes and could see her face, lightly sheened with sweat as she moved rhythmically above him.

He opened his eyes and smiled. Worked every time. Something about impending combat that wonderfully sharpens the mind, cuts through all the extraneous worries to bring into focus what was really important. And great sex was right up at the top.

Becker caught his grin in the corner of his eye, dog-eared his place in the book, stood, stretched, and yawned. His hands brushed the heavy beams of the ceiling of the bunker.

"Something funny, *Dai Uy*?" he asked.

Finn shook his head. He was unwilling to break the moment by sharing his thoughts with anyone. What was her name, anyway? Eileen, that was it. He wondered what she was doing at that moment.

Probably got herself another guy on R&R, he thought. Lucky bastard. Wish it was me.

The tactical net radio, an old PRC-25, hissed as someone keyed a mike. Finn recognized Olchak's voice, a bare whisper.

"They're coming," he said.

Finally.

Olchak saw the huge flash somewhere just inside the tree line, had just enough time to scream "Down!" and hit the floor himself before the round from the Chinese-made 75mm recoilless rifle smashed into the dirt just in front of the embrasure. Shrapnel whined through the air above them, embedding itself harmlessly in the sandbags at the back. The acrid smell of cheap explosive assaulted his nostrils.

"Stay down!" he commanded when one of the Montagnards tried to cautiously raise his head. "More coming."

Four more rounds hit, doing little more than shaking dirt down on them. Unless one of the rounds went through the embrasure and exploded inside, they were in little danger as long as they kept low.

Between the recoilless rifle strikes he could hear the steady thump of mortar rounds exploding, some in front of the bunker, some behind, and some directly atop it.

The NVA commander had gone to plan two, he surmised. The sappers had obviously failed—there were no huge explosions inside the camp as the satchel charges did their work—so now he had to do it the hard way. Lay down suppressive fire, hope that he could take out at least a few of the defenses, but mainly provide cover for the troops who would now be massing somewhere just outside the wire.

Olchak thought he had the rhythm of the recoilless now,

chanced a look outside, could see nothing but the bright explosions of the mortars.

He grabbed the handset, intending to ask for flares, but obviously Sergeant Stankow was way ahead of him. He heard the *pop!* as the mortar shell shed its cover, then saw the bright magnesium glow, shimmering slightly as the burning flare drifted down under its parachute.

The perimeter was thrown into bright relief, catching dozens of soldiers working away with their wire cutters at the outer edge. Olchak was already on the M60, feeling the comfort of the butt in his shoulder, the trigger under his finger. He fired in steady bursts, six rounds each time, directing the bullets at individual targets. None of the long chattering bursts so beloved by the movies. He pulled the trigger, and a man fell, and he went to the next man. He barely heard the roar of the other guns, so intent was he on his own targets.

The next flare was in the air before the first one burned out. He once again saw the flash, screamed to get down, hit the floor, felt the explosion, was up again. More men had rushed into the breach he'd cut in the ranks. And more and more. The sheer weight of bodies collapsing on the wire pushed it down enough that others could rush through.

Son of a bitch, he thought. We've got a problem.

Sergeant Young was giving a running commentary on the battle of the north wall. Finn McCulloden listened and tried to decide. Probe or main attack? The other parts of the perimeter were suspiciously quiet. Mortars were falling all over, of course, but as yet none of the direct-fire weapons had engaged the other bunkers.

If he rushed his reserves to the north wall and it was only a probe, they could become pinned down there while the main attack took place elsewhere. On the other hand, if this was the main attack and he didn't get the reserves there on time, the camp could be penetrated. What to do?

That's why they pay you the big bucks, he told himself. Make a decision.

He summoned up a mental picture of the camp. To the west was the runway, and beyond that the river. Terrible avenue of approach. The NVA wouldn't have had a chance to extend their bunkers any closer than the other edge of the runway, and assaulting across it would expose them to fire for at least a hundred long yards. Unlikely they'd be coming from there.

Besides, he suspected that they'd have their casualty stations there, where wounded men could be treated quickly and then shipped back across the border to the field hospitals. They wouldn't want to chance the bombardment attacking across the runway would bring.

To the east? Better terrain, just like on the north side, heavily jungled until you reached the area the camp defenders had cleared. Possibly from the east.

But he would have bet good money on the south. The ravine they'd deforested earlier still provided the best covered approach into the camp. And at night it didn't matter much that the vegetation was gone.

He decided to hold the reserve in place, at least for right now. Fight the battle as it came, worry about how it developed as it developed.

"Think we can get a little fire on this recoilless rifle?" Olchak said. "It's wearing our asses out down here."

"Roger that," Finn said. He turned to Becker. "I'm gonna go find out what happened to Epstein. He should've blasted that gun to hell by now. I'll be on the radio." He shouldered a spare PRC-25, grabbed his rifle, and headed out of the bunker.

"Tell Gutierrez," he said.

"Tell him what?"

"Tell him we're in shit up to our noses, and we're standing on tiptoe. And some son of a bitch is starting to make waves."

He was hit by the sound as soon as he left the bunker. The crash of mortar rounds impacting throughout the camp. The *plonk* of their own mortars, some shooting flares, some engaging targets outside the wire as best they could. The heavy beat of automatic weapons fire. The crack of bullets snapping somewhere close to his head. It was enough to overwhelm the senses, make you want to curl up into a ball and cover your ears and hope nobody found you.

From his vantage point he could see the steady streams of red tracers coming from the bunkers, cutting down the unseen enemy. And the answering green tracers from obviously well-emplaced guns somewhere outside the wire. Like fingers of fire reaching for each other, hitting and spinning crazily, drifting like fireflies until the tracer element finally burned out.

And for each brightly glowing tracer, there would be four more rounds seeking their target. Embedding in the ground. Richocheting off the steel flagpole just to his right in a shower of sparks. Finding soft flesh.

Crossing the open toward Epstein's 106 recoilless position

seemed little better than assisted suicide. But it would take far too long to make his way through the warren of trenches.

Screw it. He drew a deep breath, scrambled over the edge of the trench, and hit a dead run across the compound. *Unaimed fire—they're not shooting at you. Can't see you, can't hit you. Catch a bullet now and it's just pure bad luck, and you've been lucky so far. Depend on it.*

The mantra was repeated over and over as his feet hit the ground, as the mortars seemed to seek him out, as that one special bullet, the one that didn't necessarily have his name on it, but instead was inscribed "To whom it may concern," made its long way from the barrel of someone's rifle to its ultimate resting place somewhere in his skull.

Once again he wondered what the hell he was doing here, why he continued to risk his ass. And thought, Doesn't make much difference now, does it, you moron? You're here. Deal with it.

"Down!" Olchak screamed again. This time the shell hit right where he had just been, smashing the machine gun into a piece of useless junk. Shrapnel flew its whining way through the bunker, cutting sandbags and flesh alike. He felt a sharp pain, reached down to feel wetness spreading down his leg.

It wasn't spurting. Thus it wasn't important. He struggled to his feet, made his way to the back of the bunker to pick up the spare machine gun he'd stashed there for just such an eventuality, cursed at the Montagnard lying in front of it.

"Get up you cowardly bastard!" he screamed, kicking the man soundly in the chest. Realizing only then that the man would never again get up.

"Sorry," he mumbled, grabbing the gun and making his way back to the front of the bunker. The surviving Montagnards were already at their guns, pouring fire into the ranks of the screaming enemy troops now less than a hundred yards away.

Sergeant Young was suddenly there beside him, gently taking away the weapon. "Siddown, Sarge. Put a dressing on your leg. I'll take care of this for a little while."

Olchak started to protest, realized that he was swaying, and that his legs wanted to give out. Must have lost more blood than I thought. He sat down heavily, unclipped the angled flashlight from his harness and turned it on. The red-filtered light matched exactly the blood that was flowing from a hole about the size of a baby's fist, just above the knee.

"Shit," he said, pulling a field dressing from its pouch and quickly applying pressure to the wound. He ignored the hot brass raining down on him from where Young had gotten the gun into action.

He grabbed the mike with his free hand. "Goddamnit, we need some help down here," he screamed. "Somebody? Anybody?"

Finn reached the recoilless rifle position to find a bloodied Epstein struggling to right the weapon. Dead crewmen lay all around him.

As Finn helped him heave the heavy tube up and settle the tripod back into the ground, Epstein told him about the mortar round that had exploded just at the edge of the bunker.

"Hoa hadn't been standing between me and it, I'd be laying there too," he said. He gestured toward one of the Montagnards, now scarcely recognizable as human. "Good man, Hoa. Wife just had another kid. That's five."

Finn looked at Epstein's face in time to see tears stream down to wash away the blood. "Goddamnit, goddamnit, goddamn it," the sergeant kept saying.

"You need to get to the dispensary," Finn said. "Get checked out."

"My ass," Bucky Epstein said, settling down behind the sight, traversing and elevating the tube by means of micrometer dials. Satisfied, he fired the spotting rifle. They followed the tracer, seeing it hit just to the right of where the last flash of the enemy recoilless had been.

Epstein adjusted again. "Stand clear!"

Finn had already moved from behind the weapon. Bucky slapped the trigger, and the weapon roared. A gout of flame six feet long spurted out the back, and one almost as long followed the high-explosive round he had just sent on its way.

Finn had already opened the breech, removed the spent shell, and was preparing to shove a live one home when the round hit. The night lit with a flash more bright than the dangling flares, and in that light Finn saw pieces of metal and man, now inextricably fused.

He shoved the next shell in, closed the breech, shouted, "Clear." Bucky was already traversing the weapon, training it on a clump of North Vietnamese who had somehow survived the massed machine-gun fire and were now perilously close to the moat. Another roar, and the men simply disappeared.

"Target right," Finn shouted, but Bucky Epstein had already started traversing.

It was tempting to feel godlike, up here in the position with the fire and the lightning at your beck. Another shell in the tube, another *crash,* more men sent to their deaths.

But God had nothing to do with it. If God were to look down right now, Finn thought, he'd wash his hands of the whole damned mess.

Or maybe he already had.

"Think I ought to go over there and help?" Sergeant Curtis asked Washington.

"I think you better stay your white ass right here," Washington replied. "Looks like they're doin' okay on their own. And this ain't over yet."

Curtis nodded. He scanned the perimeter with the starlight scope again. He'd been seeing movement, but it was well outside the wire and thus out of the range of his weapon. Reinforcements heading for the battle on the north wall? Shock troops gathering for their own assault? He didn't know, but he did know that things didn't sound too good. If the NVA broke through the defenses on the north, they would be behind his position. The bunkers hadn't been designed for defense of the rear. They'd have to evacuate and fight it out in the trenches.

Sergeant Washington had, wisely in Curtis's opinion, picked one of the bunkers in the vee of the star, rather than on the point, for his command position. The way the camp was built, in a six-pointed star, the north and south walls each had one point, while the east and west had two. Placing the command post in the vee meant that you were in the exact center of the zone of responsibility.

Their far-left position was assisting in the north wall defenses by directing long-range machine-gun fire at the enemy attempting to penetrate Olchak's position, but that was about the sum total of what they'd been able to do thus far.

Be a hell of a thing, Curtis mused, we fight this whole damned battle and I don't get a shot off.

His thoughts were cut short by a white glare in the starlight, temporarily blinding him in the right eye. The glare was followed by the heat, felt even at this distance, of an explosion so powerful it shook the very ground they stood on.

"What the f—!" Washington started.

Through his good eye Curtis watched the glare of the explosion fade, and in its place, lit by the glare of the flares, the column of smoke go up from where the right-hand star point had been.

Looks like we've got our fight.

"Here they come," Washington said, quite unnecessarily. Curtis, sight now returning in his dazzled eye, could clearly see masses of troops storming out of heretofore concealed trenches just outside the outer perimeter. As he directed machine-gun fire toward them, several flopped down on the ground, quickly pushed their bamboo bangalores under the wire, and were consumed by the explosions as the bangalores were command detonated.

Their sacrifice cleared a path through which the assault troops stormed, more of them than Curtis would have believed possible.

He heard Washington on the radio reporting the situation, asking for help from the guns on the south side, directing the flanking fire from the remaining left-hand star. The steady streams of fire cut down dozens, perhaps more, but there were others to follow.

Another sacrificial set of sappers, and they were through the second line of the defenses. Christ, is anything going to stop them? At this rate they'd be swarming over the destroyed bunker within a few minutes.

"Stay here, keep the guns going," Washington commanded. "Got to get somebody in the backup trenches."

"Watch your ass, Sarge."

Washington grinned. "And you watch yours, cracker."

Curtis focused his attention back on the Montagnard machine gunners. They were firing steadily but not wildly, six-round bursts just as they'd been taught. The smell of cordite and the hot smoke of burning gun oil filled the bunker. Along with the fear sweat that, he realized, was coming from him.

Bullets from a heavy machine gun thumped into the top of the bunker as the enemy gunner found his range. From the heavy report just now making its way to his ears, Curtis surmised these were 12.7 millimeter, the Chinese equivalent to the .50 caliber. Hoping to suppress our fire, let the troops get through.

Sorry, Charlie. The gunners barely flinched as the rounds continued to hit, the embrasures built in such a manner that it would only be the occasional round that got through. The effect was more psychological than physical.

Bring it on, you assholes, he wanted to shout.

Instead he contented himself with observing the battle, watching as the attackers breached yet one more line of defenses.

Be to the claymores soon. He opened the improvised firing box, connected the wire leading to the nail that would serve as the contact to the jeep battery. Ready.

He stood by.

Washington, by running crouched down in the trench, reached the last surviving defender without suffering anything more than a sore back. Better than a bullet in the head, he thought.

Beyond the Montagnard gamely holding his position despite the blood that streamed down the side of his face, there was nothing but a great, smoking hole. He couldn't even imagine what Charlie had fired at it to achieve this level of destruction. For a moment he was consumed with a horrible thought. Captain McCulloden had earlier spoken about Sky Spot bombing. Had they made a run and missed? A five-hundred-pounder would do this. Clouds had been moving in all evening; now the flares gleamed against solid overcast. Could have happened.

He shook his head. The smell was different. The explosives used in U.S.-made bombs was completely different. This had a more sulfurous tinge to it. No, they'd managed to get something in here somehow—maybe a sapper not spotted through the starlight.

Doesn't matter now. Thing is, get the defenses reorganized. He pulled the wounded Montagnard from his position, pushed him forward down the trench, gathering up others as they went. A secondary communications trench cut across the star just to the rear of the destroyed bunker. They'd set up there, close the gap.

He chanced a look over the top of the trench. Holy Mary Mother of Christ, he swore. More Vietnamese than he'd seen since his last trip to Saigon, and they all appeared to be shooting directly at him!

He fired a full magazine from his M16 into their ranks, more in defiance than in hope of doing any real good, reloaded, and kept pushing the 'Yards in front of him. Within a few seconds he had them placed, their firing positions protected by sandbags to either side, their fields of fire directly across the open ground where the bunker had once stood. He rushed to the other side of the star, did the same with the troops there.

Now we wait. He checked his weapon, felt for magazines, found to his surprise that somewhere along the way he had shot up four more of them. Gettin' old, Wash. Can't remember what you're doing.

He looked up over the lip of the trench again, saw the front ranks of the enemy even closer.

Now would be about the right time, cracker, he said silently.

Curtis had come to the same conclusion. He flipped open the firing box again, grasped the nail in his hand, and quickly ran it down the series of pins that would complete the firing circuit. As the momentary pulse of electricity sped down the wire, it superheated a smaller wire in each detonator. The wire glowed red-hot, setting fire to the extremely sensitive material surrounding it. The heat produced then detonated the tiny bit of mercury fulminate, which then detonated the slightly less sensitive main charge at the tip of the detonator. The resulting explosion ran through the main charge in the claymore, well over a pound of C-4 plastic explosive.

The ball bearings in front of the explosive swathed their way through the flesh and bone of the troops standing and crouching and lying in the beaten zone, impartially cutting down private and lieutenant and sergeant alike. The power was such that weapons shattered, and the grenades they carried went off, adding to the damage.

There was shocked silence, even the troops on the north wall ceasing fire for a few moments. The carnage was complete. Where once there had been a two-company assault force—at least 150 living creatures—there was now only the mangled heap of corpses. The silence of the dead, followed shortly by the moans of those soon to be.

Then, at the edge of the perimeter, Curtis saw yet more men swarming up from the trenches.

"Keep it up!" he told the gunners. Quite unnecessary, he saw. They were happily pouring fire into the oncoming ranks. He went out to help Sergeant Washington.

"I think they're gonna need some help over there, LT," Noonan said.

"Quite right," Sloane answered.

Noonan looked at the lieutenant in something like amazement. He'd gotten on with the officer even worse than the other men in the camp and had fully expected Sloane to scoff at him, ask him what he thought he could add to the fight. He grabbed his M16 and left the bunker before the lieutenant could change his mind.

Behind him Sloane just smiled.

Now he wouldn't have to share the glory with anyone.

Captain McCulloden got to the reserve platoon just as they were getting ready to move out. He'd called earlier, told Sergeant Redmon to get ready, but to wait until he got there.

He'd come to the inescapable conclusion that, main attack or no, he had to reinforce the defenders on the east side. The loss of the bunker had sealed it. Even if the enemy had other tricks up his sleeve, he had also been known to exploit any developing advantage. If he saw he could, he would continually pour reinforcements through the gap and let other plans be damned.

"Have them carry as many grenades as they can," he told Redmon. "Bartlett, I need you to get over to Olchak's bunker, give him some blood expanders. He's fading in and out, and we need him. You get him going, take him to the command bunker. Tell him to get on the horn, call higher, beg for any damned thing they can give us."

Sergeant Bartlett didn't try to protest, though he would have liked to. Captain McCulloden's expression allowed no room for it. Besides, he thought, once I get Olchak over to the bunker, I can get back with them. Help. God knows they're gonna need it.

"Ready?" Finn asked Redmon.

"He ready, I ready," Bobby the interpreter said. Finn grinned. He'd completely lost track of Bobby in the heat of things, was glad to see him. "Kill a whole lotta goddamn fuckin' sonabitch, huh, *Dai Uy?*"

"Many as we can, Bobby. Let's go."

• • •

Captain McCulloden had managed to send over some of the Mike Force heavy weapons people before he left the recoilless rifle position manned by Bucky Epstein. They were, Bucky thought, even better than the troops he had himself trained.

They'd silenced at least one heavy machine gun, taken another recoilless rifle under fire the moment it had made its first shot, and Bucky estimated, killed probably a platoon's worth of troops in the open.

And it wasn't going to be nearly enough.

The fighting on the shattered east wall was so close that he didn't dare fire at the NVA massing there. He saw figures running toward the battle, reckoned it to be McCulloden and the recon platoon, then saw another machine gun open up on them.

Sorry about that, motherfucker, he said as he spun the weapon around.

McCulloden and the recon platoon got into the trenches where Washington and his men were desperately fighting for their lives just as the enemy mounted a company-sized attack. The next ten minutes were a blur—it was throwing grenades as fast as he could pull the pins, snatching his rifle to shoot the man who suddenly appeared atop the trench, more grenades, explosions all around as the enemy stick grenades found their own targets, the roar of rifle fire so continuous as to achieve the status of white noise.

Down the trench a squad of NVA troopers managed to reach the lip, tossing grenades down on the men inside, moving in, and mopping up the survivors. Only to be themselves wiped out when an enraged Washington turned the corner of the trench and emptied a magazine of 5.56mm rounds into them, their cramped position allowing only one at a time to shoot at him, and each one falling as Washington's withering fire cut them down.

Finn barely remembered pushing more troops into the gap, gasping orders to Bobby as yet another wave came swarming across the ruined wire. The Montagnard beside him, who'd brought a case of grenades that he'd felt were excessively heavy, but who now wished he'd brought more, started handing them to Finn with the pins already pulled and the spoons gone. Finn tossed them as quickly as he was handed the deadly little spheres, not bothering now to duck his head as they went off—if they got him too so be it don't have time to duck *oh shit here oh shit more gimme another 'nade too close gotta shoot somebody else just did here comes more oh shit.*

And even more quickly than it had started, it was over. The surviving NVA soldiers were running back toward the perimeter and were being coolly shot in the back by the Montagnards in the trenches who, when these targets ran out, started shooting the wounded men still left in the battle zone.

Finn didn't even try to stop them. He was far too busy gulping great gasps of air, wondering if he had held his breath during the entire goddamn battle or only the last part of it.

After a moment he started moving down the trench, stepping over the bodies of both the wounded and the dead.

There were many. All too many. Whole sections of the zigzag trench were now held by one or two soldiers.

They come through here again, we're screwed.

"Will you get the fuck off my stomach!"

He hastily pulled his foot back, squinted in the darkness to see Sergeant Washington's grin. "Where you hit?" he asked.

"Ain't, as far as I know. You want to help get these assholes off me?"

Finn grabbed a khaki-clad leg, yanked the dead NVA free, pulled at the arm of another only to have it come off in his hand. Washington heaved and together they pushed two more off the big man.

"Standin' right on top of the trench," Washington explained as he felt his body, checking to see if any of the blood with which he was covered was his own. "Bobby blasted 'em, and they fell right on top of me. Where's that little asshole? Don't know whether to kiss him or slap the shit out of him."

"Right here," Finn said, sadness filling him. Bobby's gold tooth gleamed in the light of the flares. His eyes were already dull.

"Well, motherfucker!" Washington said.

That about sums it up, Finn thought. That just about sums it up.

Chapter 14

"Charlie Six, this is Cowboy One One, over."

"Hello, Slats," Gutierrez replied. "Where's One Zero, over?"

"Puttin' out fires," Olchak replied. "Listen, you order a Sky Spot?"

"That's a negative, One One."

Didn't think so, Olchak mused. No Sky Spot meant no misplaced bombs. Which meant that someone inside the camp had taken out the east side bunker. Someone who might still be running around.

"Get on the tactical net," he instructed Becker. "Tell 'em we got an infiltrator. Somebody comes up carryin' anything they ain't supposed to carry, blow 'em away!"

As Becker did as he was told, Olchak got back on the command net. "We got penetration on the east. Holdin' em okay right now, but if they reinforce, we got a problem. Anything we can get from you guys?"

"FAC tells me you're solid overcast," Gutierrez replied. "He's flying right over the camp now, says he can hear the shooting, but can't see shit. He can't see, he can't direct."

"Roger that. How about some arty preplots at the following locations?" Olchak strung out a series of coded grids.

"Can do," Gutierrez replied. "Now, how about the Sky Spots?"

Might as well, Olchak thought. The high-flying bombers wouldn't be bothered by the cloud cover. Of course, all they might be doing would be bombing empty jungle. Still, it wasn't as if they were on a budget.

"Anything we can get on the north and east," he said. "South and west are quiet right now, but stand by just in case."

"Roger. You guys able to hold out?"

"Got to, don't we," Olchak said, thinking the question extraordinarily stupid. He recognized the impulse, the frustration at the other end of the line, sitting in a safe position and listening to people die and being able to do little about it.

But it was a stupid question, anyway.

He sat down heavily, grimacing in pain as the muscles flexed in his wounded leg. He'd refused the offer of morphine, knowing that he had to keep his head straight, just had to deal with it, that was all.

"You okay, Sarge?" Becker asked.

Another goddamn stupid question! "It look like I'm doin' okay?" he snarled.

"Must be," Becker said. "Still mean as a goddamn rattlesnake with a toothache."

Despite the pain, Olchak had to grin. At least my reputation's intact.

• • •

Finn assessed the damage. Severe. Out of the recon platoon, ten were dead and fully half the remainder had wounds of varying severity. The two platoons of camp strike force whose area of responsibility this was were even worse off. Fifteen dead, six more soon to be, and very nearly everyone else wounded.

Worse yet, Spearchucker Washington had taken a bullet in the upper chest, punching through the scapula and exiting in a large hole in the rear. A sniper, they surmised, waiting for his chance, seeing it when Washington had raised up high enough out of the trench to shoot at the retreating enemy. Finn had patched him up as best he could and sent him to the dispensary, still cursing that he could damned well stay there and fight, goddamnit!

And worst of all, young Noonan was dead. He'd been hit by a burst from a heavy machine gun as he ran toward the fight. He'd never gotten the first round off.

That was it. Lieutenant Sloane should never have let him leave his position. Not only was he dead, there was now one less person to depend on when the shit really hit the fan, and for what? Absolutely nothing. Finn determined to relieve the lieutenant, send him to the command bunker where he could do no more harm. That a relief for cause during combat would kill a career didn't bother Finn McCulloden at all. Son of a bitch doesn't deserve to be an officer. Should have relieved him when I first came here. My own fault for giving him a chance. Won't happen again.

But first he had to plug this gap.

A flash more bright than the sun dazzled him just a fraction of a second before the ear-pounding roar. The glow faded rapidly, replaced by a column of dirt and smoke lit luridly by the flares. Sky Spot, Finn thought. It had hit just to the east of the tree line. With any luck it had smacked one of their rally points. Five hundred pounds of explosives had a way of making you want to get far away as quickly as you could.

The bomb was followed by the sky-ripping sound of incoming artillery. Instinctively he ducked, then realized it was friendly. When he didn't hear the explosions he thought, Shit! They're still using time-delay fuse.

Where the hell did I leave the radio?

There, by the empty case of grenades. Jesus, did I throw that many? Got to get a resupply of those. Thank God Charlie doesn't have them. The casualty rate would have been far worse, if he had. The stick grenades the NVA used burst in four to six large pieces of shrapnel, instead of the thousands of bits of wire of the Americans'. If one of theirs hit you, it was certainly going to do some severe damage. But the chances of it hitting you were fairly small. If you were within the bursting radius of an American grenade, you were going to get hit, and that was it.

He pressed the push-to-talk button, was grateful to hear the hiss indicating it was still working. "One One, this is One Zero, over."

"Glad to hear you're still walkin' around," Olchak answered. "Gettin' worried about you."

"Getting worried that somebody might get a chance at my Rolex before you did, most likely." Finn was absurdly grateful for the sound of his friend's voice. Getting old, he thought. Emotional.

"That too," Olchak admitted. "That arty doin' any good?"

"Not as much as it would, they were using VT instead of delay. See if you can get our redleg friends to do that."

"Roger that. Just got a call from Inger. Spearchucker's gonna be okay. Would you believe it didn't even hit a lung? Wants to know how pissed off you'll be, he comes back over there."

Not too, Finn admitted. Ordinarily Washington should have been put under enough morphine to fell an elephant and make even the great Spearchucker feel at least a little woozy. Then they'd call in a dustoff and get him back to a nice field hospital, where he could thoroughly terrorize the entire medical staff.

But that wasn't going to happen. And right now Finn needed every hand he could get.

"Have him go over to the west side, pick up every spare body he can get," Finn said. "Get 'em back over here as quick as he can. Got a feeling Charlie ain't gonna wait long."

"Gotcha. By the way, I'm feeling just a little bit useless here right now. Sure you don't need me too?"

"Need you to keep calling in thunder and lightning. I'm gonna be tied up for a while."

With a young lieutenant, Finn thought. Maybe I ought to just shoot him. Save us all a bunch of trouble.

They were coming. He could feel it.

Massing somewhere just outside the range of the starlight scope. He could not tell how he knew—he just did.

As he'd known all along that this was what he had been

meant for. No matter where he had been sent, there it was going to be. It wouldn't have mattered if he had been in the north, in the east, or even the relatively safe west. If he had been in the west, the NVA would have made the insane assault across the airfield. If he had been in either of the other places, it wouldn't have been a probe—it would have been the main attack.

He'd had a moment of doubt, listening to the course of battle on the east side, the seesawing of the tide, the bloody and desperate fury of the fight. But, he thought, he should have known better.

They were coming. And he was ready.

Relieving Sloane was going to have to wait. First came the mortar barrage, far more furious than before. Finn estimated that they were using at least two dozen tubes, everything from 60mm all the way up to 120s. The high arc of the weapon made it a perfect means of creating casualties in the trenches with no overhead cover. He crammed as many men as he could in the surviving bunkers.

Then came recoilless rifle fire directed at those very bunkers. They were being hit on both the east and the north, the purpose being to keep their heads down, degrade their return fire, provide cover for the assault that was sure to come.

Much of the fire was being directed at their supporting weapons—Epstein's recoilless position, Stankow's mortars. Both crews stubbornly kept on firing, dropping down into cover only long enough to avoid the closest barrages, popping back up again and slamming back.

Finn could only wait, constantly monitoring the radio to hear Olchak adjusting the artillery, request yet more Sky Spots, transmit casualty reports. There would have been a lot more of those if the Seabees who had built the camp had not done such a good job.

During the lull he'd had a crew out hastily emplacing claymore mines, connecting them all to one firing circuit wired to a blasting machine that he now held. He could only hope that the mortar barrage didn't cut too many of the wires, that the mines themselves were properly placed and sited, that none of them had been raided for C-4 for cooking fires.

Also during the lull he had checked on the enemy casualties piled up in various waves where they had been cut down. He had not been entirely surprised to see that they had been armed with a motley assortment of rifles and submachine guns—mostly semiautomatic SKS carbines and PPSH submachine guns shooting the underpowered 7.62 pistol round. This meant that the NVA had sent in the most expendable troops first—punishment battalions, locally recruited auxiliaries.

Bullet soakers.

Such tactics worked well when facing a relatively poorly trained adversary. The tendency of such defenders was to put their weapons on rock and roll, firing up everything they had and all they could get within the first few minutes of the fight.

Not so well against troops like his. They husbanded their rounds, shooting only when they had a target, and then only in two- or three-round bursts. There was still plenty of ammunition, and many, many more grenades.

They would need it. The good troops would come next—the shock battalions, the battle-hardened infantry. They'd be armed with AKs, which they'd fire from the underarm assault position, RPD machine guns, B-40 rockets. And instead of human wave attacks they'd be using fire and maneuver, an element laying down a base of fire while another rushed forward, then the first rushing while the forward element laid down the fire.

It would be exactly as he would have done it. The turkey shoot was over. Now came the real nut-cutting.

Lieutenant Sloane instructed his interpreter to tell the Montagnard gunners to evacuate the bunker, get to the east wall and help repel the attack that was sure to come there. That he could handle this position alone.

The interpreter, a Vietnamese who had been a schoolteacher before the war and who was usually to be found in as safe a position as he could find, was happy to leave the exposed bunker, stuck like a finger into the eye of the enemy. He would not, he thought, be going with the gunners. There was a nice safe hole not too far from here, where he could hide and wait for the end to come. If the Americans won, they wouldn't do anything to him. And if the North Vietnamese did, he could claim he was on their side all along. It was not being traitorous, he told himself. Just realistic. The war had been going on so long, the only sensible thing to do was to survive it. No matter who won.

Sloane watched their departure, feeling both deep satisfaction that his plan was working so well, and terrible apprehension. Now the enemy had to do his part. Would he? As the minutes passed by, and the sounds of the battle behind him grew even more fierce, he was seized with doubt. Would the entire action pass him by? Had all this been for nothing?

No! Quit whining, you silly little shit. His lips curled in an ironic smile. Exactly the same words his father would use. The acorn doesn't fall too far from the tree after all.

The world suddenly lit up as the bangalore torpedoes, snaked under the wire by replacements for the sappers Noonan had killed, blew. The concertina coiled in the sky like an angry snake, snapping back in a half dozen places and opening gaps through which any number of people could come.

And any number of people were coming. He could see them, coming out of the ravine in a solid mass. The burst of fire each triggered as his left foot hit the ground provided a steady metronome, a drumbeat, a thump of a giant heart.

He glanced over at the box that contained the claymore firing device, smiled. How unsporting!

He heard the gunners in the bunker that formed the vee of the star on his right open up, watched the stream of tracers hose into the oncoming troops. It scarcely slowed them down, the living stepping over the bodies of the dead. Like some terrible khaki machine they marched, straight toward him.

He realized that he was probably a little mad. *Crazy as a shithouse rat,* he could almost hear Billy Joe Turner say. But great warriors were always a little mad. Berserk Vikings, Hun warriors howling in fury, perhaps even cavemen clubbing everything that stood in their way.

Now or never. He grabbed the M60 machine gun, coiling the belt over his supporting arm and up over his shoulder, where it dragged on the ground behind him. Too bad nobody's here to take a picture of me, he thought.

The picture will be in their minds. Forever.

He left the bunker.

I was right. Goddamn it to hell, I was right.

Finn had been busily hosing down the front ranks of the oncoming enemy when the bangalores went off to his right. The fire that erupted from that direction made that coming his way pale in comparison.

There was the main attack. I knew it and did what they wanted me to do, anyway. Now his reserve was pinned down, barely holding its own against the troops who, he now realized, intended exactly that.

He'd stripped the west wall of all the troops he dared take, and obviously taking something away from the beleaguered north was out of the question. That left only one choice.

An army of one, hero, he told himself. You.

"Gotta go, Walter," he told Washington.

The big sergeant nodded. "We'll hold 'em down here," he said. "Keep 'em out of your rear, anyway."

Finn stuffed grenades in the cargo pockets of his fatigues, replaced the two magazines he'd fired into the ranks of the force opposing them, took a couple of deep breaths, and tried to go to a zone he'd been in before. Where his mind closed to everything but the task at hand. Where there was no time, no fear, no awareness of danger.

And when that zone didn't come, said screw it, and launched himself over the back of the trench anyway.

The rounds reached for him, tugging at his fatigues, snapping by his ears, hitting the ground and whining crazily away. He ran as fast as his tired legs and heavy load would let him, which, he realized, wasn't very fast. It seemed to take forever to reach his first objective, the pile of sandbags that was all that remained of one of the ammunition bunkers hit during the earlier artillery barrage. He didn't bother to zigzag, feeling that it was largely a waste of time and energy. The bullets would find him as well on this course or that.

He was almost surprised when he made it to cover without being hit, flopping down behind the sandbags and gasping for great gulps of air. His chest heaved and his heart felt as if it were in his throat. He lay there for a moment, listening to the bullets snapping right over his head, thumping into the sandbags behind which he took cover.

Halfway there. And running into a lot more firing than he was running from.

Well, hell, Finn, did you expect to live forever?

He heard the rush of a heavy mortar round coming in, had barely enough time to throw himself flat, arms crossed over his head, legs crossed at the ankles to protect his gonads. *Whomp!*

A huge chunk of shrapnel, so big the sound cutting through the air was a low buzz rather than the high whine one ordinarily heard, sliced across his back so close it severed his web gear. He could actually feel the momentary flash of heat as the scorched metal passed perhaps a fraction of an inch from his flesh. Then actual burning as other chunks fell from their high arc and landed on his back.

Shit! Goddamn. He got up quickly, shaking his shoulders to dislodge the pieces of metal burning their way into his flesh.

And saw something that chilled his blood. Troops, lots of troops, and the lead elements had already passed the moat and were breaching the remaining barrier that kept them from the interior of the camp. Claymores! Where were the goddamn claymores?

The assault troops were cutting the wire with as much sangfroid as one could muster, considering that the Montagnard defenders in the trenches were pouring as much fire as possible into their ranks. The NVA security elements were returning fire at a steady rate, keeping the defenders' heads down and degrading the effectiveness of their aim.

It was hopeless. Time to call a retreat, get back to the inner perimeter, hole up, and try to last until daylight. Although what good the sun was going to do was problematic. He glanced up, more in desperation than in any real hope of seeing the looming clouds break. Or maybe he was just looking for God.

What good could one man do?

Got you now, Sloane said as he rose up from the shell crater like, he fancied, some avenging angel. Or a demon from hell, called to take you back there with him.

He triggered a long burst from the M60, the heavy gun bucking in his hands like something live. Center of mass, traverse left, finger off the trigger, center of mass, traverse right. At this range the heavy bullets cut through the tight-packed mass of men, each round nearly exploding the first man in line, continuing on with scarce a drop in velocity into the man behind him, tumbling now and producing mangled flesh wherever it touched, heart and lungs and arteries and nerves and bone—made no difference. By the time it finally stopped it had killed or wounded three or four.

The expressions on their faces are wonderful to see! Stunned surprise, replaced with a grimace of pain, the dull sheen of death already overtaking them as they fall to the ground, and still the bullets come, chattering through the smoking gun, links falling to the ground to join the hot pile of brass—a hundred, two hundred rounds, belts prelinked together—die you bastards die!

Security force now recovering from their stunned surprise, those still living, in any case, and returning fire. Bullets snapping by, plucking at his clothes, so close to the head that they ruffle the hair, they can't hit you!

The last round slips through the gun, drop the useless weapon, the barrel so hot it glows red, drop down in the crater, grab the first grenade you've lined up, pull the pin, throw, pulling the pin on the second as the first one is still in the air, now the third and fourth—the explosions so close they sound like a mortar barrage.

Out of the hole, scurry to the rear before they can respond, grab the weapon you've secreted there, up again and fire! Their only surprise now is your new location, and that doesn't last long. Survivors now through the wire, trying to assault, close with you and kill you just as if they've been taught, but they can't—you know they can't because this is the way it was supposed to be and nothing, no nothing, can stop you.

• • •

Who the fuck does he think he is? John Wayne? Those Japs in *Sands of Iwo Jima* were shooting blanks, you silly ass-hole, Finn wanted to shout.

But it was working! The assault troops faltered, some of them starting to fall back. Sloane kept shooting, as happily mowing down the ones who retreated as he did the ones who tried to keep fighting.

As Sloane's belt ran out, an NVA soldier who had wisely been crawling toward the lieutenant leaped up and assaulted, his tripointed bayonet in the thrust position. Almost as an afterthought, it seemed to Finn, Sloane parried the thrust with the barrel of the machine gun, then slammed the butt of the weapon into his head. Then all Finn could see was the lieutenant methodically slamming the weapon down on the fallen man, until it was covered in blood and brains and still he slammed it down.

Gone completely nuts, Finn thought.

At least a platoon of enemy troops came storming through the breach, heedlessly trampling over the dead and wounded, aiming directly for Sloane's position. But he'd somehow moved—even Finn couldn't see how he'd managed it, and when he came up with yet another machine gun, he was on their flank.

Better troops than the ones he'd already engaged—probably the exploitation force, Finn surmised—they didn't just stand there and let him kill them. They scurried toward cover of their own, the survivors of the first burst of fire, in any case, and quickly unlimbered a barrage of small-arms fire at the lieutenant. Finn saw him step back as if he'd been punched, swaying for a moment, then steadying and triggering the machine gun.

Asshole's gonna need some help. Finn scurried ten or so meters to the left, which brought him in line with their flank. Perfect position. He took careful aim at a head silhouetted over the top of a shell hole, put one round through it. Then a second, and a third. By the time they realized their danger, he'd killed six. Finn heard a shouted order in Vietnamese, and the survivors clambered out of their holes and tried to run for the wire.

It was an opportunity too good to pass up. Finn flipped the selector switch to automatic, emptied the rest of his magazine into their ranks, reloaded, and was ready to kill again when Sloane once again opened up, at least a hundred rounds, scything down what had once been the cream of the North Vietnamese assault force.

Finn ran toward him, seeing him once again sway, almost sit down, steadying only at the last moment. Sloane saw him, swung the gun in his direction.

Finn saw the look in his eyes, the one that spoke of a great emptiness, of whatever made a man having fled the body, and realized that he would soon be dead. He could almost feel the lieutenant's finger tightening on the trigger.

"Ben," he said softly, as he would have talked to a child. "Ben. It's me. It's okay now. They're gone. Put down the gun, Ben. Rest."

Sloane looked at him with eyes that did not comprehend. He raised the gun, pointing it directly at Finn's chest. Then he smiled, and there was nothing remotely human in the grimace. He pulled the trigger.

The bolt slammed home on an empty chamber.

Ought to beat his fucking brains out myself, Finn thought as he gently pulled the gun away.

He pushed the now-unresisting officer down into the bottom of the crater, out of the line of fire that was still coming their way from at least two different directions. Sloane's face was spattered with blood and bone and brain from the man he'd beaten to death. But there was more blood, and it wasn't from the enemy.

Finn pulled back Sloane's shirt, saw the neat, round hole just above his navel, the edges blackened, the blood streaming out. He ran his hand around to the rear, feeling for an exit hole, didn't find one. It meant the bullet had tumbled around in there, as the 7.62-by-39 rounds fired from an AK-47 tended to do, and was still resting somewhere in the body. Having done no end of damage, he was sure.

He took Sloane's field dressing, pressing the sterile side into the wound and using the tails to tie around the lieutenant's body. It wasn't going to do anything for the bleeding, obviously internal. Morphine?

"How bad are you hurting, Ben?"

Sloane's eyes focused on him for the first time, something like true consciousness finally returning. "Am I hit?" he asked, his voice almost childlike. "Didn't feel it."

"Not bad," Finn lied. "We'll get you back to the dispensary, let Andy Inger take a look at it. Two Purple Hearts in one day! Not too bad, LT."

Sloane smiled. "Gotta stay here. They'll be back."

All too true, Finn thought. "What happened? How come you didn't stay in the bunker, fire the FPLs, blow the claymores?"

"Not right," Sloane said, grimacing as his guts went into spasm.

Not right my ass, Finn thought. This son of a bitch is stone crazy.

He looked up over the edge of the crater, seeing the bodies lying everywhere. Maybe we all are, he thought.

Have to be. He saw movement out toward the edge of the perimeter. The second wave, he surmised, getting ready to come on in. With damned little standing in their way.

He searched around in the crater, finding several ammo cans filled with belted 7.62. He delinked the last round from a belt, lined up the empty link with the link connector of the next belt, pushed the round home to secure it, did the same with the next. He opened the bolt of the M60, flipped open the cover, laid the first round in the tray, closed the cover on it. He opened the bipods, set the weapon up at the edge of the hole, sighted it. Perfect. He had clear fields of fire out to at least a hundred yards.

"Ben," he said. "I need you to hold this position. Think you can do that?"

Sloane's shoulders squared. He crawled up next to Finn, grasped the pistol grip of the machine gun, placed his finger on the trigger. "Forever," he said.

That's what it might take, Finn thought.

"Keep your ass down," he instructed. "No more of this John Wayne shit. We're all depending on you."

Sloane turned to look at him, but he was already gone, scrambling over the edge of the crater and scurrying toward the unoccupied bunker.

This was what it was all about, he thought.

He settled down to wait.

• • •

Finn made the bunker with no more trouble than having the shit scared out of him from the mortar explosions that all seemed now to be directed at his sector of the line. Gratefully he slipped in the door, to find the interior largely untouched. The machine guns locked into their fixed positions gleamed in the light coming through the embrasures, the neatly stacked linked ammunition waiting in oiled readiness.

The bunks against the back walls were untouched, no head marks on the pillows, the blankets tucked beneath the mattresses in hospital folds.

Like something came in and sucked out the humans, leaving only inanimate machines, he thought, shuddering slightly.

Most important thing first. He opened the box containing the claymore firing circuits, found the ohm meter, ran a continuity check on the wiring. Intact. Thank God.

Gonna be some real surprised folks out there in a minute. He waited.

More of them. Even more than before. His stomach twisted, Sloane grunted with the pain. All for nothing?

No. No matter what happened now, men would remember this. They would tell the tales that would be a part of the history of this place, and of his part in it, from now on. It was enough.

If any of them survive to tell of it, he corrected himself. His stomach twisted again.

They will. They've got to.

He pulled the trigger.

• • •

Finn heard the roar of Sloane's machine gun, watched the tracers as they reached out for the front ranks of the oncoming soldiers, inwardly cheered as they started to fall. My turn, he thought.

He triggered his own long burst from the gun mounted in the center embrasure, ran over to the left-hand gun, fired; back to the center; now to the right. Enough to make them think the bunker was fully manned? He could only hope so. He wanted them headed directly for it, rather than the breach in the inner wire.

Like water seeking a new channel, they changed direction, coming right toward him. Long bursts from the guns now, killing many, but not nearly enough. Sloane's gun was now at their flank, cutting them to pieces but still not enough.

Bullets whacking into the bunker, passing through the embrasures and embedding in the sandbag walls. The flash of a B-40 rocket, the gunner obviously not taking the time to aim it properly because the missile flashed over the bunker and impacted somewhere inside the camp.

Smoke filling the bunker from the hot gun oil, the burnt powder. Fear sweat so profound it soaks your fatigues, eyes burning and wincing but not daring to blink. No sense in changing guns now, they're coming directly this way. Through the first barrier, now in tatters. On to the second, some of them stumbling in the tanglefoot but most high-stepping right across. A chunk of razor-wire concertina that hadn't been blown away by the bangalores slows them only slightly, the front rank soldiers throwing themselves full length on it and the ones behind trampling over their backs. Impossibly brave, completely mad, it doesn't matter. They will come, and they will not be stopped.

B-40 flash again, the gunner having reloaded his launcher, and this time he's taken the time to kneel, taken a proper sight picture, held steady as the heavy missile has left the launcher in a burst of light, a cloud of smoke, a pall of dust. Finn can see it coming, his eyes now so focused that he thinks he can see the bullets, and he can certainly watch the relatively lazy trajectory of the missile.

Down! As it hits just below the embrasure, the jet of pure energy produced by the shaped charge inside the warhead punches through sandbags and timber, bouncing the gun just above it halfway out of the bunker.

No matter. He is already scrambling for the box, the lovely box. He flips open the cover, toggles the safety, grabs the flat piece of copper attached to the one terminal of the battery, the other terminal being connected to the pins that stand like little soldiers in one long rank. How many? Does it matter?

Run the copper connector across the pins, like running a stick along a picket fence when you were a kid, achieving the shouts of the enraged homeowner just as you intended, teach him to yell at you for stealing peaches!

No shouts. No curses. Just the world ripping apart as each mine blasts one after another in a ripple that spreads across the front ranks of the oncoming enemy, from one end of the assault to the other.

A stunned silence after the thunder.

Where once men stood there is nothing but the charnel house.

About exhausts that bag of tricks, Finn thought. Time to get the hell out of here.

Chapter 15

Finn tested the command radio still in the bunker, was happy to see it was still working. His transmission to the other elements was simple—withdraw. Get yourself and your troops to the inner perimeter.

He figured he had only a few minutes until the NVA sent in the next assault force. That they were coming he had no doubt. They'd been hurt, but not enough. The Vietnamese commander had almost unlimited assets outside the wire, could afford to lose a few hundred or even a thousand. Whereas the forces he had at his command were being whittled down past the point where they could maintain defenses on the extensive bunker system that marked the outer perimeter.

Before leaving the bunker, he opened a red-painted ammunition can that had been emplaced in one of the walls. Inside were four fuse lighters attached to lengths of time fuse. He pulled the pin safety, grasped the rings at the end of the lighters, and yanked hard. With a pop each ignited, and soon the fuse was bubbling from the fire inside. Now he had about five minutes to get clear before the cratering charges placed in the walls blew the place to kingdom come. You didn't leave a perfectly good bunker for the enemy's use.

He left the bunker to the light of Stankow's flares, still burning brightly above them, throwing everything on the ground into alternating shadow and light. He could see men streaming from the trenchline, those who had suffered only minor wounds helping those who couldn't help themselves. There were pitifully few of the former.

Sloane was slumped over the machine gun. Finn checked the pulse in his neck. Very rapid, thready. Shock from blood loss. Nothing to do for it now.

He hoisted the lieutenant, intending to put him in a fireman's carry, finding that he couldn't. Didn't know I was that tired, he thought. Okay. Drag his ass it is.

Sloane came to, looking up groggily at Finn. "We get 'em?"

"We got 'em," Finn replied. "Can you walk?"

"I can try." Finn placed the lieutenant's arm around his shoulders, stood up. Sloane struggled to help, managed a wobbly upright position.

"Gotta get back to the inner perimeter as quick as we can," Finn said. "Place is gonna blow any second."

He noticed that Sloane did not object. No "Leave me behind, I'll hold 'em off" stuff. Finn was glad. He had no intention of leaving a live American behind, and it would have been much harder to drag a resisting subject the long way to the inner perimeter.

They stumbled forward, Finn half-dragging the semiconscious Sloane. By fifty yards Sloane had slipped back into wherever it was that people went at times like these. Now it was a full drag.

The bunker explosion caught Finn by surprise, blowing them flat on the ground. Bits of sandbag, chunks of support beam, and pieces of pierced steel planking rained down. From outside the wire came a renewed burst of small-arms fire, some of it from heavy machine guns. B-40 rockets were impacting among the fleeing men, the shrapnel adding to their already severe losses.

Not gonna make it, Finn thought. The bunkers that marked the inner perimeter were still at least a hundred yards away. Gonna die right here.

No, goddamnit, I'm not, he swore to an unheeding sky. And neither are you. He grabbed Sloane by the web gear and, half-crawling, half-stumbling, kept going.

Then strong hands were lifting the lieutenant, pulling him away. Finn rolled over to see DiUlio and Wren supporting the unconscious man between them.

"Figured you could use some help, *Dai Uy,*" DiUlio said. "Goddamn it, Bobby," he said to Wren, "you want to do your part here?"

"Already lifting more than you are, you greaseball mother-fucker," Wren said. "We gonna screw around here all night?"

"Like I said earlier," Finn said laughing, getting up and following the two sergeants as they made their quick way to safety, "you two ought to get married. Want me to perform the ceremony?"

On the north side of the camp, Sergeant Young took stock of his situation. He'd pulled the fuse lighters for the bunker demolition almost two minutes before. That meant he had perhaps a minute before it blew, and with it, him. The NVA had got a squad inside the wire and in the connecting trench, and now they were blocking his way to safety. Every time he raised his head up above the trench, a heavy machine gun tried to take it off.

Behind him in the bunker lay Bartlett, the junior medic who'd patched up Olchak, then stayed to help defend the position. A B-40 rocket had hit the machine gun he was manning, the resulting explosion and shrapnel taking his head off at the neck. The spray of blood hosing out of the stump had washed the bunker in red. Young had covered him as best he could and left him.

Die here with him or die there in the trench, he thought. Through his fatigue jacket he touched the gold Saint Christopher medal his wife had given him when he'd left for Vietnam. It'll bring you through, she had said, return you to me.

"Gonna have to do a lot of work tonight, Chris," he said. "Hope you're up for it."

He pulled a nicked bayonet from its sheath, clicked it onto the lug at the end of his rifle. The only thing he'd ever used it for had been to open cans of C rations, had thought it largely useless. Who did bayonet charges in today's army?

Now or never. He pulled a grenade from its ammunition pouch keeper, tried to yank the pin with his teeth, felt like all he was going to get for his trouble was a broken tooth. Remembered that he'd bent the ends of the pin back for safety, straightened them, and this time pulled the pin with his finger. Much easier. Guess the movies had it wrong.

He let the spoon fly, the click as the striker hit the cap loud in the trench. One one-thousand, two one-thousand, three one-thousand, he counted, then tossed the little orb around the bend in the trench. He heard shouts in Vietnamese, then the explosion, more shouts and moans.

There was little that happened next that he could remember, even years later. A confused melee of shooting until the bolt locked back, trying to reload, being rushed by a soldier, jabbing the bayonet through his throat, yanking back only to have the man follow his movement, the bayonet stuck in bone. He kicked the man full in the chest, trying to pull the blade from resisting flesh, another onrushing soldier! The blade comes free just in time for him to jam it into the next man. Smarter this time—slam a full magazine home so quickly it frees the bolt catch, pull the trigger, and the bayonet comes free from recoil, shoot two more behind this one, feel a punch as a bullet hits the floating rib, angle such that it glances off and traverses beneath the flesh to an exit point in the rear, only by this missing the liver, another one—shoot!

Then a long, wheezing run through the now clear trench, reaching the inner perimeter just in time to see Sergeant Olchak limping along, coming to get you.

"C'mon," Olchak says. "We were waitin' for ya."

Sergeants Washington and Curtis were making a fighting retreat. The breakthrough on the east side had put enemy troops right up against the trench, where they continued to throw grenades and shoot at anything that moved. Crossing the open ground was suicide. The NVA had set up at least two RPD machine guns in the ruins of the old bunker and were sweeping the open ground with steams of tracers that ran about knee-high.

Luckily, the trenches that led to the inner perimeter were thus far clear of enemy troops. Washington and Curtis alternated rear guard, at each twist in the trench throwing a grenade back over into the area they'd just left, then cutting around the corner and hosing down any survivors with a full magazine of 5.56. Rush back to the next twist, where one or the other would be waiting to do the same.

Curtis drew his last magazine from its pouch, reloaded, waited for Washington to get back to him. "I'm out," Washington said as he squeezed past.

"Then get the hell out of here," Curtis said. "I'll be right behind you."

No false heroics. No "I'll stay here with you." Washington shuffled off down the trench, turning the corner just as he heard a burst of fire behind him. Then a much heavier fusillade, from at least three AK-47s.

Shit! he said. Shit.

Stankow realized he was going to have to leave the mortars, and it broke his heart. The guns had been his joy for so long, he almost felt they were alive.

But they were no good to him now. The enemy was so close that he couldn't elevate the tubes high enough to reach them.

He set the charges that would destroy the guns and the ammunition still in the bunker, told his two surviving Montagnard crew members to get to their secondary positions in one of the bunkers that protected the inner perimeter, and started the firing train.

He made it to the command bunker just as they blew, the big 120 tube making a beautiful arc in the sky.

"You look like shit" were the first words from Olchak.

"You don't look so good yourself, you Nazi prick," Stankow replied.

Olchak looked down at himself, the blood, the embedded dirt, the pieces of flesh not his own hanging from his clothes, and then back to Stankow, who was bleeding from at least a dozen places, including one slash across his face where his cheek had been cut away from his jaw.

"It's a draw," he said.

Bucky Epstein had come to the same conclusion as had Stankow. He'd used up all his beehive rounds on the North Vietnamese troops who were now running around in the compound, mopping up this or that pocket of Montagnard resistance. All he had left was high explosives, and the enemy was so close the arming mechanism wouldn't work in time to set the rounds off. What he now had was a big, single shot rifle. Hit someone with the round, it was certainly going to spoil his day, but that wasn't a particularly effective use of the weapon.

He opened the breech, pulled the pin that held the breechblock in place, removed it, and threw it into the ammo bunker. He searched for the red-painted box that held the demolitions firing circuit, finding only a smoking hole where it had been.

He grabbed a grenade, pulled the pin, and tossed it into the bunker, then scrambled over the sandbag wall, holding his head as the explosion went off. For a moment there was complete darkness as the wall collapsed on him. He dug his way to the surface and limped toward the safety of the inner perimeter. The North Vietnamese gunners followed him with tracer.

Can't get me, he taunted them, as he fell into the hole and safety.

Finn McCulloden took stock of his assets. Of the men who had been there when the battle started, three—Noonan, Bartlett, and Driver—were dead. Curtis was missing and presumed dead. Sloane was being worked on by Inger, might live if they could get him to a hospital within the next twenty-four hours, would certainly die if they did not.

Olchak, Stankow, Washington, Young, and Becker had suffered wounds that would have gotten them evacuated under normal circumstances, but they could still fight. Becker had gotten his when, after a mortar round had destroyed the antenna for the Collins radio, he'd gone outside and erected a spare. That had made him a target for every sharpshooter in the area, and he'd taken a hit in the fleshy part of the right buttock, the round transiting that and the left buttock, strangely leaving an exit hole not much bigger than the entrance. DiUlio was now giving him a ration of shit about not keeping his big ass down.

DiUlio, Wren, Epstein, and Redmon had suffered smaller wounds—cuts and scratches mostly, though on closer examination it seemed that Epstein was peppered with tiny bits of shrapnel.

The reports had come in from the platoons, and they weren't good. Fully half the Montagnards that had made up the camp strike force and the Mike Force company were dead or missing. And Finn hadn't even started to tally the wounded.

Only he and Inger were untouched, Inger because he'd been steadily working on the wounded in the dispensary bunker—and him? He didn't know how he'd escaped. His canteen had been shot away, as had his hat, and after a moment Olchak came over, poked his finger through a bullet hole that cleaved through his fatigues right across his chest, and raised a shaggy eyebrow.

"Been livin' right, have you?" Olchak said.

"Clean mind, clean body," Finn replied. "Take your choice."

"Must be the mind, 'cause you stink! So, what's the plan, fearless leader?"

"Get ammo and grenades redistributed," Finn replied. "Make sure there are no big gaps in the line. Everybody under overhead cover. Charlie's got a smaller target for his mortars now, we can expect a lot of them. Go through the dispensary, put everyone who can still hold a gun on the line."

The NCOs left to do his bidding, leaving him there with Becker. "Need a shot of morphine?" he asked the commo sergeant.

"Already had one, can't you tell?" Becker was in great good humor. The wound no longer hurt when he sat down, there was no serious bleeding, and he felt fairly certain he wouldn't again have to go outside.

"Empty Syrette?"

Becker produced it from his shirt pocket. Finn pushed the needle through Becker's collar and bent it over, leaving the empty Syrette as a signal to anyone who might in the future treat the sergeant. Too many times medics up the chain of evacuation, not knowing that the casualty had already had Syrette after Syrette, gave their patients more and more morphine, the casualty finally expiring from an overdose.

Finn then turned to the radio, got Gutierrez, and quickly brought him up-to-date on the tactical situation.

"That matter we talked about earlier?" Finn said.

"Roger."

"Think it's about time."

"Agreed. Inbound in thirty minutes. Can you hold out that long?"

"Got to, don't we?" Yeah, Finn thought, we've got to.

A joke currently making the rounds of the combat troops ran through his mind. Like all the black humor that came out of Vietnam, it contained more than a grain of truth.

"War exacts a heavy toll," it went. "Please have the correct change."

At Pleiku air base a hundred miles to the south, the crew of the C 130 got the word they'd been waiting for. Preflight checks were done quickly—hell, Crew Chief Danny Williams thought, they'd already done them about ten times before getting the word to take off. The gas turbine engines started to whine, the big props whirling the heavy, moisture laden air. Williams looked up at the sky, shook his head. Still solid overcast. IFR takeoff and landing tonight. Lots of fun, considering the mountains all around.

He and Airman Gus Martinelli pulled the chocks from the wheels, heaving them through the open rear doors, and scrambling on board just as the plane started its ponderous roll.

The C-130 Hercules four-engine transport plane had been the workhorse of the Vietnam War almost from the beginning. Ferrying troops, hauling everything from ammunition to water buffalo, flying paratroopers to combat jumps, carrying USO entertainers to spots they'd never heard of, couldn't find on a map. You name it, the Herky-Bird had done it.

The Air Commandos had outfitted some of them with so much electronic equipment they could barely take off, electronic equipment that played havoc with North Vietnamese antiaircraft radar. Blackbirds, they called them, instantly recognizable by the folded-back prongs attached to the nose of the aircraft. These prongs, when extended, were designed to snatch the rope attached at one end to a balloon, at the other to a man on the ground strapped into a Fulton recovery rig. Designed to rescue downed pilots, the rig allowed the man to be picked up off the ground and reeled into the back of the aircraft. Not a pleasant experience, but far better than spending your time in the Hanoi Hilton.

This particular bird was also heavily laden, but only partially with electronic gear. Spectre, they called it. General Electric 7.62mm miniguns, electronically fired Gatling guns, protruded from firing ports on the pilot's side. A 20mm automatic cannon supplemented the Gatling guns. And from the opened tailgate, a low-recoil 105mm cannon completed the weaponry.

Spectre was the outgrowth of a program that had started with placing just the miniguns in an old C-47 Dakota, called alternatively Spooky and Puff the Magic Dragon. The old birds had done good service at dozens of places, proving their worth by saving the lives of hard-pressed ground troops about to be overrun. To a country where bigger is always better, the thought that if a C-47 was good, a C-130 must be wonderful, was a logical conclusion.

And Spectre too had proved its worth. It was able to loiter for hours above the battlefield, the guns so precise they could engage an enemy literally at buckle-grabbing distance from the friendly troops, the rain of fire so thorough and so deadly that, it was said, a one-second burst from one of the miniguns placed a bullet in every square inch of an area the size of a football field. It had been used in support of infantry operations throughout the war zone, as a truck-buster on the Ho Chi Minh Trail, and had saved the bacon of more than one SOG recon team.

That the North Vietnamese hated it was attested to by the well-known fact that the aircrew knew they would never survive a shoot-down. The NVA had let it be known that their deaths would be the most merciful thing that would happen.

That Spectre was respected and loved by the Americans was attested to by the fact that hard-bitten infantrymen who would ordinarily have scoffed at a crew of "pantywaist zoomies" wouldn't allow a Spectre crewman to buy his own drink in any club in the country.

The bird, loaded with so much ammunition it squatted on its tires, lumbered down the taxiway, turned onto an active runway, and sought permission from the tower to take off. Given clearance, the engines were run up, swirls of moisture streaming back so thick from the propellers they looked like minitornadoes.

Slowly the plane moved forward, gaining momentum with each yard until finally it achieved takeoff speed, way past where an ordinary Hercules would already have been in the air. The pilot, Major Charlie Hackett, lifted the bird just in time to avoid the trees, skimming over them so low the prop wash whipped the branches into a frenzy.

Within seconds he was in the clouds, visibility effectively zero. He depended upon the air traffic controllers below to vector him past the mountains, up over the—luckily—low overcast until he came out into a starlit sky.

He relaxed enough to release the puckered ass that, he suspected, threatened to cut holes in his seat, turned the aircraft on a heading to the north.

The FAC, orbiting unseen somewhere up ahead, was already calling him.

Give her the juice, the FAC said. We need you.

Darkness, interrupted only by the flickering of a few fires from destroyed bunkers, blanketed the camp. With no stars, no moonlight, and especially no flares from Stankow's guns, the North Vietnamese felt free to mass their troops for the final assault. They'd taken grievous casualties, but none that they could not afford. The planners had never expected this to be an easy nut to crack.

Now the very best troops they had, the ones whom the commander had held back for just such a mission, were ready. They would roll over the pitifully meager defenses that marked the inner perimeter, the defenses of which the commander had full information provided by spies placed inside the camp long ago.

They would take even more casualties, but in the end they would win. Just as they always had, always would. The Americans suffered from the fact that they had to limit their losses. On the lower levels of command, excessive losses would get you relieved, your career shot to ribbons. On the higher levels, it would lose the war for you as the people back in the States, obviously less dedicated and far less controlled than were the people of North Vietnam, rose up in protest when too many body bags came back.

For the commander, any and all losses were acceptable, as long as the job got done.

His last units were in place. It was time.

DiUlio watched them through the starlight scope. "Call the cap'n," he told Wren. "Tell 'im they're comin'."

Wren complied, for once not bitching that he wasn't a goddamn radio operator, that if DiU wanted to talk to somebody, he ought to get off his greaseball ass and do it himself, that just because he was an Indian didn't mean he had to follow the white devil's orders.

He was far too scared to make any jokes at the moment. From the occasional glint off a rifle, from the smell of unwashed flesh, from the sensing mechanisms buried in the back of his brain that no one could explain, but everyone had, he knew they were coming too. This time no easy ride, the enemy not attacking portions of the camp where he wasn't. They'd be right on top of his bunker, shooting down into the ports, dropping grenades, shoving satchel charges up against the door. Killing anyone who came out.

Upon receiving a roger from Captain McCullodcn, he

dropped the handset for the field phone that was hardwired to the command post and went to the machine gun that covered the wide-open space between the inner perimeter and the trenchline where the enemy was massing. They'd have to come up and out of there—the connecting trenches had been blown—and cross a killing field that would have daunted the over-the-top boys of World War I. But they would come. Of that he was sure.

A strange calmness settled over him. "DiU," he said.

"Yeah, Bobby."

"Tell me again what it was the gladiators said."

"You mean, 'We who are about to die salute you'?"

"Yeah. That was it." Wren was silent for a moment. "That's pretty fuckin' stupid, isn't it," he finally said.

"Yeah." DiUlio grinned over at his friend. "But better than 'It's a good day to die.' "

Finn was getting reports from his men stationed on the perimeter, the gist of which seemed to be that the enemy was going to attack from two sides—the north and the east. Just as he would have done. A slight elevation to the east would let the NVA support weapons shoot over the tops of the assault troops, and to the north some of the bunkers that had been imperfectly destroyed by the demolitions charges provided a bit of cover.

They wouldn't try to attack from more than two complimentary directions for fear of shooting their own people on the other side. But there would be reserve troops in covered positions stationed to the south and west to exploit any breaches, and more important, to block any escape.

Not that there would be any attempts at organized break-out. The only chance, should the positions be completely overrun, would be to take advantage of the confusion and escape by ones and twos. A very slim chance indeed.

The field phone hissed. "Here they come!" came Wren's voice.

The fire that erupted from both sides made the message moot. Okay, Finn thought. Let's see how this is going to work.

Stankow and Epstein were side by side, the big Polish sergeant manning a 1919A6 machine gun while the diminutive Epstein steadily worked an M-79 40mm grenade launcher—called the blooker from the sound it made when firing grenades the size of a juice can. Stankow was sweeping the onrushing assault troops with long, sustained bursts, ignoring the return fire that seemed to be pinpointed at his head. Bucky Epstein mechanically inserted round after round in the blooker, aiming at knots where the NVA bunched up, the high-explosive grenades shattering among them and downing everyone within bursting radius.

A screaming berserk broke from the ranks and rushed toward them, wildly firing his AK-47. Bucky took careful aim and shot him directly in the chest. The Vietnamese was so close that the round didn't have time to arm, instead embedding itself in his chest. That'll teach you, Epstein thought.

He chanced a glance down the covered trench, seeing the Montagnard soldiers pouring steady streams of fire into the enemy, not a one of them cowering, not a one trying to run. Beyond the squad that helped defend this section of the trench was the key bunker defended by DiUlio and Wren. Streams of tracer reached out from the embrasures like searching fingers.

Those who have not been there cannot imagine the level of noise, the smoke, the smells, the confusion of combat. The mind shuts it out, completely overloaded, and movement becomes dreamlike, seemingly suspended in time. Actions that take only seconds seem hour-long. There is no sound of individual shots or explosions, only an ongoing roar made up of the reports of thousands of rifles and machine guns, punctuated by ear-shattering blasts of grenades, B-40 rockets, satchel charges.

Holes are blown into the line of defenders, smoke whirling away momentarily to expose shattered bodies, men crying for help, their mouths moving but no sound coming forth. Only the ugly rictus of oncoming death.

Epstein glanced down to see that he had fired up almost all his grenades, and the enemy was still coming. He dropped the blooker, grabbing up his M16 and emptying a magazine into the closest ones. They fell, but there were more behind them. Just too many.

He unsnapped the strap holding his pistol in place. Checked to see that his K-bar knife was still in its sheath. Reloaded the M16, his movements as sure as those of a robot. Just too many.

Charlie Hackett keyed the intercom to the fire control officer in the back of the plane. "FAC says first run should be two hundred meters on an azimuth of two seven five degrees from Sky Spot Bravo Tango Five," he said.

The FCO looked out the window to see nothing but pure overcast below, then checked his charts. "Hell," he said, "that's right on top of them."

"Roger that," the pilot replied. "Guy down there says, we're underground. Victor Charlie isn't. Requested miniguns and twenty mike-mike only. You copy?"

"I copy. Standing by."

The pilot turned the big plane on its wing, setting up an orbit that would circle the target below. "You may fire when ready, Gridley," he said.

From the skies came a great moan, as if a dragon had bestirred itself and was roaring in anger. And his anger was ferocious.

An ordinary machine gun putting out sustained fire puts out a tracer round for every four ball, and you can see them flying at regular intervals at perhaps a tenth of a second. Measured intervals, as regular as a metronome.

There is no interval in the tracer stream coming from the minigun. It looks like a garden hose pouring out liquid fire. The ground where the stream strikes looks as if it were a live, churning creature in its death throes.

And there were three of the guns firing.

Epstein watched in wonder as the enemy troops now within feet of his position were struck down as if by the hand of God. Where there had once been living creatures, there was now nothing but flesh mangled and bleeding. The beat of the incoming rounds rattled against his overhead cover like the staccato of monsoon rain. The finger of fire moved on, simply erasing everything in its path. Behind it the point-detonating 20mm cannon fire simply mangled the dead bodies even more.

The only enemy troops who survived were those who had already breached the defenses on the north side, and they were quickly dispatched by the defenders rushing into the gap.

Epstein stared, fascinated, as the miniguns continued to work their deadly mission, now moving outward toward the enemy troops who had not perished in the first assault. They tried to break and run, but were tangled in pieces of wire, fell into holes, gathered in confused knots as the men in front of them hesitated for a long, fatal instant. The fire swept over them, and they were gone.

I asked for a miracle, he thought. And I got this. Close enough.

"Bucky?"

He turned to see Stankow slumped in the bottom of the trench. Blood flowed from a bullet hole in the side of his neck. Epstein dropped down, checked the wound. Ah, shit. He pressed his finger into the pressure point just beneath Stankow's jawbone, trying to stop the flow from a severed jugular vein.

"Medic!" he screamed. "Goddamnit, get a medic over here!"

Spectre kept its orbit, the FCO slowly working his guns outward in an ever-expanding circle. The electronics warfare officer (EWO) monitored the high-tech consoles that jammed enemy radar, popping a magnesium flare every time his radar indicated a handheld SAM had been fired. The flares, far hotter than the exhaust from the Hercules engines, pulled the heat-seeking warheads inevitably away from the plane. They'd been through this routine many times before, and the air defenses here were far less sophisticated than those they ran into across the fence, where the largely unmolested NVA had set up so many guns and missiles to protect their precious trucks.

"I've got heat signatures, moving toward the camp in a vee formation," one of the operators told him.

The EWO read the data, concluded that the heat signatures could have been trucks, but were most likely tanks. He passed the information on to the FCO.

"Targets," the EWO told the gunners for the 105mm cannon sited in the back of the airplane. "Engage."

The 105 gunners, who had been feeling very left out, adjusted the weapon according to directions given by the FCO. About time, the gun chief thought.

Chapter 16

"Choppers comin' in, sir," DiUlio said.

Finn completed the sutures he'd been putting in the shrapnel-ravaged body of a young Montagnard soldier, washed his hands, and stepped outside the medical bunker where he had been helping Andy Inger treat the casualties. He looked down at his fatigues, covered with blood and bits of flesh, shrugged his shoulders. They expect somebody looks like he stepped out of a bandbox, he thought, they'd better go back to the States.

The first lift brought in Captain Charlie Secord and one of the Mike Force companies. The other would soon follow. The troops fanned out, alert and ready, facing outward toward an enemy that was no longer there.

The NVA had pulled out after the slaughter of their best troops by Spectre. Back across the border to regroup, lick their wounds, treat their wounded, bury their dead. The ones they'd managed to carry off, at any rate. It was a measure of just how badly they'd suffered that the camp was littered with bodies stiffening in the sun.

"You okay, Finn?" Charlie asked, gesturing at the blood.

"Belongs to somebody else. Dustoff on the way?"

"Be in as soon as we call the place secured. Fourth ID commander said he wasn't going to risk his pilots until we do."

Which thoroughly pissed off some chopper pilots, Finn was sure. Dustoff had a habit of flying into anything, anytime, to evacuate casualties. Which saved a lot of lives. Which got a lot of dustoff crews killed. Worth it? Hell if he knew.

Any more than if it was worth it, the dead and wounded in the camp.

Stop that! he told himself.

"I think it'd be about time, wouldn't you?"

Captain Secord immediately got on the radio. "Be here in five," he said after a moment.

The second lift came in, carrying the remainder of the Mike Force battalion. Sergeant Major Mike Hauck was with them. He sent his troops to reinforce B company, then joined the two captains.

"Had yourself a minor pissing contest here, it looks like?" he said.

"Little fight," Finn admitted. He looked out over the camp, seeing the shattered bunkers, the ripped barbed wire, and everywhere the bodies. Hundreds, maybe even thousands. Friend and foe alike, wrapped in fraternal embrace, forever together. Blood trails so wide the ground was slippery with it leading out of the camp where the NVA body-recovery teams would have used their hooks to drag people away.

The sound of helicopters grew loud again, and within a few moments he could see the big red cross on the nose of the first bird. It sat on the flat space where DiUlio had spread a panel, and from the medical bunker came a stream of patients, some walking on their own, some supporting others, and many, many carried in litters.

Lieutenant Sloane was one of the first ones aboard. Weak from loss of blood, pumped full of serum albumin and saline, in and out of consciousness, he was nevertheless still very much alive. He waved weakly at Finn as they put him on board. Finn waved back.

Washington, Olchak, Stankow, Young, and Becker also went out. Stankow was protesting that he could stay, they ought to get some of the more seriously wounded Montagnard soldiers out first; Olchak was telling him to shut up; Washington was watching in silent amusement; Young and Becker just looked glad to leave.

Bird after bird came in, taking the wounded Montagnard soldiers to the Sixty-seventh Evacuation Hospital (Semi-Mobile) in Pleiku, the same hospital to which the Americans were being taken. Back in the old days there had been huge arguments about this, the brass in Saigon and Long Binh insisting that indigenous soldiers be treated in Vietnamese hospitals. After a few occasions when Special Forces soldiers visited their wounded troops and found them in absolutely filthy conditions, largely untreated, with infections that would have responded immediately to even the most basic antibiotic therapy but which now suppurated and turned into gas gangrene, that had changed. Particularly when the SF had let it be known they weren't completely averse to tossing a grenade into the next medical command conference.

It took over an hour just to get the more severely wounded on their way, eight at a time. If a company had taken over 10 percent casualties, most military planners considered it as combat ineffective, ready to be pulled off the battlefield. Alpha company of the II Corps Mike Force had suffered 60 percent casualties—with 2.2 percent dead. The camp strike force had suffered even worse. Out of the three companies at the beginning of the battle, they could muster at most a reinforced platoon.

But the North Vietnamese had suffered worse. Much worse. God knew how many had died in the pre-attack bombardment from the 175s. Sky Spot had accounted for more. Bodies still hung from the wire and protruded grotesquely from the ground in the outer perimeter. Three PT-76 light amphibious tanks still smoldered on the other side of the runway. Wren and DiUlio were just now organizing a body removal squad to clean up the hundreds caught in the Spectre strike.

A great victory, someone would call it. Body count for this week would go through the roof. Politicians would cite it as an example of the wisdom of the policy of Vietnamization— after all, this had largely been a fight between Vietnamese forces. Instead of dozens, scores perhaps, of American troops filling the casualty lists, there would be only four, Curtis, Bartlett, Driver, and Noonan.

"I'm gonna try to find myself a cold beer," Finn said, turning away from it all.

Hauck gestured toward the sky, at a shiny helicopter that

bore the insignia of the Fourth Infantry Division. "Looks like the muckety-mucks finally decided to come out and see what's going on. Maybe get themselves another air medal."

"Fuck 'em," Finn said. "They want me, tell 'em I'm taking a nap."

"Mind if I come in, Finn?" Sam Gutierrez asked.

McCulloden was sitting in what was left of the team house. The roof was almost completely blown away, there were holes all through the walls that hadn't been sandbagged, and worst of all, the refrigerator had been blown to shit. No cold beer. No beer of any kind.

But he'd found a bottle of Jim Beam, so things weren't completely bad.

"Want a drink?" he said.

"Don't mind if I do." Gutierrez accepted the proffered bottle and took a healthy swig. It burned all the way down and through his stomach. Too late, he remembered he hadn't eaten anything in the last twenty-four hours.

Couple more swigs, and he'd be telling the general who had given him the ride out here to go fuck himself too.

"Did a good job here, Finn," he said.

"Suppose so," Finn took another shot. He handed the bottle back.

What the hell, Gutierrez told himself. He took another drink.

"You want a ride back to Pleiku? Wash up, get some food, maybe a little sleep? You know they're gonna be on your ass like stink on shit. After-action reports, write-ups for medals, all the normal happy horseshit."

Finn nodded slowly. "I reckon Sccord and Hauck can handle it from here on out. They gonna rebuild?"

"Doesn't look like it. Vietnamese say it'd cost too much, camp's too exposed anyway."

"So Charlie gets what he wants." Finn's voice was flat, unemotional. He knew better than to let go, to scream and rage over the incredible stupidity of letting people die for something you were going to give up anyway.

"Yeah. But it cost him." Gutierrez reached for the bottle.

"He's willing to pay. Are we?"

Epilogue

Two days later, in starched and pressed jungle fatigues with all appropriate badges sewn in place, Finn reported to the division commander and his staff. His boots were shined, his face clean-shaven, he'd even gone to the barber and had him reduce at least some of the accumulated shag.

"We're accepting your recommendations," the general said. "Citations are being prepared for the Silver Star for Sergeants Olchak, Stankow, Epstein, and Washington, Bronze Star with V device for all the other defenders. Colonel Gutierrez has recommended you for the Distinguished Service Cross, and I agree. And in line with your recommendations, we're beginning the investigation that should lead to Lieutenant Sloane's being awarded the Medal of Honor. Congratulations, Captain."

Finn shook his hand, and the hands of all the remaining staff, and kept his tongue. Just as Sam Gutierrez had told him to. He rendered a salute, received one in return, and did a smart about-face and left the command center.

Outside it was raining, as it had been for the last two

days. The monsoons were finally here. He stood for a moment and watched the hustle and bustle of the camp, the men ignoring the rain in their haste to pack up equipment, get the base ready for turnover to a Vietnamese division, get the hell out of this benighted country.

He shook his head. Made his way toward the club. Gutierrez was waiting and had promised him a steak dinner and all the wine he could drink.

He and Gutierrez had argued, that day in the shattered team house. Sam had told him that the people in USARV, down in their plush trailers in Tan Son Nhut air base, had followed the battle with great interest. And had decreed, once it was over, that someone out of the team should get the army's highest award. Surely, someone would have deserved it.

"I think it should be you," Sam said.

"Nope," Finn replied, looking a little forlorn when the bottle of bourbon was passed back to him with only a tiny little swig left in the bottom. "Let me tell you about Lieutenant Bentley Sloane."

"Already heard," Gutierrez said, his voice curt. "Right now I'm trying to decide if he should undergo court-martial. What he did endangered the entire camp."

"You could read it that way. But you could also claim he thought up a brilliant tactical maneuver, sucked in the first wave to be wiped out while saving our best weapon for the assault troops in the second wave. And that's the way it worked."

"I don't see it," Sam said. "Suppose there's any more bottles back there?"

They interrupted their argument long enough to search, finding a whole bottle of Scotch. Finn wasn't fond of Scotch, but it was alcohol. Good enough.

"No question he was brave," Finn said. "Even heroic. Risked his life probably more than anyone else in camp. Wounded, kept on fighting."

"Wolverines do that," Sam said. "We don't give 'em medals for it."

"One more reason. The most important one."

"That being?"

"I think we can agree that he should never lead troops in combat again. You try to court-martial him, he's going to beat it. And someday, somewhere, somebody will suffer. Because he'll try again. And again, and each time some poor innocent bastard will die. You want that on your conscience?"

"And if he gets the Big Blue, he'll stop?"

"You know the army," Finn said, grinning. "Not gonna put a bona fide hero back down where the rest of us grunts are. He's gonna be a general's aide, a staff officer, a nice little icon they can sit on a shelf somewhere and bring out when they want to impress the great unwashed."

Now it was Gutierrez's turn to smile. What Finn was saying was true. A Medal of Honor winner would have to fight to ever again see combat. The army would make sure of that.

Then Gutierrez sobered. "We're probably creating a monster here."

"Yeah. Probably. Pass that bottle, willya?"

Visit
❖ **Pocket Books** ❖
online at

www.SimonSays.com

Keep up on the latest new
releases from your favorite
authors, as well as author
appearances, news, chats,
special offers and more.

SIMON & SCHUSTER
A VIACOM COMPANY
www.SimonSays.com

Pocket
Books